BETRAYAL

By Danielle Steel

DANIELLE STEEL

BETRAYAL

A NOVEL

DOUBLEDAY LARGE PRINT HOME LIBRARY EDITION

Delacorte Press New York

This Large Print Edition, prepared especially for Doubleday Large Print Home Library, contains the complete, unabridged text of the original Publisher's Edition.

Published in the United States by Delacorte Press, an imprint of The Random House Publishing Group, a division of Random House, Inc., New York.

DELACORTE PRESS is a registered trademark of Random House, Inc., and the colophon is a trademark of Random House, Inc.

ISBN 978-1-61793-766-8

Printed in the United States of America

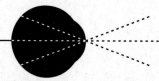

This Large Print Book carries the
Seal of Approval of N.A.V.H.

To my beloved children,
Beatrix, Trevor, Todd, Nick, Sam,
Victoria, Vanessa, Maxx, and Zara,

May those you trust never betray you.
And may those you give your heart to
always treat it well, with tenderness
   and respect.
And may the love you give to others
come back to you tenfold.

   With all my heart and love,
         Mommy/d.s.

"In each loss there is a gain,
As in every gain there is a loss,
And with each ending
 comes a new beginning."

—*Buddhist proverb*

BETRAYAL

Chapter 1

The two men who lay parched in the blistering sun of the desert were so still they barely seemed alive. There had been shattering explosions in the distance earlier, and one of them was covered with blood. Although they had been enemies, one of them now held the other's hand, as the lifeblood trickled from him. They looked at each other one last time, and then the injured man gave his last breath and died, just as there was the cracking sound of a gunshot nearby. The survivor of the pair looked wide-eyed and terrified as the man who had fired the gun appeared from behind them, seemingly out of no-where, as though he had dropped from the sky like an avenging angel.

"Cut! . . . and print!" a voice rang out in the stillness, and within seconds, everything was action, a flock of men with cameras and equipment entered the scene, the dead man stood up as the blood ran down his neck, and a pro-duction assistant rushed up to him with a cold drink and he guzzled it gratefully. The man who had been holding his hand an instant before walked off the set to get something to eat as soon as he was told that they were finished shooting for the day.

Two dozen people were talking, shouting, and laughing, and a tall, thin blond woman in ragged cut-off denim shorts, high-top sneakers, and a torn man's undershirt conferred with the camera crew with an enormous grin on her face. Despite her fair coloring, she had a deep honey tan from being out-doors, and a mass of long, uncombed blond hair piled up on her head. A mo-ment later, she braided it into a disheveled pigtail, and helped herself to a bottle of icy water as someone passed them out. There was an enormous catering truck nearby, and a still photographer shot the actors as they left the set. Four of Hollywood's biggest stars were in the film, which was always the case on her pictures. "It's going to be the best scene in the movie," the blond woman assured the head cameraman, as people came and went around them and checked with her, and the sound technician confirmed that he was happy with the scene too. Everything had gone smoothly. *The Sand Man* was going to be her best movie yet.

They were making her new film, sure to be an instant hit, like all the others Tallie Jones had made. Her films were box-office gold. She had been nominated for two Oscars and six Golden Globes. There were two Golden Globes on her desk, but no Oscars so far. And her pictures were an enormous success because she included both the kind of intense action men wanted in a film, just enough violence to suit their bloodlust without exploiting it excessively, and the sensitivity and emotional insights that made her films appealing to women. She offered the best of both worlds. Tallie had a Midas touch. At thirty-nine, she had been directing movies for seventeen years, and she hadn't made a lemon yet.

There was already a smell of victory on the set, and Tallie looked happy as she walked to the trailer that was her office on location with her dog-eared copy of the script under her arm. It included all the changes that the screenwriters had made the night before. Tallie was always honing and fine-tuning, she was a perfectionist, and people who worked with her accused her of micromanaging, but it was worth it. She turned her BlackBerry on as she walked into the air-conditioned trailer, and saw that she had two messages from her daughter, who was a freshman in college at NYU in New York, studying prelaw. Maxine, or Max as they called her, had no interest whatsoever in a career in films, only the law. She wanted to be a lawyer like her grandfather, Tallie's father, Sam Jones. He was Tallie and Max's hero, and they were the only two women in his life. Tallie's mother had died of leukemia when Tallie was in high school, and her father had been supportive of everything she did. Tallie had taken him to the Oscars with her as her escort, when she was nominated, and he was fiercely proud and protective of her.

It was Tallie's mother who had made her fall in love with movies. She had taken her to every imaginable movie as a child, watched every classic with her, and was fascinated with films and actors herself. She had named Tallie Tallulah, after Tallulah Bankhead, who she thought was the most glamorous woman who had ever lived. Tallie had always hated her name, and shortened it to something she could live with, but she had loved every film she'd ever seen with her mother, who had wanted desperately to be an actress, and wanted her daughter to fulfill her dreams. She hadn't lived to see Tallie's career or the wonderful films she made. Tallie always hoped her mother would have loved them and been proud of her. Tallie's mother had married her father at twenty-one, when he was already a successful lawyer at forty-five. It was his second marriage, but Tallie was his only child. He was eighty-five now, retired, and suffering from poor health. They called each other every day, and he loved hearing how it had gone on the set. She was his link to the outside world now, since he rarely got out anymore. Crippled with arthritis, it was just too hard.

Tallie's marital career had been a checkered one, not surprisingly in the world she lived in, where unstable relationships and quick turnover were the norm. She always said that it was impossible to meet normal, decent guys in the film industry. Max's father had been another story entirely. He was a cowboy from Montana she'd met at USC, and she'd gotten pregnant at twenty. She had dropped out of school for a year to have the baby, and her father had insisted they get married. They were both barely more than kids themselves, and by the time Max was six months old, her father had gone back to Montana, and they got divorced. Tallie had gone to see him a few times, to see if they could maintain the relationship, but their lives were totally different. Since then, he'd been on the rodeo circuit for twenty years, married a girl from Wyoming, and had three other kids. He sent Max a birthday card every year, a souvenir from the rodeo for Christmas, and Max had seen him four times in her life. He wasn't a bad guy, he just had no connection to Max, and came from another world. He'd been a handsome boy, stunningly so at twenty, and Max was even more beautiful than her mother, a six-foot-tall blonde, long and lanky with sky blue eyes. Tallie's eyes were green, and she was slightly shorter than her daughter. When they went out together, they made a striking pair, and looked more like sisters than mother and daughter.

Tallie's only other foray into marriage had been with an actor in one of her films. She never got involved with actors on the set of her movies, but had made an exception for him. He had been a major heartthrob, a big British star, and had swept her off her feet. She was thirty and he was twenty-eight, and he had cheated on her very publicly six months later when he was on location on another film. The marriage had lasted eleven months, they only spent three months of it together, and it had cost her a million dollars when she wanted out. He drove a hard bargain, and she paid the price.

She was alone for five years after that, and concentrated on her work and her daughter. She had no desire to try marriage again. And she'd been startled when she met Hunter Lloyd, a successful producer, and they started dating. There was nothing wrong with him, he wasn't a cheater, a liar, or a drunk. He'd had his own bad experiences with two failed marriages that had cost him a fortune too. They had started dating four years before, and lived together for the last three. He had moved in with her after a year, and had given up his own house, a palatial home in Bel Air, to his last wife. And for both of them, the arrangement worked. Tallie and Hunt loved each other, Max loved him too, and he was great to her.

Hunt was a big, kind teddy bear of a man, and the picture Tallie was making was the second one she had produced with him. The first one had been a record-breaking box-office hit. Together they were even more successful than either of them had been alone. And Tallie was happier than she'd been in years. She didn't want anything more than they had. Hunt Lloyd and the solid, quiet, stable relationship they shared were perfect for her. She was a modest person, despite her vast success, and liked leading a quiet life. She had no time to go out anyway, she was either shooting, preparing a film, or in post-production. There was rarely a time when she wasn't working.

At twenty-one, after she had Max, Tallie had been "discovered" by a Hollywood agent, in a supermarket. He had gotten her a screen test and into a film. She had only done it for the memory of her mother, and because she knew what it would have meant to her. She did fine, and the film did well, but she had hated every minute as an actress. It wasn't for her, nor anything that went with it. Much to her agent's annoyance, she turned down all the offers she got after that, and there had been several. The camera had loved her looks, and with some coaching she had been a decent actress, but what she had fallen in love with was directing. It was what she wanted to learn, and when she went back to college after having Max, she enrolled in USC's film school and applied herself. Her senior project had been a small low-budget film that she had made on a shoestring, financed with her father's help, and it had become a cult film, *The Truth About Men and Women*. It was the start of her career as a director. She had never stopped or looked back since.

Her first few movies did well and got rave reviews, and they started making big money by the time she was in her late twenties. She had become a Hollywood legend and a huge success in her seventeen years as a director. She loved what she did. What she didn't love, and never would, were all the trap-

pings that went with it, the fame, the attention, the press, the premieres, all the
opportunities to show off and be in the
limelight. As far as she was concerned
that was for actors, not for her, which
was why she hadn't wanted to be an
actress and loved being a director, and
contributing to each actor's performance and interpretation of the script.
After her one film as an actress, she
could see what would happen to her if
she pursued acting as a career, and she
wanted none of it. Tallie was a worker, a
creator, an artist. She was willing to
work endlessly on everything she did,
but not be a star. It was the one thing
she didn't want, and she was very clear
about it.

She'd had to go out and buy a dress
for her first Golden Globes when she
was nominated; she didn't own one. All
she had were the clothes she worked
in, which made her look like a homeless
person most of the time. Tallie didn't
care. She was happy just the way she
was, and Hunt loved her that way too.
He was smoother and more worldly
than she was, and more involved in the

Hollywood scene, but it never went to his head, and he was always content to come home to Tallie, sprawled out on the floor or the couch, poring over scripts. And when she was on location, he joined her whenever he could. He was more of a businessman than someone involved in Hollywood. Pictures were big business to him, and it didn't get much bigger than a film produced with and directed by Tallie Jones. And whether she bothered to comb her hair or not was immaterial to him.

They were near Palm Springs, in the location they had set up. She had a hotel room there for when she wanted to spend the night, but most nights she tried to get back to her house in L.A. to be with Hunt, if she didn't have to work too late, or he came out to be with her.

Tallie wanted to look at some of the day's takes, particularly the last one, before she left the set for the day. She had three pencils and a pen stuck in her hair as she made notes and answered e-mails, and she was just leaving her trailer to go look at the day's rushes when a cloud of dust appeared on the road leading to the set, with a shiny silver Aston Martin causing it.

She squinted into the remaining sun as the sports car approached, spinning up a cloud of dust around it. The car came to a rapid halt near where Tallie stood, and she grinned as the driver got out. The woman emerging from the car was a spectacular-looking girl in a micromini skirt, with endless sexy legs, a striking figure, and a mane of blond hair. She looked rushed and windblown and like something in a movie as she climbed out of the car. She had an enormous turquoise bracelet on one wrist, diamond studs in her ears, and was wearing towering high heels.

"Shit, did I miss the last take of the day?" Brigitte, the beauty who owned the Aston Martin, looked annoyed, and Tallie grinned.

"It went great. You can watch the dailies with me. I was just going to look." Brigitte looked relieved.

"The traffic was unbelievable. I got stuck for half an hour twice." Brigitte looked every inch a star. In her platform stiletto sandals, she was taller than Tallie, her makeup was perfect, she never went out without it, and her outfit suited her to perfection, showed off her incredible body, and made her look irresistibly sexy. She was the opposite of Tallie in every way. Everything about her had been carefully thought out to catch the eye, as opposed to Tallie, who preferred to think of herself as invisible, and liked it that way. Her whole business was to show off others, not herself. Brigitte Parker loved the attention she got and had none of Tallie's subtlety and shyness. The two women had similar looks, both tall, thin, and blond, but did entirely different things with the attributes nature had given them. Tallie hid them, and Brigitte shone a spotlight on them. Tallie honestly didn't care how she looked and never thought about it. Brigitte put a lot of thought and effort into her dazzling appearance.

They were the same age, but Brigitte had knocked ten years off her looks, although Tallie had done so inadvertently too. By looking as though she dressed out of a rag bag, in high-topped Converse sneakers, torn jeans, and T-shirts, she looked like a kid. Brigitte had had her eyes done, was proud of her breast implants, got Botox shots regularly, collagen in her lips, and spent time every day at Hollywood's most exclusive gym. She worked hard at how she looked, and the results were great. She was as beautiful as any star.

They had met at film school at USC seventeen years before. Brigitte had wanted desperately to be an actress, and was determined to learn everything about films she could. Everyone knew she was a debutante from San Francisco and didn't have to work, but all she craved was an acting career. Like Tallie, she had lost her mother at an early age. Her father had remarried a much younger woman very quickly, and the prospect of dealing with her "evil stepmother" had driven Brigitte to L.A. Tallie had hired her to help her with her first independent film, while she was in school, and Brigitte had been so efficient, so organized, and such an enormous help to her that she had asked her to work on her next film too. Brigitte made all aspects of Tallie's life easy, and she loved doing it. In the end, she had given up her dreams of becoming an actress, and had been Tallie's assistant ever since. She was everything that Tallie didn't want to be or do. Brigitte was the perfect front man, protected Tallie fiercely from the press, and shielded her from all she could. She liked to say that she would have taken a bullet for her. There was such a naïveté and simplicity about Tallie in some ways that she needed someone to run interference for her and protect her. Brigitte was Tallie's representative in the world, and she thrived on every part of that, and she took all the tasks off Tallie's hands that she could, which gave Tallie more time for her work, or to spend with her daughter. She was grateful for what Brigitte had done for her in the past seventeen years. It was an arrangement that worked perfectly for both of them, and met both their needs, and the time they had spent together had made them best friends. As hard as she worked, Tallie never had time to have many friends. Brigitte was always there, protecting and pampering her in every way she could, and she took great pride in what she did for her. No task was too difficult, too challenging, too time-consuming, or too menial for her.

They walked side by side to the trailer where Tallie could view the dailies, and chatted animatedly about the day's takes, as Brigitte minced along the rocky path in her towering stiletto heels.

"You need to get yourself a decent pair of shoes," Tallie teased her with a grin. It was a comment she often made. Brigitte never wore anything but stiletto heels, as sexy as she could get them, and they looked great on her. She acted like they were running shoes.

"Like Converse maybe?" Brigitte chuckled. Tallie never wore her newer ones, but only the ones that were torn, stained, and full of holes. She could have looked as sexy and fabulous as Brigitte did if she wanted to, but it interested her not at all, and Hunt didn't care. He loved her as she was. Her scruffy look was part of her charm, and what he admired most about her was her brilliant, creative mind. It was what

Brigitte appreciated about her too. They both knew that Tallie would be recognized as one of the greatest filmmakers of her time one day.

They got to the trailer and watched the dailies together. Tallie was silent and intense, observing every minute detail. She had them stopped several times and made comments to the editors who would work on them in post-production. She had a keen eye and saw nuances that no one else did, which was what made her great. And she had a discussion with the assistant director and the editors before she left. It was after seven when she walked back to her trailer with Brigitte. Tallie looked tired but pleased.

"Are you going home tonight?" Brigitte asked her. She had an overnight bag in the trunk of her car in case Tallie wanted her to stay. She always put Tallie's needs and plans first, and made her own around her. It never bothered her to take a backseat to Tallie's life, which was one of the things that made her so valuable to Tallie. She was the perfect personal assistant in every way.

"I don't know," Tallie answered. "Did you see Hunt before you left?" She wanted to be at home with him, although she knew they wouldn't get back to the city till nine or ten.

"He said he'd cook dinner for you if you come home, or he'll drive out if you prefer. I told him I'd let him know." Tallie hesitated for a minute, and realized she wanted to go home. Even if they only had a couple of hours together before she went to sleep and had to get up at four the next morning, she liked being in her own house with him, and he was a terrific cook.

"I think I'll go back."

"I'll drive you. You can sleep on the way in." It had been a long day for Tallie, it always was on location. She was used to it and enjoyed it.

"Thanks," Tallie said, and picked up a canvas bag she had been using as a handbag for months. She had found it at a garage sale, it was meant to carry plumber's tools, and was perfect for the scripts and notebooks she carried everywhere, to study whenever she had the time and opportunity. She was al-

ways working, and making notes of
new ideas, either for the scenes she
was currently shooting, or for her next
film. Her mind was constantly racing at
a hundred miles an hour.

Brigitte texted Hunt that Tallie was
coming home, as she had promised
him she would. She had made a dozen
calls for Tallie earlier that day, taken
care of several errands, ordered some
things for Max in New York, and paid
the bills. Brigitte was the most efficient
person Tallie had ever met, and Hunt
agreed with her. He always said that
Tallie was lucky that Brigitte had the
kind of personality to do the job. She
was perfectly content to live in Tallie's
shadow and be her emissary to the
world. And it had perks for her as well.
Every time Brigitte admired some new
outfit, fur jacket, or piece of jewelry, the
stores gave them to her, and she
gloated victoriously. It was one of the
best perks of her job. Jewelers and designers sent her gifts either for Tallie, or
to induce her to convince Tallie to wear
their creations, which Tallie had absolutely no interest in. She was only too

happy to let Brigitte keep their gifts. Brigitte was delighted to accept them and looked fabulous in everything she wore. She had even gotten a great deal on her Aston Martin, and owned a gorgeous house in the Hollywood Hills with its own pool. She lived well, and had a lot of fun being Tallie's assistant. It had been a great blessing for her for seventeen years. And even if she came from money and didn't need the advantages Tallie offered her, she enjoyed them anyway, and didn't have to deal with her father and stepmother. She liked being independent of the family money, although she admitted that she had paid for her house out of her inheritance from her mother, but it had been a great investment, and was now worth two or three times what she had paid for it. Between what she had on her own, and the handsome salary Tallie paid her, along with a constant flow of complimentary gifts and perks, Brigitte lived a golden life, better than Tallie in many ways, or at least it looked that way.

Tallie was naturally more discreet, although she had grown up comfortable too, but not on the scale that Brigitte described her childhood. Brigitte went to see her family from time to time, and always complained about it when she did. She thought San Francisco was dreary, still hated her stepmother, and hadn't gotten along with her father since he'd been married to her. Tallie had been her family, the one she really cared about, for seventeen years, and Tallie felt the same way about her. Brigitte had become the sister she'd never had, and a benevolent adopted aunt for Max, who adored her, and told her everything about her life as she was growing up, sometimes even more than she did to her mother, particularly if Tallie was busy or on location with a film.

Tallie got into the passenger seat of the flashy Aston Martin, put on her seat belt and settled back against the seat. She'd been on the set since five o'clock that morning and suddenly realized how tired she was. They had handed her new script changes just before she left, and she took them out to read them on the way, but she was exhausted as they drove off the set.

"Why don't you just sleep?" Brigitte suggested. "You can read the changes tomorrow morning. I'll drive you back. You don't have to read them tonight." Tallie was unfailingly conscientious.

"Thanks," Tallie said gratefully. She couldn't imagine what her life would be like without Brigitte to do everything for her, and hopefully she'd never have to try. She hoped that they'd be old ladies together, and Brigitte always teased her and said that would be the case. She assured her she wasn't going anywhere, she was never tempted to move on, or take any of the offers she frequently got trying to steal her away to work for someone else. She was quick to confirm that this was the job and employer she loved, and after so many years together, Tallie was also her best friend.

And then suddenly out of nowhere, Tallie chuckled as she glanced at herself in the mirror on the visor. "You look like you picked up a hitchhiker. I'm a mess."

"Yes, you are," Brigitte said, laughing as she glanced at her. "Maybe you should try combing your hair once in a while." Brigitte added extensions to hers, which made them look even more similar. Tallie's long mane was natural, and the big difference between them was that Brigitte's was always combed. She couldn't have gone to work looking the way Tallie did, but she wouldn't have wanted to anyway. And Tallie's work was more physically arduous, she was always climbing ladders, or riding up on cranes to get a better view of the shot. She sat for hours in the sun, without bothering to put sunblock on despite Brigitte's dire warnings about how wrinkled she'd get. Tallie would crouch on the ground behind a camera, or lie in the dirt to see the angle better. Tallie was a workhorse in every way, but even when she looked disheveled, she was beautiful, in a natural shining way. She seemed almost lit from within. Brigitte's looks were more studied and took far more work to maintain. Tallie would never have the patience or the interest to look that way or invest the time and effort it took.

"Thanks for driving me back," Tallie

said gratefully with a yawn. Now that she was relaxing, she realized how tired she was.

"Close your eyes and go to sleep," Brigitte ordered her, and Tallie did what she said with a peaceful smile. And five minutes later, as they got onto the freeway to L.A., Tallie was sound asleep, as Brigitte drove her home.

Chapter 2

Brigitte shook her gently when they got to the house in Bel Air. Tallie didn't like obvious shows of wealth, but she had a beautiful home that was simply decorated, with stark, modern open rooms, and a peaceful feeling to it. Tallie had no need for clutter in her life. She had a house in Malibu she rarely had time to use, the apartment in New York for Max, and a small apartment in Paris that she had bought with her first big success. It was something she had always wanted, although she hadn't been there in two years, but she loved knowing she had it, and loaned it to friends occasionally. Brigitte had used it for her last vacation, and loved being there. Tallie had been in Africa on location while Brigitte had gone to Paris for a week. The perks of Brigitte's job were nothing less than fabulous, which was what being a personal assistant was all about. You shared your employer's life, and gave up your own to do it, and Brigitte's own life fit easily into Tallie's or around it. She had a date that night at ten o'clock, and if it turned out to be midnight because Tallie needed her for something, that was fine with her too.

"You're home," Brigitte said softly as Tallie opened her eyes. The script changes were still on her lap, unread. But Brigitte was right, she could do it in the morning. She felt refreshed after she'd slept. For a minute, she didn't know where she was.

"Wow, I slept the whole way," Tallie said with a grin, and looked like a kid sitting in the front seat of the Aston Martin outside her house. She still had all the pens and one pencil stuck in her hair. She added them one by one throughout the day.

"Hunt texted me and said he has dinner ready. You're a lucky woman," she said, as Tallie opened the door of the car.

"Yes, I am." But they both knew that an arrangement like Hunt and Tallie's had never been what Brigitte wanted. She liked her freedom and a variety of men, usually younger than she was, for only a short duration in her life, and most of them were actors working on Tallie's films. She had a weakness for young actors who had the potential for behaving badly. She never kept them around long enough to give them that chance. She slept with them during the filming of the picture, and after that they both moved on. It worked for her.

"I'll pick you up at four-thirty tomorrow morning," Brigitte called out to her, and Tallie waved as she got to her front door. She wanted to be back on the set by six. As usual, it would be a short night, and before she could unlock the front door with her key, it was opened by a tall, handsome man with dark hair and a beard wearing an apron over a T-shirt and shorts. He kissed Tallie hard on the mouth, and the door closed.

Brigitte drove away. One of the actors from Tallie's current movie was waiting for her at her house. She had told him where the spare key was. Tommy was twenty-six years old, and when Brigitte got home, he was naked and waiting for her in the pool.

"Well, isn't that a pretty sight." Brigitte smiled as she admired him, and then stepped out of her skirt, and stood there in her thong and high heels, and then she pulled off her shirt and unhooked her bra. The breasts she had invested in several years before stood in sharp relief against the spotlights as the young actor gazed at her appreciatively. She had an amazing body, and made good use of it.

"Come on in," he said invitingly, thoroughly enjoying the warm water and the prospect of a night with her. They had been having an affair for the past six weeks, during the making of the film. No promises had been exchanged and wouldn't be. The kind of night they were about to spend with each other was all they wanted and all it would ever be. Brigitte wanted nothing more. She dove into the pool and came up between his legs, and he laughed. She was an incredible woman, and he had a great time with her. And he was hoping she'd help get him a part in another of Tallie's films after this. She hadn't promised, but she had implied it. And even if she didn't, he was having a ball with her. She was one of the most important women in Hollywood, as far as he and others were concerned, she had total access and the confidence of Tallie Jones. The one thing you could never do with Brigitte was say anything bad about Tallie. Brigitte was instantly ready to kill you if you did. She was the most loyal woman he had ever met. And offered the best sex.

Hunt handed Tallie a glass of wine as she walked in. She put her canvas bag and the script down on a kitchen chair, and smiled at the great smells all around them. The kitchen led out into the garden, and they wandered out onto the deck together and sat down. She was happy to see him and glad she had come home to him instead of staying in Palm Springs, and he was happy too. He was an easygoing person, and their lives had meshed perfectly for the past four years. There was rarely any friction between them, he had never disappointed her, and she loved sharing her work with him.

"Good day?" he asked, as he took off the apron and tossed it on a chair. He was taller than she was, and slightly round since he enjoyed eating well, but he was a handsome man. He was forty-five years old, and the beard gave him a more mature look than his years.

"Very good," she confirmed with a smile about her day. "When are you coming to Palm Springs?"

"I can't tomorrow. I've got meetings. Maybe the day after. How'd the death scene work out today?" He tried to keep up on the script changes, but with Tallie there were many of them, and sometimes she altered the script as she went along. She was always sensitive to how the dialogue was working, and let her actors add something more to it, if they could. The results were often breathtaking.

"It was perfect," Tallie said, looking pleased. "I'm starving. What's for dinner?" He often made Japanese food for her, Chinese, and Thai. He had a gift for Asian cuisine, and French, and sometimes made Mexican on the weekends. Hunt loved cooking, and everyone devoured what he made. It was fun coming home to the surprises he prepared, and the dinner he served her that night was no exception. They spent a relaxing evening, talking and eating on the deck, and he had gotten a bottle of her favorite white wine, Corton-Charlemagne. It was like going out to dinner whenever she came home, only better, because they were alone and she didn't have to get dressed up or even comb her hair.

He was already working on putting together their next joint venture. They would be on location in Italy for it, and he was planning to spend a lot of the time there with her. They wanted to rent a villa in Tuscany for the duration of the film. He was already lining up the cast, and working with their insurers and investors to secure the film. It was what he did best, while Tallie did the directing. And he set it all up meticulously. He had enlisted an important Japanese investor to back the film. It was easy raising money for a movie directed by Tallie Jones, but all the conditions had to be right. Hunt was great about it and as meticulous a perfectionist as Tallie.

"I think we're all set," he said about the Japanese investor as they cleared the table together after a wonderful meal. She had thanked him with a kiss. "The only thing he wants is an audit of our books on the project, and our personal ones as well. I guess he wants to make sure we're both solvent and won't run off with his money." He was smiling as he said it. "You don't have a problem with that, do you?" he asked her as they cleaned up the kitchen.

"Of course not. I'll tell Victor Carson to give him whatever he wants." They both knew he was a solid investor, and they wanted his money for their next film.

"He's using some very fancy independent accounting firm, run by a couple of ex-FBI guys. I hear they're pretty thorough, but that way everyone will be happy. We'll have his money, he'll know we're honest, and we can lock everything in." He'd been talking to all the big agents in Hollywood about who he wanted to star in it, and once they had the money, they'd be ready to move ahead very quickly with contracts.

"I'll have Brigitte call Victor tomorrow," Tallie said as they turned the light off in the kitchen and went upstairs to the large master bedroom with the enormous movie screen in it. They loved lying in bed and watching movies. But not tonight. It was midnight by then, and she had to get up in four hours. She was used to living on very little sleep when she was working.

She had wanted to call Max that night, but it was too late in New York by the time she thought of it, and she'd have to call her in the morning. And then Hunt mentioned that her father had called right before she got home and he'd forgotten to tell her.

"He has to have some tests tomorrow," Hunt told her, and she looked instantly concerned. "He said it's nothing important, just routine stuff. He was wondering if you were working tomorrow, and I said you were."

"I can have Brig take him, or his housekeeper Amelia," she said thoughtfully. Her father always said that her assistant was a Hot Mama, which made her laugh. He thought Brigitte was gorgeous and the sexiest woman he'd ever seen.

"I told him I'd drive him," Hunt said easily. "I can make the time. It's not a big deal. He was fine with it, if that's okay with you."

"You're a saint," she said, putting her arms around him and he pulled her close.

"No, I just love you. Thanks for coming home tonight."

"Thank you for cooking me dinner. Do you want to come to Palm Springs tomorrow night?" she asked him again, thinking that they'd have more time together without the long drive back to L.A., and the hotel they were staying at in Palm Springs was very nice, and had a terrific spa. She liked it when he came out there to spend the night with her. And sometimes it was easier for her than coming home if she had long shooting days.

"I've got some things I really need to do tomorrow, and a meeting tomorrow night. I think I'll come out the day after. Why don't you stay out there for the next couple of nights, so you don't have the long drive after work, and I'll spend the night with you the day after tomorrow?"

"Sounds good to me," she said, and then went off to take a shower, and a few minutes later she was in bed next to him, and cuddled up close to his body. She noticed that he was naked, and she peeled off the T-shirt she had worn as a nightgown, and they lay pressed against each other as he kissed her, and she was even happier that she'd come home.

"I miss you when you're on location," he whispered to her, and she kissed him again. Palm Springs was hardly a hardship location. There were films she had made where she'd spent six months in the jungle, three months living in a village in Africa, and they had been in places where civil war had broken out while they were there. Palm Springs was a piece of cake, and it was only two hours from home. They'd be coming back from location soon anyway, and it was a little bit like a vacation when he came out to spend the night with her.

"I miss you too," she whispered as he started to make love to her, and after that she forgot everything but him.

Afterward, they lay in each other's arms and talked for a few minutes, and she had to fight to stay awake. She was so peaceful and at ease, she couldn't keep her eyes open. She put an arm around him, and while he was still talking to her and stroking her hair, Tallie fell sound asleep.

Chapter 3

Brigitte was in the driveway at four-thirty the next morning, right on time, as always. No matter what she did the night before, she always came to work on schedule, whatever the hour. She texted Tallie that she was there, and she came out of the house barefoot and carrying her shoes, and closed the door silently behind her. Tallie ran to the Aston Martin and got in. She had showered again and her hair was wet, and if possible she looked an even bigger mess than she had the day before. She was wearing another pair of ratty, torn denim cut-off shorts with a T-shirt that was in shreds.

"Is that fashionable and you paid a fortune for it," Brigitte asked, referring to the shirt with fascination, "or did you get it at Goodwill?" There were in fact items of clothing that looked like that, wrecked by trendy designers who tore the clothes before they sold them. Max was always buying things with that look at Maxfield's. Tallie usually created hers for free, but with her you never knew. She rarely spent much on clothes. And designer anything was of no interest to her.

"No," Tallie said happily, "I got this shirt out of the garbage. Hunt threw it away, but I hated to waste it. It looks like it still has some life in it." She seemed pleased.

"As what? A rag at a car wash? You're the only woman I know who makes the kind of money you do and dresses out of the garbage." Brigitte laughed as they drove down the street.

"If I told you it came from Maxfield's, would it be chic?"

"Of course," Brigitte said without hesitation.

"Okay, then pretend it did. I don't have time to worry about the way I look." She never did. It wasn't on her priority list. She cared about what was in her head, not on her back, unlike most of the women she knew, and Brigitte certainly, who wore new designer clothes almost every day. Brigitte spent most of her salary on jewelry and clothes. She liked to say that she had an image to keep up, since she represented Tallie Jones. But Tallie didn't give a damn about that herself.

She called Max in New York on the way to Palm Springs, and caught her just as she was leaving for school. Max said she had just been calling to check in the day before, to see how she was and how the movie was coming.

"It's going great. We're pretty much on schedule, and we should be back in L.A. in a few weeks. What's happening with you? How's school?" Tallie loved talking to her, and called her as often as she could.

"It's okay. I met a new boy in the library last week. He seems pretty cool. He's in pre-med." Her romances always worried Tallie, realizing that she'd only been two years older when she fell for the cowboy from Montana and got pregnant with Max. But it didn't seem like the kind of thing she would do. Max was less naïve than Tallie had been at the same age, and Tallie felt now that if her mother hadn't died a few years before that, she wouldn't have gotten pregnant and had a baby. She was pretty lost for a while, although her father had always been there for her. But she was sure her mother would have handled it differently, and probably wouldn't have insisted she get married, which her father did. The whole event had been a big mistake, except that she had gotten a terrific daughter out of it, and was grateful for that. Max was a wonderful kid, and had never caused her mother a moment of grief. And her aspirations to be a lawyer like her grandfather sounded good to Tallie. She didn't want her in the movie business. It was too hard a life, full of unstable people, and a crazy world. She had never encouraged her to hang out with movie stars' children, although Max had met several at school. But she was a level-headed girl, and some of the stars' children were surprisingly nice kids too. Max had always avoided the bad ones, and had a knack for gathering wholesome young people around her.

"Have a nice day, Mom," she said cheerfully after a few minutes, and they hung up, and then Tallie remembered to tell Brigitte about the audit for their Japanese investor. Tallie asked her to call Victor Carson, their accountant, and ask him to cooperate fully with them, and give them whatever they wanted.

"At least you don't have to do the work on it," Tallie said to her, looking relaxed as she pulled out the script.

"I'll give Victor whatever he wants, if he needs anything from me." Brigitte was good with figures and kept impeccable track of all of Tallie's bills. There was never a problem about not having bills or receipts for whatever she paid for. After the first several years of chasing Tallie around to sign the checks,

they had set up an account where Brigitte could sign them to pay all her bills.
It saved Tallie the time and headache,
and Brigitte kept meticulous accounts
of everything. She had a charge card
she used for Tallie's expenditures as
well, and she handled everything for
Max, who lived in the apartment Tallie
owned in New York.

She and Victor worked well together,
and Tallie counted on both of them to
keep her financial life in order. With Brigitte at the helm, it ran like a Swiss
clock. Hunt always said he was envious
of her and wished he had an assistant
like Brigitte. She was even helpful to
him too, and never minded assisting
him with anything.

Tallie read the script changes on the
way back to Palm Springs, and they
had faxed several more to Brigitte at
midnight the night before. She had
brought those with her too, and Tallie
went over all of it, while making copious
notes. She wanted more changes when
they got to the set, which did not surprise Brigitte. That was how she
worked, vigilant about the tiniest detail.

"So what did you do last night?" she asked her assistant as they approached Palm Springs.

"Nothing much. Took a bath, read, answered some e-mails. I went to bed pretty early. I need my beauty sleep," Brigitte said innocently. The one thing she never told Tallie about was the actors she got involved with on the set. Once in a while Tallie found out, and she didn't say anything about it. She had a don't ask, don't tell attitude, and figured that it was one of the perks of Brigitte's job, if that was what she wanted, and it seemed to be. Tallie didn't think it was worth the trouble commenting on it since Brigitte's on-set romances never lasted longer than the making of the film. It was fine with her, as long as she didn't put Tallie in a compromising position of some kind, or promise favors she couldn't deliver, but Brigitte was too smart for that, and never stepped over that line. So Tallie figured that whoever Brigitte slept with was none of her business. She looked a little too innocent to her employer and old friend as they drove along, and Tal-

lie smiled, wondering who it was. Un-
doubtedly someone very young, one of
the extras or young actors. That was always Brigitte's style.

Tallie's day on the set was as busy as
the one before. Brigitte stuck around
and brought her cold drinks and hot
ones, and saw to it that she got something to eat. Otherwise Tallie never took
the time, she was too impatient and had
too much to do to stop for meals. It was
the same reason why she didn't bother
to dress decently and comb her hair.
Tallie was obsessed with her work, and
hated anything that distracted her from
it or took a moment of her time away.

Brigitte answered e-mails, and made
several calls for her. She called Victor
Carson and told him about the audit,
and when she had nothing else to do,
she sat and watched the action on the
set. She often gave Tallie very valuable
critiques. She had a great eye, and she
always knew exactly the nuance and
impact that Tallie was trying to get. Tallie respected her candid opinions much
of the time. Brigitte had learned a lot
about the business over the years.

It was another good day, and Tallie talked to Hunt when she finished work. He was on his way to a meeting at the Polo Lounge, and told her about what he'd done all day. He said he missed her, and after a few minutes they hung up. She liked that neither of them felt they had to be together all the time, like Siamese twins. They lived together but had their own lives, with joint projects as a common bond. But he never got antsy or jealous when she was away, and she didn't worry about him. After four years they trusted each other and knew each other well.

Hunt was an entirely different kind of man from the ones she'd been involved with before, all of whom had eventually cheated on her. Her second husband had been the most glaring case of that, but the others hadn't behaved much better. It was the kind of men she met in the film business. She liked the fact that Hunt was honest, true, and solid. He wasn't as exciting as the other guys in some ways, but she wasn't looking for excitement, she wanted a man she could love and trust. Otherwise, why

bother? She had come to that conclu-
sion a long time ago, and had learned it
the hard way, after being burned too
many times. He was essentially and
profoundly a kind man. He mentioned
to her before he hung up that everything
had gone fine when he took her father
for his tests, although he thought he
was looking a little thin.

"I know. His housekeeper says he
doesn't eat enough," Tallie said, sounding worried.

"I should go over and cook for him
sometime," he said thoughtfully.

"As though you have nothing else to
do," she said.

"I can make time. I love your dad,
he's a great guy. We had a good time
today. I think he was a little nervous before we went. I told him all my new
jokes, and he was fine by the time we
got there."

"Thank you for doing that," she said,
genuinely touched. These were the
things that made her love Hunt, and
there were a lot of them. He was an extremely thoughtful person, and he had
always been equally good to Max. The

two of them got along very well. Max had been fourteen when Tallie started dating him, and after a little initial resistance, she had relaxed. And by the time Hunt moved in a year later, it seemed like a natural evolution to all of them, even Tallie's father, who was a little more old-fashioned about things like that. He called Hunt his "son in love."

Tallie settled in at the hotel in Palm Springs that night. She was happy that things were going well on the film. None of the usual nightmares had happened, like problems with insurance, investors, actors who got sick or tried to break their contracts, hated each other, or got injured on the set. Those things didn't happen to her often, but when they did, it was a mess. Tallie always tried to avoid problems by hiring actors with reputations for being reliable, and getting all the kinks in their contracts worked out beforehand. Hunt was brilliant at handling those details, which was why their joint productions were such a success. She loved working with him. He was the best producer she'd ever had. And Tallie drove herself hard, was tireless in her efforts to get the best performance possible out of each actor, and the best writers and scripts she could. She deserved the remarkable reputation she had.

And she was content relaxing at the hotel that night. She and Brigitte went for a swim at the pool, and Brigitte had arranged for a massage for Tallie in her room, which Tallie said afterward was heavenly. She suggested Brigitte get one too, which was a perk Brigitte thoroughly enjoyed. The lifestyle that Brigitte shared with Tallie, and benefited from because of her, suited her to perfection. Thanks to Tallie, she led a star's life.

Victor Carson was staring at a mountain of papers, files, and spreadsheets on his desk. He had been Tallie's financial adviser for fifteen years, and other than the details Brigitte handled, his firm did all the accounting for her. And when Brigitte called to tell him about the audit for the investor, he almost groaned aloud. It was a headache he just didn't need. His life was complicated enough as it was. His own problems were precluding everything else. He didn't know why they were requiring an independent audit. All he needed were a bunch of hostile auditors taking all his records and files apart and demanding explanations for them. Tallie's affairs were in good order, but an audit would be incredibly time-consuming, even with someone else doing it, and possibly more so, if he had to explain everything to them. Normally, he and Brigitte handled everything and it was smooth as silk. He just didn't have the time to spend on this, but there was no way he could say that to Hunt or Tallie. He was having personal problems, although he would never have admitted it to them. He now handled Hunt's taxes as well as Brigitte's. But right now, he had his hands full at home.

Women had always been Victor's nemesis. His first wife had cost him a fortune in alimony and a settlement twenty years before when she discovered that he had a mistress, a beautiful Italian model. He left his wife for her and married her. He had had two children with his first wife, and had twins with the second. Two years later she adapted to the American ways he had taught her, left him for someone much younger than he was, and took him to the cleaners. She'd eventually gone to Paris, married someone there, and he hadn't seen his twin daughters in eighteen years. They were strangers to him, and he had been paying child support for them until that year. Fortunately his two older children were now adults and employed, and their mother had remarried, but for several years he had been supporting two ex-wives and four children.

And more recently, some bad investments made by his own financial adviser had lost him a considerable amount of money. He took far better care of his clients than he did of his own affairs. And at sixty-two, he had fallen madly in love with a young aspiring actress, and married her after a sexually charged weekend in Las Vegas. He had promised to use all his connections in Hollywood to help launch her career, which had turned out to be not as easy as he'd thought. As it turned out, Brianna had no talent, her screen tests had been a disaster, and the only work she'd been able to get was as a bathing suit model at trade shows, which was not what she'd had in mind.

Victor had just turned sixty-five, Brianna was twenty-nine and threatening to divorce him if he didn't make good on his promises to establish her career in either movies or TV. She was great in bed, but not on the screen. And she hadn't slept with him in six months anyway. She spent all her time getting plastic surgery, shopping up and down Rodeo Drive, and demanding money from him. She had threatened to leave him only the week before, and he didn't want her to. As impossible as she was, she was a breath of excitement and glamour in his otherwise dull life and he was crazy about her. She seemed like the perfect trophy wife to him. He loved going out with her on his arm, and watching other men look at him with envy, or so he thought. Anyone who had spent an evening with her would

have pitied him instead. But he was be-
sotted and didn't want to lose her,
whatever it took. And the truth was,
with his recent financial losses, he
couldn't afford her anymore, and he
didn't want her to know. He could
barely cover her shopping habit. She
was constantly angry at him and demanding things, or trying to improve on
body parts she had already had altered
before. She had had her first set of implants redone, a tummy tuck, a buttock
lift, and recently had liposuction on her
thighs. But whatever it took to keep her,
he was willing to pay the price. It was
cheaper than alimony and a settlement.
But he didn't know where to get the
money from anymore. He felt like a ma-
gician pulling rabbits out of a hat.

He was much too busy juggling his
own money to want to spend time on
Tallie's audit, which would be time-consuming. He had just promised to take
Brianna to Europe, and if he reneged on
that now, he was sure she'd leave him.
She wanted to go to Brazil to check out
a plastic surgeon there. His life had
been a descent into hell for the past

three years, and losing a large amount of money recently was putting his life and marriage at risk. There was no question in his mind that if Brianna knew, she'd leave him. Flat. His children would be happy if she did, but Victor would be devastated.

He left his office at eight o'clock that night and went home. Brianna was waiting for him, and the result of her day's catch was still in shopping bags near the front door. He winced when he saw the familiar names. Dolce and Gabbana, Roberto Cavalli, Neiman's, and Chanel. It was a full-time job for her, and as far as she was concerned, the only reason to be married to a man his age. Victor Carson was not an exciting man, and he looked older than his age. He wasn't attractive, and Brianna was only interested in what he could do for her. He always meant to diet but never got around to it, and had never been to a gym in his life. And he had lost his hair in his early thirties. But he adored his beautiful young wife and was totally dazzled by her. Other men longed for expensive cars, or large blocks of real estate, or dreamed of success. All Victor ever wanted was a beautiful young woman in his bed. It had cost him two marriages and some very heavy debts so far, and he was well on his way to the same fate again. Unless he won the lottery, there was no way Brianna was going to stay with him.

"You're late," she said petulantly when he walked in.

"I had a lot to do today," mostly trying to figure out how to pay her bills, but the upcoming audit for Tallie had caused him additional work. He had to get his assistants working on organizing her files.

"I want to go out to dinner," she pouted at him. She had had her lips modeled on Angelina Jolie's and had a fearsome pout.

He didn't want to tell her he was exhausted and wanted a quiet evening at home. "Where did you have in mind?" He never denied her anything, and now wasn't the time to start.

"Mr. Chow," she said with a gleam in her eye. She loved seeing the stars who went there, and the paparazzi gathered outside. It was loud, trendy, expensive, and the food was very good. It was definitely the place to be and to be seen.

"All right. I'll call and see if we can get a reservation," he said quietly.

"I already did," she said with a broad smile. "We have to be there in ten minutes. I invited Carla and John to join us." They were her friends, not his, ordered the most expensive things on any menu, and fancy wines, and never reached for the check. And they were her age.

All of her friends expected him to be their sugar daddy, and so did she. His own friends had disappeared long since. The women he went out with, and now Brianna, made their wives uncomfortable. Victor felt they were just jealous. It never occurred to him that they thought he was a fool, and Brianna unbearable. She never talked about anything but plastic surgery and the gossip she read in movie magazines. He wasn't looking forward to an evening of hearing about which Hollywood couple had broken up, who was sleeping with or cheating on whom, and

whose facelift or new breasts looked
the best. But it was the life he had cho-
sen for himself, high-stakes marriage
with a gold digger half his age. He never
thought about it that way, although her
insatiable appetite for his money had
begun to frighten him. None of his
clients had ever met his wife, although
Brigitte had run into him at a nightclub
one night and told Tallie she looked terrifying. She would never have expected
somber, sedate, mousy Victor Carson
to be married to someone like her. And
he had looked proud when he introduced her to Brigitte, which was even
worse. Brigitte thought he should have
been embarrassed to be seen with her.
She was expensively dressed, but it
didn't help. The obvious designer labels
and flashy diamond necklace and ring
didn't alter the fact that she looked like
someone he had rented for the night,
not invested in for a lifetime. To Brigitte,
Brianna looked like a colossal mistake.

Brianna's friends were already waiting for them at Mr. Chow when they arrived, and they had brought another
couple with them whom Victor had

never seen before. They ordered every-thing that appealed to them on the menu, two expensive bottles of wine, cocktails before that, and champagne with their dessert. Victor could feel his credit card straining when he paid the bill, but Brianna looked happy when they went home. She sank into a bub-ble bath and thanked him for a nice evening, and then she asked him when they were leaving for Europe.

"I haven't made the reservations yet," he told her honestly from her bathroom doorway. She had remodeled his apart-ment when she moved into it, which had also cost him a fortune, and she had a gigantic pink marble bathroom. "I just heard about a big audit I have to cooperate with for one of my clients. I don't think I can get away until that's been taken care of." Otherwise he would delay the start of Tallie's next movie or lose her investor, and he would lose an important client, which he could not afford to do, and he was too conscientious to do that anyway. Victor was meticulous about his work.

"Are you saying we're not going?" She looked instantly suspicious.

"No, I'm just saying that I won't know when for a few weeks. But we'll go, I promise."

She nodded, mollified for the moment, and he felt as though he'd gotten a momentary reprieve from the pressure she always put on him. And just as he was about to leave she announced that she wanted to redo their bedroom. It was a new idea, and yet another way for her to spend his money. "I heard about a new decorator I want to try. She did J-Lo's bedroom," Brianna announced with a determined look. Victor didn't answer, he just quietly disappeared into his closet to undress and put on his pajamas. He sat on a stool he had in there, and thought about what lay ahead if he was going to try and keep Brianna with him, and he wanted to cry when he thought about it. Other than robbing a bank, or winning the lottery, he had no idea where to find the money to satisfy her. Her demands were getting bigger, and the funds he had left were dwindling day by day.

Chapter 4

Hunt came to Palm Springs to stay with Tallie the day after. They spent a nice evening at the hotel, although Tallie finished late, but Hunt never minded. They lay out by the pool for a long time late that night and chatted. He told her that everything was in place for the audit to begin the following week, and then he asked her if she'd talked to Victor Carson.

"Not lately," she answered. "I usually have Brig talk to him. She called him about the audit. Why?"

"Nothing. He sounds incredibly

stressed about something. Maybe he's insulted that we're doing the audit. It's a smart thing to do anyway." Hunt was sensible and cautious about business, although he spent a considerable amount of money, but he could afford it.

"My father always said that too. He's been bugging me to do one for years. He never trusts anyone. He was a lawyer for too long." And then she remembered what Brigitte had told her about meeting Victor's wife at the nightclub. "Apparently, he's married to a real bimbo, half his age. Maybe she's giving him trouble." Hunt laughed when she said it.

"He doesn't look the type. He looks so dull and respectable, I figured he'd be married to some nice conservative old lady." He assumed Victor was older than he actually was. Tallie always had too. He looked ten years older than his age.

"Maybe that's the one he left for this one. Sometimes guys go a little crazy at his age. Just warn me if you ever decide to dump me for a bimbo or a younger woman."

"I'm not that old yet," he said, smiling at her from a deck chair. "Besides, I love what I've got."

"You never know," she teased him. "Give it a few years, you might want some twenty-year-old bimbo too."

"I hope not. If that ever happens, just shoot me. Besides, I can't afford one." He could, but he didn't want to.

"Maybe he can't either. Maybe that's why he sounded stressed. I can never understand why guys do that. Someone half my age would just make me feel older."

"Men think it makes them look young and virile, instead of old and foolish," Hunt explained. It was a phenomenon they saw a lot in Hollywood, but Tallie had never known Hunt to lust over young women. He was totally focused on her, and devoted to her. She thought not being married kept their relationship alive and fresh, and that was how she intended to keep it, and Hunt had never objected. He didn't want to get married again either. They shared that point of view.

He told her about the agents he'd

talked to that day, about the potential
stars of their next film. They had two
locked in already, the biggest ones, and
two who were almost sure. The last hur-
dle they had to get over was the audit,
and they both knew it wouldn't be a
problem. Their finances were in good
shape, and their last movie had made a
fortune. The audit was just a formality to
satisfy their investor, and not a concern
to either of them.

After shooting the next day, Tallie had
given the cast the weekend off, and she
and Hunt drove to Santa Barbara. He
had rented a beautiful house in Mon-
tecito for the weekend, and they were
both looking forward to it. Brigitte went
back to L.A., and Tallie was going to
drive back up to Palm Springs with her
on Monday morning. It was going to be
a treat to have a weekend to relax and
get away from the film. Tallie always got
new ideas when she got a little distance
from it. She would wake up in the middle of the night, and make notes on a
pad she kept next to her bed. And this
weekend was no different. But most of
all, she and Hunt enjoyed each other's

company. They walked on the beach, slept late, and went out to dinner, and by the time they got back to L.A. on Sunday night, Tallie felt as though she'd had a vacation, not just a weekend.

She felt alive and fresh when she left for Palm Springs with Brigitte at four o'clock on Monday morning. She chatted with Brigitte all the way there and told her about the weekend. Brigitte said she'd had a couple of dates but didn't volunteer with whom, and Tallie assumed they couldn't have been important, or Brigitte would have said more about them.

And she reminded Brigitte to call Victor Carson a couple of times that week and see how the audit was going. She was expecting everything to go smoothly, and Brigitte assured her she'd do it.

Tallie and Hunt both had a busy week ahead, and he warned her that he didn't think he'd be able to come to Palm Springs. She promised to come back to L.A. when she could, but she had a lot to do too. She didn't want the location shoot to fall behind.

And by six o'clock that morning, Tallie was off and running, and she didn't stop till midnight that night. The cast was utterly worn out by then, but Tallie was still going strong. Brigitte smiled as she watched her in action. There was no one in the world like her.

The independent audit got under way as planned. The firm that was doing it was based in San Francisco, and they were cool and businesslike when they went to Victor's office, and asked for what they needed. They used his conference room to spread out Tallie's books and accounts, and they had brought their own computers. There were two accountants, and they had brought two assistants with them. And they kept to themselves all week. Now and then they asked Victor for an explanation or some substantiation as they pored over her general ledger, and they offered very little comment. But Victor found it stressful anyway. He felt as though they were checking his work and questioning his competence. They were a very high-flying firm, and he was sure they were charging the Japanese investor a fortune for the audit, but apparently the investor thought it was worth it.

On the second day of the audit, Brianna had a surprise for him when he got home, looking nervous and exhausted. She'd been to see a lawyer, she explained, and she said she wanted a postnup from Victor. She looked very pleased with herself as she said it.

"A postnup?" He looked shocked. "What exactly do you mean?" A cold chill ran down his spine as he said it.

"You know, a postnup. Like a prenup, but after the marriage."

"We already have a prenup, Brianna. We don't need a postnup too." He didn't like the sound of it at all. It sounded like blackmail to him, or a serious threat at the very least. He had done a prenuptial agreement with her, and she had insisted that he put a sum of money in an account for her before they married. He had been so desperate to marry her that he agreed.

"I've already spent most of the

money you gave me in the prenup, Victor. I need more. My attorney says that you can give me an amount now, and pay me an additional sum for every year we stay married." It was like paying her to be married to him, and something told him that the amounts weren't going to be small.

"Why did you go to an attorney?" he asked her somberly. He wondered if she'd been asking about a divorce but was afraid to tell him. He had given her seven hundred thousand dollars when he married her, and she had spent it in three years, in addition to what she had cost him. He couldn't imagine what she had spent it on, but she went through money like water. Despite his careful accounting, she constantly slipped through his fingers.

"I just don't feel comfortable without money of my own," she said, whining at him. "I don't want to ask you for everything. If you give me a lump sum now, and pay me an amount every year, I'd feel a lot better," she said, sidling up to him.

"I honestly don't think I can afford it

right now," he said sadly. "Some of my investments haven't been doing well. I'd rather just pay your bills and take care of you, than put a set amount in an account every year."

Despite the Angelina Jolie–lookalike pout, Brianna set her mouth in a firm line. "I don't think I can stay married to you if you won't do that for me," she said with a nasty undertone in her voice. "If you love me, you'll do it. You didn't do anything you promised for my career. This is the least you can do for me. I wouldn't feel secure without it."

"And if I don't, or can't?" he asked, feeling discouraged and frightened. It was a race he couldn't keep up with. He had nearly ruined himself for her, and she was insatiable in her demands and need for money. It was why she had married him in the first place. That was finally coming clear even to him now, with her demand for a postnup.

"I'll have to discuss it with my lawyer and let you know," she said with something very hard in her eyes. "Think about it, Victor. You don't have any choice." She was making her position clear, and he felt desperation clutch his throat. He was sixty-five years old and he didn't want to lose her. And despite her ulterior motives with him, he had grown attached to her. And how many more women who looked like her were there going to be for him? He felt suddenly tired, defeated, and old.

He sat in his study alone that night, thinking about what she'd said, and he drank too much Johnnie Walker. Brianna went out with her girlfriends and came home at two o'clock in the morning. Victor was passed out on the couch in his study. She looked at him from the doorway and went to bed alone. She didn't wake him or try to get him into bed. She was sure he would give her what she was asking for. He had no choice if he didn't want to lose her, and she knew he didn't. She had him by the throat, or worse.

She heard him in the shower the next morning and left for the gym. And by the time she got back, Victor had left for the office. The independent auditors were still in his conference room, and he was using the opportunity to go over

Tallie's accounts himself. It never hurt to double-check things. And late that afternoon, he came across several entries that confused him. Brigitte paid all of Tallie's bills, and she was always very organized and careful about it. She recorded the entries in the general ledger, and then turned over the accounts to him. Brigitte signed the checks, and had been doing it for years. What was puzzling him were regular stays at several hotels. It was none of his business what Tallie did and how she spent her money, but he wasn't aware of why she was staying at various hotels in L.A. And if they were business related, he wanted to take them as deductions.

There were a few stays at the Bel-Air, and quite a number at the Chateau Marmont and the Sunset Marquis. The same hotels appeared in Hunt's accounts as well. Brigitte didn't pay his bills—he had a bookkeeper he'd had for years. And Victor wondered if they spent romantic nights at hotels, or used the hotels for meetings, but he just wanted to confirm that with Tallie, as long as he was going over her books. He was sure it was nothing important. He also noticed that she was spending a considerable amount of cash, which he didn't like, because whatever she spent it on, he couldn't use as a deduction for her taxes, and he wanted to tell her that too. He wanted her to use her credit cards instead of cash.

Victor tried not to think of Brianna as he went over Tallie's books. What she had said about the postnup was very upsetting. He knew he wasn't going to be able to give her large amounts, and he was afraid that what he could give her right now wouldn't impress her. And her request for a postnup had sounded like an ultimatum to him. His personal life was in turmoil. But he had to get this audit taken care of for Tallie and Hunt. He didn't want to hold up their next picture, or frustrate their very precise Japanese investor. Tallie was counting on him to do it promptly, but it was hard to concentrate while he worried about Brianna.

Victor carefully went over Tallie's accounts for two weeks and made a list of

questions. There were expenditures relating to her daughter, some of which
the IRS could have viewed as gifts, in
which case Tallie had to pay taxes on
them. He didn't think they could take
the Paris apartment as a business-re-
lated deduction since she never went
there anymore, and up until then they
had been. She hadn't made a film in
France in years. And he had a list of
other expenditures that he wanted clar-
ification on. The independent audit was
to establish her solvency and net worth,
but the one Victor was doing was just to
make sure that her accounts were in
good order, and they were taking deductions properly. Victor was conservative in his approach. He never liked taking too many deductions, if they were
questionable, and he wanted to be able
to defend all of their positions if they
were ever challenged by the IRS. He
didn't want to get anyone in trouble, or
let his clients stick their necks out too
far. Some of them wanted him to be
more aggressive than he thought reasonable, although Tallie never had, but
this was a good opportunity to reevalu-

ate their positions, and he was doing the same for Hunt.

Hunt's bookkeeper's accounting system was less precise than Brigitte's. A lot of money came in and a lot went out, but he spent most of it on his credit card, so they had a good record of it. Victor met with him and asked him several questions. It was all very straightforward. And when Victor asked him about the local hotel stays, he said he'd stayed there with Tallie, and once in a while he rented suites at hotels for meetings with out-of-town investors so those were business deductions, and Victor wanted to know which charges were for business if Hunt remembered, and most of the time he did.

It all made sense and Victor was comfortable with the deductions they were taking for him, and they hadn't put Hunt at risk for an audit. Victor was satisfied with Hunt's answers, and the accounting firm of the Japanese investor seemed pleased too. They were almost finished at the end of two weeks, and very happy with what they'd seen. It looked like the deal would go forward.

All Victor had left to do was ask Tallie similar questions to those he had asked Hunt, just for the sake of clarity in their ledger. And in Tallie's case, he thought they should be taking more deductions. He also wanted to be sure that they were up to date on her California Use Tax, for things she had purchased out of state or abroad. He checked diligently that Tallie was keeping track of it, and Brigitte was recording it correctly, so Tallie didn't get hit with penalties later. Most of his questions were about that, money spent on Max, and the considerable amount of cash that Tallie was spending, instead of using her credit cards, which he would have preferred.

He called her on her cell phone on Friday afternoon on the set. She sounded busy and he apologized for bothering her, and told her he had a number of questions to go over with her, to be sure that everything was in order and that he fully understood her expenses in the ledger.

"Can you talk to Brigitte about it?" she asked, sounding distracted. They had fallen slightly behind that week due to bad weather and a lot of changes in the script. She was worried that they were going to go over budget on location.

"I can," Victor answered her cautiously. Sometimes he drove her crazy, he was such a nitpicker, but that was what she paid him for. She just didn't have the time to spend on it with him at the moment, or she really didn't want to. "But I'd rather ask you. You're the one who's responsible for your taxes, if Brigitte or I make a mistake. I'd rather hear it from the horse's mouth. When will you be back in L.A.?"

"This weekend. But I'll be back here on Monday morning."

"Would you like to meet on Sunday?" he offered, and Tallie sighed, thinking about it. She wanted to spend her time off with Hunt, not Victor, but she knew he'd drive her crazy till she agreed to meet with him. She might as well get it over with, and figured she could do it on Sunday morning when Hunt played tennis. It wasn't how she wanted to spend her Sunday, but she agreed to meet him at ten-thirty at his office to answer his inquiries. He promised he'd make it quick. Brianna liked to go to the Polo Lounge at the Beverly Hills Hotel for Sunday brunch, and she wouldn't be happy about his working either.

When Tallie went back to L.A. that night, Hunt had good news for her, and he was making a wonderful dinner.

"Well, we passed the audit with flying colors." Hunt beamed at her. "Mr. Naka-mura is happy with everything, and they're going to draw up the papers next week. I guess that means that nei-ther of us is going broke, nor a crook." He kissed her and she smiled too, and told him about her meeting with Victor on Sunday. "I had one of those meet-ings with him this week too. I swear, he wants to know everything I ate at every restaurant and was I talking business while I did." They both laughed about their persnickety accountant, but Tallie commented that she was sure he was why she had never had an audit by the IRS, because he was so precise and so honest, and Brigitte kept such good track of her books. Problems with the IRS would be a headache, and she had always assiduously avoided them by being honest and cautious. So it was worth putting up with how thorough Victor was, and sometimes how annoying.

"I'll meet with him when you play tennis," she told Hunt. "He said it would be quick. The last thing I want to do is spend my Sunday with Victor." They both laughed at the idea.

Hunt and Tallie spent a relaxing weekend. Tallie caught up on some errands and things she wanted to do. It was nice to have some time in the city before she had to go back to Palm Springs again. She visited her father on Saturday afternoon, and spent several hours with him. He wanted to hear all about how the film was going, and they sat in his garden and chatted while she filled him in. And on Sunday, when Hunt went to play tennis, she went to Victor's office for the meeting she had promised him. He was waiting for her in a suit and tie. Tallie was wearing torn blue jeans, her high-tops, and a faded sweatshirt whose only virtue was that it was clean.

"Thank you for coming in on Sunday,

Victor," she said politely. "My schedule is crazy right now while we're on location. It sounds like everything went great with the audit. Our investor notified us on Friday that he's satisfied. I really appreciate everything you did."

"That's my job," he said, as he adjusted his glasses and sat down. He had a list in front of him on his desk. The questions that applied to the California Use Tax were on the top of his list. He reminded her that it applied to her daughter too, and that anything she bought in New York and brought back to California had to have state tax paid on it. It seemed like a terrible burden to Tallie, but it was the law. And she said that Brigitte kept a careful record of everything they bought out of state and reported it to him. Victor was relieved and said that many of his clients forgot and got in trouble for it later on. He had questions about employees, several independent contractors that he wanted to verify with her. And as he droned down the list, Tallie found herself thinking that he could have done a lot of it with Brigitte. He had recategorized

the apartment in Paris as a personal
rather than a business expense, and he
reminded her that she could only take
Max as a dependent as long as she remained a full-time student, which Tallie
already knew. He had told her several
times. And then he scolded her for the
amount of money she spent in cash
every month.

"I can't use it as a tax deduction
when I don't know what you spend it
on," he complained.

"Ice cream, parking meters, Starbucks. I don't think you're missing any
big deductions, Victor," she said with a
rueful look.

"You must drink a lot of Starbucks
then. From what I can tell, you're
spending about twenty-five thousand
dollars a month in cash." He tried not to
look disapproving, but he was unhappy
about it. That was a lot of deductions to
miss.

"Twenty-five *thousand*? That's impossible, I don't think I spend more
than two hundred a month in cash,
maybe one. I use my credit card for
everything I buy, even if it's just sham-

poo," and Brigitte usually bought that for her too. She bought all of Tallie's personal supplies for her. There was very little that Tallie had to do herself. Brigitte took wonderful care of all her needs, and often thought of them before Tallie did herself. "Victor, that's crazy. You must be looking at the wrong amount or the wrong column or something. There's no way I'm spending twenty-five thousand a month in cash."

"That's what I show. There are checks made out to cash, and they're being cashed at the bank. Do you leave the cash lying around the house?"

"Of course not. Half the time I have to borrow money for coffee, especially when Max is here. She helps herself in my bag, but not to twenty-five thousand dollars. That has to be a mistake." She was certain of it.

"No, it's not," he insisted. "That's why I wanted to have this conversation with you. I'm concerned about the lost deductions, and even more so if you don't know what you're spending it on, or don't know what you spent." He made it sound as though she were irresponsi-

ble and careless and couldn't keep
track of her own money.

"Look at my credit card statements.
For anything over five or ten dollars, I
use my card."

"Then how would you explain a
twenty-five-thousand-dollar cash ex-
penditure every month? Is Brigitte using
that much cash for you?"

"No, Brigitte uses a credit card too.
We have a joint card for anything she
buys for me." He knew that, he saw it in
her accounts. "I don't think she uses
much cash either."

"Well, somebody is spending it. You
need to find out who, if you're not." He
was visibly worried about it on her behalf, and Tallie was concerned too. To
Victor, it was a black hole in her accounts. "If you round that up, annually,
over the last three years, it comes to
close to a million dollars. You can't just
lose track of that kind of money."

"Obviously," she said, mystified. "I'll
talk to Brigitte. Maybe she's paying for
something in cash that I don't know
about. Since she pays the bills, I don't
know what she's using the credit card

for, or checks, or maybe cash. I'll ask her," Tallie said, although she looked less concerned than Victor. She was certain that there was a reasonable explanation for it. And Brigitte kept a very careful record of her accounts. Victor had always been satisfied before. But the recent audit had allowed him to do some fine-tuning, and look at the overall picture more carefully, and he never liked to press his clients about what they were spending unless they were in financial trouble, which Tallie certainly wasn't, but he didn't want her to lose track of that much money either. It was a very large amount. He didn't like his clients using cash for just that reason— no one could ever remember what they spent it on, and Tallie was no different. Victor was sure the money had been spent legitimately, but he wanted to know for what, and by whom. Tallie promised to find out. She knew without a doubt that Brigitte would have the answer to his question.

After that, he ran down a list of bills that he wanted to verify with her, to double-check that they sounded accurate. Clothing for Max, some artwork Tallie had bought in New York, and several gifts for Hunt, among them a gold watch. He was always very generous with her too. And at the end of the list, several travel expenses, airfare, and the local hotels that he had also questioned Hunt about.

"Hunt explained to me the other day about the local hotels." He was no longer concerned about that, but he had wanted to be sure. Victor could see from her accounts that they frequently stayed at several local hotels, although they had stopped showing up on her credit card statements for the past year. They had been on her credit card bills for about three years before that, and now they were only on Hunt's. Apparently Hunt was paying for the hotels now since the charges still showed up on his statements right up to the present, and no longer on Tallie's.

"What local hotels?" Tallie asked in answer to what he'd said.

"The ones where you stay with Hunt." Victor was prepared to move on. He was meeting Brianna for lunch, and he had covered all the ground he wanted to with Tallie, particularly the cash.

"I don't stay at local hotels with Hunt," she said simply. "I only stay at hotels out of town, when I'm traveling or on location, like right now in Palm Springs. I have a room booked there for a couple of months, but that's a business expense."

Victor looked surprised. "You have a few charges at the Bel-Air, and quite a lot of them at the Chateau Marmont and the Sunset Marquis. I've got three years of charges there on your statements, although none for this year. And Hunt has them on his statement too. He says he rents rooms sometimes for meetings with foreign investors, and that he stayed there with you."

"He must have misunderstood. We've never stayed at any of those hotels, except once we stayed at the Bel-Air when I was having work done at the house. That has to be a mistake." And then suddenly Tallie wondered if Brigitte had used their joint credit card for some of her racy little flings. She knew that Brigitte had a fairly active romantic life, and Tallie was sure that if she had used the card for that, maybe because she didn't have her own card with her, she would have reimbursed it in some other way, which Victor might not be aware of. "Maybe it's Brigitte. I'll ask her about that too," although she didn't love the idea of Brigitte using the credit card for her romantic trysts.

She was sure Brigitte wouldn't let her pay for it in the long run, but she might have used the card initially, which she really shouldn't. It didn't sound like her. She was so diligent and businesslike, and so careful with Tallie's accounts. There had never been any question about it before. It was the investor's audit which had brought it to light. Tallie said she would get the explanation from Brigitte about the hotel charges and the cash. Victor dropped the subject of the hotel charges. He didn't want to press it. Hunt had been absolutely clear that he had stayed at those hotels with Tallie, and she was saying they never had. It sounded like delicate ground to Victor. It wasn't the first time that something like that had come to light in one of his clients' accounts, and it could be extremely awkward. He didn't want to insist, but he definitely wanted to know about the cash, which was of much greater concern to him and a far larger amount than the hotel stays. He reminded Tallie about the cash again before she left.

She wasn't worried about it as she drove back to the house, but she wanted to check it out to satisfy Victor. Brigitte would know, and she seriously wondered if Brigitte had been charging her little hotel stays to their joint credit card account. If not, Tallie wondered if it was a case of identify theft. That had happened to her before too, where someone got her credit card number and was running around to stores, and charging things to her account. She had had to change her credit card numbers several times because of that. At least there had been no local hotel charges on her bill for the past year, so they must have straightened it out. And she had no idea why Hunt had said he had stayed at those hotels with her, since they never had. She was sure that Victor was confused.

Other than that, it sounded like everything was fine and her accounts were in good order.

Hunt got home from his tennis game five minutes after she walked in. He was hot and sweaty, and she was making a big salad for lunch. Despite her lack of skills in the kitchen, even she could do that. He was in good spirits, he had won. He was very competitive on the tennis court, and at most games. He played hard, and usually took it badly when he lost. From the grin on his face, it looked like it had been a good day.

"How was Victor?" he asked, helping himself to some Gatorade in the fridge.

"Fine. The poor thing asks a million questions and worries about everything. And he's a little confused about some of it. He says I'm spending too much cash, and I don't spend any. I always use my credit card. I have to make sure Brig isn't using cash to pay for things or for bills, because that way we lose deductions. That's what he was upset about. I'm sure Brig has the explanation. I don't." And then she wanted to mention the hotel bills to him, but she didn't know how to do it without sounding accusing. She thought that maybe she should ask Brigitte first, in case she had been charging hotel bills to her when she stayed there with her boyfriends. If so, Tallie was certain that she had reimbursed her, probably by depositing a check or cash to one of Tallie's accounts. And Victor wouldn't have known what it was for. And there again, there was surely an explanation. So she didn't say anything to Hunt. She was sure that the confusion was at her end. What she needed to do was check it all with Brigitte and get back to Victor with the simple explanation.

They spent a cozy, relaxed afternoon together and sat chatting in the garden after lunch. Tallie was loving being home. She was getting tired of being on location, but she reminded herself that it was a lot less arduous and unpleasant than some of the locations she'd been to in the past, like India during a monsoon, or Africa during a civil war. Palm Springs certainly couldn't be considered a hardship and at least it was close to home.

And as Tallie and Hunt were relaxing in her garden, Victor was having lunch with Brianna at the Polo Lounge at the Beverly Hills Hotel. She had been annoyed when he kept her waiting for half an hour, but he explained that he had had to finish his meeting with Tallie. And Brianna was irritated that he had to work on a Sunday. She thought he looked like an undertaker in the suit and tie. She had suggested he wear jeans and a button-down shirt, but Victor wouldn't do that, out of respect for his clients, whether it was Sunday or not.

Victor and Brianna had been passing like ships in the night for several days. She seemed to be out a lot these days, and he had been tied up with the audit.

"I'm sorry I've been so busy lately. It should calm down now," he said apologetically. She looked beautiful in a tight white dress with a low neckline she had bought that week at Roberto Cavalli. Her cleavage looked remarkable in it.

"It's okay," she said quietly. She

waited until they were having coffee to drop the bomb. She took a breath and leaped in. "I want five million dollars," she said bluntly.

"What for? So do I," he said with a smile.

"To stay married to you," she said coldly. She was suddenly all business, and not nearly as inviting as she looked. "And an amount every year that we can negotiate. But I want the five million up front."

"What is this? A business deal or a marriage?" he asked, looking upset. "I don't have that kind of money," he said, looking her in the eye.

"You used to."

"I don't anymore." And if he did, he still wouldn't have paid her to stay married to him. That was pure blackmail. "Pay, or I'll leave" was the message to him loud and clear.

"What about three million?" she asked. She was willing to negotiate with him. "But if you don't pay it, I'm leaving. I can't sit there penniless all the time. I need to know that there's some money in the bank, just for me. It will make me feel secure." Her secure, and him broke, Victor thought to himself.

"Brianna, I just don't have it." He didn't know why her lawyer had put the idea of a postnup into her head, but it was destroying their marriage overnight.

"If you don't give it to me," she said coolly while he paid the check, "I'm going to leave you. I can't be married to a man who doesn't want me to be happy." Her happiness came at a high price. She had made herself clear. Victor looked pale as they waited for their car outside the hotel, and they drove home in silence. He could see where this was headed. Either he paid the postnup, or he paid alimony and a settlement. He was so upset that he ran a red light and they nearly had an accident. He had never felt so panicked in his life.

Chapter 5

On the way to Palm Springs with Brigitte the next morning, Tallie mentioned her conversation with Victor about the cash.

"Are you paying some of the bills in cash?" Tallie asked her as she sipped a light vanilla latte from Starbucks on the way. They had stopped for it as they left town.

"Of course not. What's he talking about?" Brigitte looked annoyed. "I pay all the bills by check, or credit card. He knows that."

"That's what I thought. I don't see

how he can think we're spending that much in cash. I knew we weren't. Maybe he screwed up the accounts." Anything was possible. Maybe it was a bookkeeping mistake at his end. Tallie thought that was more likely than she or Brigitte spending twenty-five thousand a month in cash, which would have been astounding and sounded utterly impossible to her.

"He seems so distracted to me lately," Brigitte commented. "Maybe he's sick. Or too old to do his work and keep the numbers straight." She sounded annoyed.

"Yeah. I don't know. It sounded crazy to me too. I'll tell him it's a mistake of some kind." And then she thought about the hotels. Maybe that was a mistake too. But she had to ask her anyway, just to be sure. "He showed me a list of hotel bills too, for the Chateau Marmont and the Sunset Marquis." There was a momentary silence, and feeling slightly embarrassed, Tallie went on. "I hate to ask you this," she said apologetically, "but did you happen to stay there and accidentally charge it to the joint card?"

"No." Brigitte looked puzzled. "I've never stayed at either hotel. Why would I? If I were going to sleep with someone, I'd go to my own house, not a hotel right here in L.A. That sounds crazy to me too. Maybe it's identity theft again."

Tallie had thought of that too.

"That's what I thought, or I figured you stayed there, charged it to our joint card, and reimbursed me later."

"I'm not that sloppy," Brigitte said with a broad smile.

"I know you're not." Tallie smiled back at her apologetically. "Especially if you've never stayed at those hotels. It must be a mistake then." Tallie knew there had to be a reasonable explanation for it, whatever it was. And without thinking about it further, she pulled out the script and read the new changes on the way to Palm Springs. The incorrect hotel charges were the furthest thing from her mind.

* * *

She called Victor from her cell phone that morning from her trailer on the set, while Brigitte went to get her coffee. They had an espresso/cappuccino stand set up by catering that was as good as Starbucks. Tallie told Victor on the phone that she had no explanation for the cash or the hotel bills. She sounded unconcerned about it, and he sounded surprised.

"Hunt said he goes to those hotels with you," Victor said clearly, and Tallie suddenly felt her stomach curl itself slowly into a knot like a boa constrictor in her belly. Had Victor misunderstood? Was he senile?

"I think you misunderstood him, Victor," she said firmly. If Hunt had said it to him it simply wasn't true, and Brigitte had denied that the charges were hers. So who had been charging hotel bills to her?

"It must be identity theft again," Tallie said simply, as the boa constrictor in her belly relaxed.

"I'll check it out," Victor said cautiously, "and I'll call you back. The credit card company should have a record of who signed at the hotel."

"Probably no one we know," Tallie said quietly. Victor said nothing and hung up a moment later, as Brigitte came back to the trailer with Tallie's coffee. It smelled delicious.

"Everything okay? You look pissed," Brigitte commented as she handed Tallie the cup of steaming latte. Tallie laughed when she said it, and felt instantly better.

"Not pissed. Just annoyed at Victor. He's so ridiculously stubborn sometimes. He's like a dog with a bone when he gets something in his teeth. He's all worked up about the cash he says we're spending, and I'll bet you anything, it's some kind of clerical error on his end when his assistants put our entries into the general ledger."

"I'm pretty precise about them," Brigitte said calmly.

"I know you are. I'm not worried about it. He's being a pest, although I know he means well. But they probably screwed up and we didn't. I don't want to get upset about it. And he keeps harping on the hotel bills he claims I charged, and I agree with you on that too. I'm sure it's identity theft again. The last time someone stole my credit card number, they went to a sex shop in Detroit, and about thirty bars. I'm sure the hotel charges are the same thing. He claimed that Hunt said he stayed at those hotels with me, and I'm sure he didn't say that. Victor gets so nervous, he gets it wrong sometimes. For about an eighth of a second I got nervous about Hunt when Victor said that. And then I realized that's just me being crazy. Victor will get it straightened out, tell me it was a mistake, and I'm not going to accuse Hunt of staying in hotels because Victor got a bee in his bonnet. Shit, I hate accounting. Thank God, you do it for me. He makes me crazy." Brigitte laughed as she said it, and Tallie grabbed the script and stood up.

"I don't love the accounting either. He's such a nervous Nellie," Brigitte said as she handed Tallie her Black-Berry.

"I know. Well, I've got to get to work." Tallie finished her coffee, put the script under her arm, and slipped her Black-Berry into a pocket of her shorts after putting it on vibrate, and a moment later she was riding a cherry picker with the cameraman, setting up the shots with him for that morning, and her irritation with Victor was already forgotten.

It was another long shooting day to make up for lost time. Tallie worked straight through lunch, and it was midafternoon before she took her BlackBerry out of her pocket and checked it for messages. She had felt it vibrate several times. She had four messages from Victor and rolled her eyes as she sat down in a chair on the set and cracked open a bottle of water. As she called Victor back, Tallie noticed Brigitte talking and laughing with one of the actors, and she wondered if he was the man of the moment. While Tallie was watching them, Victor answered.

"I wanted to get back to you about the Sunset Marquis and the Chateau Marmont," her accountant said without preamble, and Tallie was reminded of the image of a dog with a bone again.

"It's probably identity theft, Victor,

just like all the other times we couldn't explain charges on the cards. And you said there have been no charges for those hotels on my card for the last year anyway. What's the problem?"

"I don't like unsolved mysteries," Victor said sternly, "not when it's about your money."

"I appreciate that, but it's not recent anyway, and it can't be a very large amount." Tallie was trying to be casual instead of worried.

"I still have an obligation to explain it. I called the credit card company this morning. They keep the signed charge slips on microfiche, and I had them fax them to me to see whose signature was on them."

"Don't tell me I signed them," Tallie said, almost laughing at the absurdity of it.

"No. Brigitte did. Her signature is clearly on all the hotel charges, at both hotels. Yours is on one from the Bel-Air, but you already explained that. The ones I mentioned to you are all signed by Brigitte Parker."

"She said she's never stayed at either

hotel," Tallie said firmly, far more willing to believe her assistant than her accountant. She still believed that the mistake here was his, not Brigitte's, or any improper use of the credit card on her part.

"Maybe she's forgotten. It's been a while," Victor said calmly.

"I don't think so, Victor."

"Maybe she's embarrassed to tell you that she used the card for personal reasons, and she reimbursed you without our knowledge." He was willing to believe that she had made it up to Tallie, although he couldn't prove it, but he was entirely unwilling to believe that she'd never been there and checked into the hotels. Her name on the charge slips said otherwise. "It's clearly her signature on the charge slips."

"Maybe someone forged it," Tallie suggested coolly.

"I doubt that."

"I never look at things like that, Victor. Brigitte handles all the statements when they come in. I don't have time. That's why I have her. And you check the accounts and the general ledger."

"Yes, I do. This only came up because of the recent audit. And we still have no explanation for the twenty-five thousand in cash you're spending every month and can't account for. I'm much more concerned about that than the hotel bills we can't explain."

"So am I. If you don't mind, I'd like to show the accounts and the spreadsheets to my father. He's a lot better at this kind of thing than I am." She always relied on her father's advice and wise counsel.

"Of course, I have no problem with that."

"Thank you, Victor. I'll call you later."

She sat thinking for a minute after the call to Victor, wondering again about the hotel bills. And then she called her father. As always, he answered on the first ring.

"Hi, Dad," she said, trying to sound casual, but he knew her too well for that.

"What's wrong?" He went right to the point.

She laughed at his question and tried to sound unconcerned. "Some stuff came up in the audit that I'm confused about. Maybe my accountant made a mistake. Would you look at it for me?" Her father was good with spreadsheets and figures, and his mind was still sharp. His body had failed him, but his brain was still operating at full speed.

"I'll be happy to take a look. Send it over whenever you want. What's the problem?"

"My accountant says I'm spending twenty-five thousand dollars a month in cash. I'm not spending it, Brigitte says she isn't. I can't figure it out."

"Do you have a joint account with Hunt?" he asked her bluntly, although he liked Hunt immensely, and Hunt certainly had more than enough of his own money and didn't need Tallie's, and he'd been very generous with her and Max.

"No, I don't. We haven't commingled anything. But I can't imagine that twenty-five thousand dollars is disappearing every month. I think it's got to be a mistake, and I don't want to get upset about it till I know."

"Have your accountant send me the

spreadsheets and I'll take a look," her father said in a concerned voice.

"Thanks, Dad." He was always there for her. She didn't mention the hotels to him, there was no point. It was either identity theft, or one of them was lying, and her father couldn't know that. But he might be able to figure out the cash or see where Victor Carson had made a mistake. She called Victor back afterward and asked him to messenger copies of the spreadsheets to her father. He promised to do it immediately. And she felt better after that when she went back to work. She was sure that the mystery of the missing cash would be solved with another pair of eyes on the spreadsheet.

Brigitte drove her back to town that night. They chatted amiably on the way home, but Tallie was distracted, thinking about her conversations with Victor, and the conversation between them felt a little strained, which was unusual for them. She wanted to ask Hunt about the hotels, but when she got home, he was out with investors that night. He'd left her a note telling her he loved her.

And she sat down on the couch, thinking about the hotels again.

She called Max in New York then just to chat. They talked for half an hour and then Max said she had reading to do for school, and Tallie reluctantly hung up. Tallie's father called her as soon as they hung up.

"He's right," Sam Jones said, sounding disturbed. "You've got twenty-five thousand going out the door in cash every month, give or take a thousand. Can't Brigitte account for it somehow? She's always so organized and efficient. That's a lot of cash to lose track of." Her father sounded as concerned as Victor had.

"I know, Dad," Tallie said. "I can't account for it either. And I'm not sloppy with my money."

"I know you're not." He was disturbed about it.

"She pays all the bills and signs the checks, and there's never been any slippage before, or I thought there wasn't. But Victor says it's been going on for a few years." The same length of time that Hunt had lived with her. But he

had no access to her money that she
knew of, so that didn't solve the mystery either. She knew just enough to
scare her now, but not enough to figure
it out. And there had to be an answer
somewhere. "And I know it's not Brigitte, Dad," she added. "Her family has
a ton of money, and she makes a big
salary from me. She doesn't need to
steal cash from me." It hurt to even say
it, but she wanted to get to the bottom
of this. "Besides, she is the most impeccably honest person I know. I've
never had a problem in all these years."
She had been paying Tallie's bills for
sixteen of the seventeen years she'd
worked for her, and there had never
been a concern or an issue about
money. Tallie trusted her completely,
and Brigitte had earned that by how reliable and trustworthy she was.

"Well, somebody is taking money
from you, if you're not spending it yourself," her father confirmed. "What are
you going to do?"

"I don't know," Tallie said, sounding
distressed. She had been hoping he
would tell her that Victor had made a

mistake, but he hadn't, which complicated everything now.

She had no idea where to turn or who
to ask. And the issue about the hotel
bills was upsetting her too. Brigitte
claimed she'd never been to the two
hotels, yet she had signed the credit
card slips, and Hunt had told Victor that
he went there with Tallie, if Victor had
understood him correctly. Neither of
them was telling the truth, and she had
no idea why. Or someone else entirely
had gone to the two hotels and charged
it to her, which was also possible. There
had to be an explanation, but maybe it
was one she didn't want to hear. She
lay in bed wide awake, torturing herself
that night. She had been turning it
round and round in her mind. And she
always came out in the same place. Brigitte and Hunt were the two people she
trusted most in the world, other than
her father and daughter, and for the first
time ever, in both relationships, she had
the feeling that they weren't telling the
truth. It felt awful. She had never had
any reason to doubt either of them before.

When Hunt came home, he slipped into the darkened bedroom, careful not to wake her, and she pretended to be asleep. She didn't know what else to do. She didn't want to talk to him about it and question him at that hour. And what if he denied going to those hotels? She didn't want to catch him in a lie. She was afraid to ask him and hear what he'd say. She lay wide awake long after Hunt fell asleep, and she'd only had two hours of sleep when Brigitte picked her up in the morning. Tallie looked terrible, and Brigitte looked serious as they drove away. There was very little conversation between the two women, which was rare for them. Brigitte didn't say anything all the way to Palm Springs after they picked up coffee at Starbucks, and then just before they got to their location, Tallie was startled when Brigitte pulled off the road. She glanced at Tallie with an agonized look, as Tallie watched her. Something was very wrong.

"I have to talk to you," Brigitte said in a shaking voice. "I always wondered what I would do in a situation like this, and I hoped I would never have to find out. I have to talk to you about Hunt. And I have a small confession to make too." The two women were sitting in the car, and Tallie dreaded what she was about to hear. Whatever it was, she already knew it wasn't good. It was written all over Brigitte's face. She looked as though she hated what she was about to say. For an instant, Tallie wanted to run away before she heard it.

"About three years ago," she went on, "right after he moved in, Hunt asked me for some cash. He said you had asked him to pay for something. I can't even remember what it was, but whatever it was, it sounded believable. He had just moved in with you, and you seemed madly in love with him." Tallie had never been madly in love with him, it was something that had grown over time. But she had certainly been in love, enough to want to live with him and they had been happy and still were. Brigitte went on. "It kept happening. He kept asking me for cash. It wasn't a lot at first. Just small amounts. He would tell me that he'd forgotten to cash a check, or that you'd asked him to get cash from me. It just kind of snow-balled, and eventually I realized he was doing it all the time. I didn't know what to do or say. I didn't want to mess things up for you, after all you've been through, and he really is a nice guy. It's just gone on and on and on. I had no idea how much it came to until you told me the other day. I don't know what he does with the money. I guess he spends it on himself, or socks it away, or what-ever. I figured if I said anything to you, it would be all over, and I didn't want that for you, so I've been going along with it for all this time, worried sick about it and scared for you, and mostly sad. I think he's a nice guy, but maybe not an honest one. Tallie, all that cash is going to him." She looked mortified as she said it, because she had been giving it to him. "Now he just expects it."

"And you just gave it to him and didn't tell me?" Tallie looked horrified. The man she lived with and loved had been stealing money from her for three years, and her assistant and best friend hadn't told her? Worse, she'd been giving him the money? Tallie felt like a total fool, and she was angry at Brigitte for not telling her sooner and hiding it from her. Three years was a long time to remain silent. Brigitte had become his unwilling accomplice, but his accomplice nonetheless. Tallie felt betrayed, by both of them.

"How could you do that and not tell me about it?" Tallie asked with a shocked look on her face.

"I didn't want to screw up your romance. You need someone in your life, Tallie. You can't do it all alone. And the picture you made together was such a big hit. I didn't want to jeopardize that for you either." There was a lot riding on their relationship now. Tallie knew it too.

"So you let him take money from me and didn't tell me? Whose side are you on?" Tallie accused her.

"Yours," Brigitte said without hesitation, with tears in her eyes. "I made a terrible mistake. I let him manipulate me, and I didn't tell you. I didn't realize until yesterday how much it had cost you. It's always a few hundred, a thousand here and there or two, but I guess it adds up in a hurry." It was a lot. Twenty-five thousand dollars a month was a huge amount to her.

"And he's been doing it for three years?" Brigitte nodded in answer. "Do you realize that it cost me nearly a million dollars in the past three years? And why would he do such a thing? He makes more money than I do." It just didn't make sense, but Tallie believed her. The story was too ugly not to be true, and she knew Brigitte wouldn't make that up. She still trusted her, although her faith in Brigitte had just taken a heavy hit. "Did he tell you not to tell me?" Tallie wanted to know everything now, down to the last word and detail, although she didn't know what she was going to do, or what to say to him. Victor had been right. She was losing a huge amount of cash. And now she knew how, why, and to whom.

"Eventually, he told me not to tell you. He knew what he was doing, and so did I. Stealing from you, and it makes me feel sick that I helped him."

"You call that a 'small confession'?" Tallie looked appropriately shocked.

"That wasn't what I meant." Brigitte looked profoundly distressed, as well she should be. It was the most upsetting thing Tallie had ever heard about a man in her life, worse than discovering that her British movie-star husband was cheating on her with his leading lady, and reading about it in the press. What Hunt had done was profoundly dishonest. It was stealing. "My 'small' confession was that I did go to the Chateau Marmont once, and charged it on the card. I didn't have my credit card with me. I'm not even sure now who I went with. I think it was that cameraman I was so crazy about. He was married, and you didn't want me to sleep with him, so I didn't have the guts to tell you. I paid back the money though, in cash, to the petty cash account, every penny."

"Victor says there was more than one credit card slip with your signature on it from the Chateau Marmont and the Sunset Marquis," Tallie said sternly. "He checked."

"I may have gone twice, but I always reimbursed it. Maybe someone forged my signature on the other slips. Maybe even Hunt. And that's the other thing I have to tell you." She took a breath and plunged in. "I think he's been seeing someone for about a year now. I suspected it at first, and I have a friend who works in his office. He confirmed it when I asked him. She's some young secretary, very young I think. She has an abusive ex-husband and a child, a three-year-old boy. I think she's about twenty-five or twenty-six. My friend says that Hunt must have been sorry for her, and tried to help her. Her ex came back to beat her up, and the kid, after she left him. Hunt was very sympathetic, and helped her find a place to live, and I guess it all started from there. They've been having an affair for about a year. He stays at hotels with her, mostly when you're away, I think. And the maid says he never sleeps at the house now when you're gone. Apparently that's true. I checked." Brigitte looked devastated as she told Tallie the details.

"The maid told you about this? Does everyone know except me?" He had played her for a fool, while stealing money from her and cheating on her. She never would have suspected it of him in a million years. Instead of being the best man she had ever had, he had turned out to be the worst one.

"What are you going to do?" Brigitte asked, looking desperately worried and remorseful. "I didn't want to hurt you. I'm always trying to protect you. I knew you'd be upset about the money, but I thought maybe you'd think he was worth it, and I thought the affair with this girl would blow over. But it hasn't. They say it's very serious, and she wants to marry him as soon as her divorce comes through."

"And when was he going to tell me that little piece of news? After their honeymoon? Jesus, he's a shit." Tallie looked as though the bottom had just fallen out of her world.

"And so am I for not telling you all this before. I only heard about the affair with the girl about six months ago. I should have told you then. And about the money before that. I really made all the wrong decisions on this one." Her confessing it now made Tallie feel a little more benevolent toward her, but she was badly shaken. Brigitte had hidden important information from Tallie, because she didn't want to hurt her. But she had hidden Hunt's cheating on her and stealing money from her. Both were serious offenses, and Tallie didn't deserve it. Brigitte had never been in such a tough position in her life. She was crying as she sat in the car looking guilty and devastated.

"I have to figure out what to do," Tallie said, looking shell-shocked. "I need some time to digest this before I confront him." There were tears in her eyes as she said it, and they were both crying as they looked at each other and Brigitte hugged her in sympathy and remorse. She felt terrible about the news she had delivered.

"I thought you'd want him around, at any price," Brigitte said as she blew her nose.

"I don't want anyone that badly, no matter how much I love him. I don't want anyone enough to let them cheat on me and steal my money." She was most hurt by his cheating on her, even more so than the money. Money could always be replaced, but her faith in him couldn't. She couldn't imagine ever trusting him or any man again. He was the last of a long, checkered career of bad men. And she no longer trusted her own judgment.

"I'm so sorry, Tallie," Brigitte said as she sat there and cried, and finally Tallie looked at her watch and said they had to go to work. She didn't reach out to comfort Brigitte. She was much too upset at her for not telling her the whole story sooner, and at Hunt for what he'd done.

Tallie had no idea how she was going to work today, but she had no choice. Even with her heart breaking, she had to continue working on the film. She wished it were already over. And she wanted to confirm the two stories first, for her own peace of mind, before she accused him. She had to figure out how to do that and who would help her. It was going to be agonizing living with him in the meantime.

"Are you going to fire me?" Brigitte asked her with a look of terror.

"Maybe. I don't know." It was as honest as she could be with her. "I don't want to. Let's let the dust settle on this and see what happens." It was the best she could do for now, and Brigitte was grateful that Tallie was taking some time to think about it. It was a terrible shock and an ugly story. They drove to the set then, both of them with heavy hearts and in silence, wondering what would happen. Tallie felt as though her world had just come to an end. Again.

Chapter 6

Tallie stayed at the hotel in Palm Springs the night of Brigitte's confession. She didn't want to go home to Hunt, and didn't want to say anything to him yet. And she was keeping her distance from Brigitte too. She understood that Brigitte's motives had been good, but what she'd done was so wrong, not telling her about the money Hunt was taking, and about the affair. She still couldn't understand why he was taking money from her, he had so much of his own. And she was just as disturbed about Hunt cheating on her. If it was true, and it probably was, he had destroyed the last bit of faith she had. Tallie lay in bed in her hotel room that night feeling sick. She wanted to call Max in New York, but she knew Max would hear it all in her mother's voice, and there was no need to upset her too, and Max was crazy about Hunt. It would be a blow to her too.

Tallie didn't bother to eat that night, all she did was cry, after working hard all day. And finally at nine o'clock she called her lawyer. He handled mostly contracts for her, but had taken care of a few personal matters too, and had managed to avert several lawsuits. She called him at home, and he came to the phone immediately after one of his children answered. Greg Thomas was an excellent attorney, and she knew he was discreet.

"Hi, Greg," she said in a mournful tone.

"Hi, what's up?" He sounded surprised to hear from her at that hour of night. Tallie wasn't the sort of client who called him at home. She was always respectful of him, and called him during business hours, so he was worried this was an emergency of some kind, and to her it was. "Something wrong?"

"Possibly. Our big investor for the new film wanted an audit, and we've been dealing with that for the last two weeks. And some things came to light as a result. Our investor gave us a clean bill of health, but I'm concerned about a couple of matters that surfaced."

"That's too bad." He was concerned for her. She sounded terrible to him. "What can I do to help you?"

"I'd like the name of a private investigator. I want to check this out, for my own peace of mind. I don't know who or what to believe right now. I've heard some pretty bad stories, and I've got a lot of cash going out the door that I can't explain. It's probably what I've been told, and none of it is pretty. It looks like Hunt is stealing money from me and cheating on me, but before I confront him, I want to be sure."

"Hunt?" He sounded shocked. He had met him several times, and knew about the movies they had worked on together. He had done a limited partnership agreement between them for the last two, and he liked him a lot.

"Yeah, Hunt. You never know about people."

"I think you're smart to check it out before you confront him. Who told you all this?"

"My accountant pointed out the missing money, and Brigitte just admitted that she knew about it, he's been pumping her for money for three years, and she knew about the affair too. She thought she was doing me a favor by not telling me."

"How well do you know her?" Greg asked coolly. He had heard stories like this before over the years.

"As well as I know myself. She's like a sister to me. She's worked for me for seventeen years, and I've never had a single problem or reason to doubt her. She comes from money, so she has no reason to steal from me, or to lie about Hunt. I would trust her with my life, my kid, and everything I have." And she had only known Hunt for four years, as opposed to Brigitte for seventeen.

"There's no telling about people. Human nature is a fearsome thing. Sometimes people who have no reason to be dishonest are pathologically unable to do the right thing." That applied to Hunt, from what she had just heard. "I'm sorry, Tallie. I know how distressing this must be." He had been through it before with clients, and it was heartbreaking to see the damage it caused, to all concerned. "I actually use a very good woman when I need an investigation done. She has her own firm, she's an ex-FBI agent. She's smart, nice, and tough as nails. I think I have her home number here. I'll give her a call right now. I'll call you back." She gave him the number at the hotel in Palm Springs, and they hung up, and while she was waiting to hear back from him, Hunt called her, and her stomach did a double flip. She didn't want to talk to him, given everything Brigitte had said, but if she wasn't going to confront him yet, she had to pretend that everything was fine. Her hand was shaking as she held the phone.

"I miss you," he said, as soon as she answered the phone. Since he was on his cell phone, she had no idea where he was and didn't trust him anymore. For all she knew, he was waiting for his girlfriend at a hotel, and planning to spend the night with her.

"I miss you too," she said quietly. Her words had a false ring to her own ears, knowing all she did now.

"How'd it go today on the set?" He sounded happy and relaxed.

"Okay. We're moving along. We should be shooting back in town again in a few weeks." But for now, she was suddenly glad they were there. It gave her a chance to breathe and figure things out away from him.

"I'll come up tomorrow, if you want," he said, sounding affectionate, and she didn't know what to say.

"Sure, that would be great, but we might have a night shoot tomorrow. If that's the case, it wouldn't be worth it, because I'll be on the set all night. I'll call you tomorrow and let you know."

"That's fine," he said easily, and then sounded rushed, as though he'd gotten to his destination and had to go. "I'll call you later," he promised, and hung up just as the phone in her room rang, and it was Greg. She was feeling ill after talking to Hunt. Everything they had had for four years suddenly seemed spoiled.

"I got her," Greg said immediately. "She said she'll make time to see you whenever you're free. I know you're on location. Can you come into town?"

"I'll do it. I think we have an easy day tomorrow." She had lied to Hunt about the night shoot to keep him away. Now she was lying too, she thought with despair. She had always thought their relationship was impeccably honest. And all Hunt had done was lie. "I could probably be in the city by six or seven, at the latest. Do you think she'll see me that late?" Tallie wanted to get the investigation started as soon as possible. She wanted to know the truth. She was miserable with it all up in the air.

"She said anytime you want. She's a kind person, and I gave her an idea what this is about. She said you can call her tonight at home. I'll give you the number."

"Thanks, Greg."

"Don't worry about it. I'm sorry you have to deal with this. Call her—she's at home right now." They hung up, and she did. Her name was Margaret Simpson, and she had a young, warm voice on the phone, but she was businesslike in what she said. Tallie gave her a brief rundown of the problem, and Meg, as she called herself, asked her a few questions that seemed run-of-the-mill to Tallie. They made an appointment to meet at her office at six o'clock the next day. There were no important scenes being shot the following day, and she was going to leave the assistant director in charge when she left, which would be a thrill for him. It was rare for Tallie to leave the set before shooting ended, but this was important. She thanked the investigator for being available to her.

"Could you bring me a couple of photographs of the subjects?" Meg asked her. "It's not vital if you can't. But it would help."

"There are good photographs of Hunt on his website, if you look it up." Tallie gave her the address. "And I've got a bunch of Brigitte at the house." She didn't want to go there before the meeting and risk running into Hunt, but then she remembered a few she had on her phone, that she had taken recently of both of them. "I can forward you a few candid shots I have of them on my phone."

"That 'll work fine," Meg assured her. "It'll give us a start. I take it you're going to want surveillance on both of them, or just Hunter Lloyd?" Tallie nearly gulped. This seemed so invasive and so mean somehow, but so did cheating and taking money.

"I don't have any reason to suspect my assistant of anything. She wouldn't take money from me, and I think all she's guilty of is not telling me what she knew about Hunt." But she had denied all the hotel charges except one or two, which didn't make sense to Tallie.

"It's up to you, but it might be smart to check them both out, and figure out what's going on. You've got a money issue happening, and a romantic issue with your man. The two aren't related, but you've got concerns about two important people in your life. You might as well know what's going on with both of them."

"I guess you're right. I think she meant well not telling me about him. She's very protective and she didn't want to upset me. But she kept it from me for a long time. She's very sorry about it now," as well she should be, Tallie thought to herself. "What do we do with the information once we have it?" Tallie asked the investigator. She was feeling overwhelmed. She had expected none of this to happen, and since Sunday her whole life had been upside down and her mind was in a whirl. She didn't feel like she was thinking clearly. The only moments of sanity she had had were on the set, when she was occupied with her work and not preoccupied about them. The rest of the time, she felt distracted and confused, and suddenly afraid of what she might learn.

"That's up to you," Meg answered. "How you handle the personal side of this is your decision. People react differently. Some of my clients find out terrible things about their mates and decide not to do anything about it. They don't want to rock the boat, and they just use the information to keep an eye on things in future and be more alert. Others make some major changes after they find out. The money is a different story. You'll probably want to confront that, and depending on what we find out, you may want to involve law enforcement. It really depends if it falls into the criminal realm or not. And you'll be the best judge about your assistant, and all of it. All I do is give you the information and enough backup so you know it's reliable, and no one is lying to you. But you're in charge."

It sounded reasonable to Tallie, given how uncomfortable the situation was. Meg would give her what she needed to make her own decisions, depending on what she heard. She couldn't imagine allowing Hunt to continue his affair, if it was true, without saying anything to him about it. If it was true, she was going to ask him to move out. And then she'd have to figure out what to do about their work together. It was all so complicated and felt like such a mess to her. But as much as this was a relationship and a person she cherished and was important to her, it wasn't a marriage, with young children involved and the kind of situation where she might want to close her eyes to his having an affair. That sounded inconceivable to her. And there was obviously nothing criminal happening. Even if he had been taking money for the past three years, she would never bring criminal charges against him. She would ask him to return the money. He could afford to, and she was sure he would. This was entirely a private matter, not a criminal one. And if Brigitte had gotten sloppy about charging things to her, like hotel stays, she would have to deal with her about it, and decide what to do. In that case, it was more about poor boundaries on her part, which wasn't okay. But that was hardly a criminal matter either.

"I don't think we'll need law enforcement," Tallie said quietly. Just a doctor for her broken heart and shattered faith. Both felt injured beyond repair right now, and no one could fix that, only time. "I don't think this is a criminal matter."

"You never know," Meg said reasonably. "We're talking about a lot of money here. You can't always tell what that will lead to, and what kind of discoveries you'll make." Tallie wondered if she should ask Meg to check Victor out too, but that seemed a little extreme. She was sure that her accountant was honest, even if he seemed distracted and over the hill, but he had picked up on the missing cash, so he wasn't completely out to lunch. But she wondered why he had never noticed it before. That seemed somewhat negligent to her. But they could always investigate him later. First, she wanted to find out what was happening with Hunt, and possibly Brigitte. "I'll see you tomorrow," Meg promised, and they hung up. As soon as they did, Tallie forwarded her the three photographs she had on her phone of Brigitte, and two of Hunt. And as soon as the photographs went through, her cell phone rang and told her it was Brigitte.

Tallie answered, and it sounded to Brigitte as though Tallie had been crying.

"Is there anything I can do for you?" Brigitte asked, sounding miserable.

"No, I'm fine." Tallie sounded sad and distant.

"I know you're not. If it's any consolation, I feel terrible too. I'm sorry I handled this all wrong. I'll never do anything like it again. My first instinct is always to shield you from everything. It was entirely the wrong thing to do here." They both knew that was true, and Brigitte wondered if Tallie would actually fire her. She wasn't going to ask again, and just prayed that she wouldn't, and could eventually forgive her so they could move forward together. But there would surely be changes now with Hunt. It didn't seem to either of them as though there were any other choice. Tallie didn't tell her about the investigator, thanked her for the call, and lay on her bed, thinking for a long time. Hunt didn't call her back that night, and she didn't call him. He texted her that he loved her and told her to sleep tight, and she wondered if he was with the girl from his office that Brigitte had told her about. Maybe that was why he hadn't called. Tallie just read the text message with tears rolling down her cheeks and didn't answer him. There was nothing left to say until she knew what was going on. She was relieved to be going to see the investigator the next day. And in her room, Brigitte was crying too.

Chapter 7

Tallie quietly told the assistant director on the set the next day that he'd be taking over for her when she left at four o'clock. They were reshooting some minor scenes that day and doing reverses, where the cameraman had to shoot the actors' backs for a variety of camera angles in important scenes. She didn't need to be there for that, and the assistant director was pleased to take over for her. She didn't say anything to Brigitte until right before she left.

"I'm going back to town," she told

her. There was a definite distance between them at the moment, but no one
else had noticed. It weighed on Brigitte
every time she looked at her. For the
first time in seventeen years, Tallie was
being distant and aloof. She was trying
to process all that had happened, and
make her peace with Brigitte's silence
for so long. Brigitte understood it, but it
hurt anyway.

"Do you want me to drive you?" Brigitte offered, assuming that she would.

"No, I'm fine. I need some time to
myself right now," she said, and Brigitte
nodded. "I'm taking one of the SUVs
from the set till Monday." Brigitte nodded her understanding. "You can go
back to town now if you want," Tallie
told her, and Brigitte said she was staying in Palm Springs for the weekend.
She didn't tell Tallie, but she had been
planning to come back anyway, to
spend the time with the young actor
she was having the affair with. They
were going to hide out together until
Monday, although a few people already
suspected their involvement, and Tallie
had heard about it too. But she hadn't

said anything to Brigitte. Her sex life was her own business, and one of the perks she enjoyed about her work, an unlimited supply of young actors for her personal entertainment. Tallie never paid attention to it, nor acknowledged that she knew.

Tallie left quietly and drove off in the SUV, after telling the head writer to be sure and fax her the script changes at home over the weekend. She wasn't in the mood, but she told herself she couldn't get sloppy or lazy about work just because her home life was falling apart. She was always conscientious and diligent and disciplined, even if her heart was breaking.

It took her two hours to get back to the city, and she was at Margaret Simpson's office on the dot of six o'clock. She had worn a torn T-shirt, jeans, and a pair of disreputable-looking old sneakers. It had never even occurred to her to dress for the appointment. She had too much on her mind to care, and she had come right from the set, and the investigator didn't seem to notice. She noted silently how beautiful Tallie was and wondered if she dressed that way because she was so upset about her boyfriend and assistant, or because she was working. She didn't know it was her personal style.

Meg was wearing a navy pantsuit with a white blouse, her long dark hair sleekly pulled back in a smooth pony- tail, and very little makeup. She looked like a doctor or a lawyer, and it was easy to believe she had been an FBI agent. She had a very official way about her, and an air of authority. She was forty-two years old, and had been in private practice for ten years, since she'd left the FBI, gotten married, and had children. She had spent ten years in the FBI before that, she explained to Tallie, to assure her of her skills and cre- dentials. But what Greg had told her was enough. Tallie trusted her com- pletely.

Meg asked her a long list of ques- tions about Hunt and Brigitte, mostly about the places they went and their personal habits. Tallie gave her the de- scriptions of their cars, and Hunt's li- cense plate number. She didn't have

Brigitte's, but her car was distinctive, and would be easy to follow. And Meg knew how to get all the information she needed from the DMV. It wasn't a problem. She had Brigitte's home address from Tallie, and then Tallie remembered to tell Meg that Brigitte was planning to stay in Palm Springs for the weekend, with a man, she assumed. She gave her the names of the institutions where they both did their banking, the names of the two hotels that were on her credit card and Brigitte had signed for. And then she told her what Brigitte had told her about the young woman in Hunt's office. She didn't know her name. All she had to go on was what Brigitte knew about her. But it was more than enough for Meg to get started and assign private investigators to them. Tallie agreed that they were both to be under surveillance until further notice, whenever Meg felt she had enough information for Tallie to come to some conclusions.

Meg explained to Tallie what her rates were, which sounded reasonable. She had expected it to be expensive, and it was, but it was worth it to her. She wanted to know everything she could now. She suspected that the surveillance on Brigitte would be useless since her personal life and who she was sleeping with didn't interest Tallie. It was Hunt she was concerned about. But she also told her about Brigitte's history, the wealthy family in San Francisco, her trust fund, and all the perks she derived from being Tallie's assistant, which made her even less likely to be stealing money. She had no reason to. And Brigitte received everything she could possibly need as gifts in the job, everything from designer clothes to jewelry and complimentary weekends at fancy hotels. Brigitte had as little need to steal from her as Hunt did, although she didn't make nearly as much money, but Meg wanted to get all the background on them she could, in order to do a thorough investigation.

Tallie reminded her again before she left that her main focus of interest was Hunt, and whatever Meg could find out about another woman, and whether or not he was really having an affair. The missing money was important too, but harder to explain since neither of them had any reason to be stealing from her. It made no sense, but neither did his cheating, since they were happy. She wondered now if he had only stayed with her in order to protect the movies they made together. Maybe that was his only interest in her, and why he was having an affair. The whole thing was incredibly hurtful, and she wanted to get to the bottom of it as soon as she could. She knew that Meg wasn't going to be able to tell her Hunt's motivations, but at least she would know if he was involved with someone else, how long it had been going on, and how serious it was. She didn't want to just trust Brigitte's information. And Brigitte had told her two small lies initially about the hotels, although her lies where harmless, but they were lies.

Meg said she would get in touch with her, and call her to give her a progress report in a few days. Tallie trusted her complete discretion, and Meg looked reassuring as she walked Tallie out of her office. It was just after eight o'clock.

Tallie wondered if Hunt was already at home, but didn't want to call him. He hadn't called her so far that evening. She had gotten a text from Brigitte saying that she hoped she had gotten home safely, and wishing her a nice weekend. Clearly, Brigitte was running scared, which saddened Tallie too. Her two most important relationships, other than her father and daughter, had taken heavy hits that week, possibly fatal ones. It remained to be seen in the coming days how great the damage was.

She felt numb as she left Meg's office, and on the spur of the moment, she stopped at her father's house on the way home. Amelia, his housekeeper, came in to take care of him during the daytime, and the rest of the time he still managed on his own. He had been a tall, handsome man in his youth, and looked a great deal like Tallie, but at eighty-five, riddled with arthritis, he appeared old and bent as he came to the door with his walker. But his eyes were as fiery and alive as they had ever been. His spirit was the same as it had been when he was in command of his cases in the courtroom. He looked worried when he opened the door to his daughter and saw how sad she looked.

"Well, isn't this a nice surprise," he said, smiling at her, and moved his walker aside so she could come in. He had just finished the dinner that Amelia had left for him. He led a lonely life, was rarely able to get out, and a visit from her was always a treat. "What brings you here?"

"I was on my way home. How are you, Dad?" She leaned over to kiss his cheek and sat down in the living room with him. It pained her to see his struggle to lower himself onto the couch, and she worried about him too. Her worst fear was always that he would fall and hit his head or injure himself in some other way, but he was stubborn and insisted on living alone.

"I'm concerned about you. What have you found out about those spreadsheets I looked at?" They were a grave concern to him. If someone was stealing from her, the cash that seemed to have gone missing represented a great deal of money, and he knew how hard she worked for it. He had never been a rich man, but he had done well and was comfortable and had helped her whenever he could, particularly in the beginning, but her real success was only thanks to herself and her own hard work and enormous talent. He was immensely proud of her, and now her daughter Maxine. And he knew how thrilled Tallie's mother would have been with her too. The look of pain in Tallie's eyes as she gazed at him made his heart ache for her.

"I just hired a private investigator," she answered him. She took a deep breath. "I don't know anything yet. I hope I do soon. Right now, none of it makes any sense. Brigitte says that Hunt is involved with another woman. I've got some hotel bills they're both lying about, although Brigitte finally confessed about that. And there's no reason for either of them to be stealing money from me. They don't need it. I just don't get it." She looked tired and depressed. The whole thing was immensely distressing, and he was distraught about it too.

"Could it be anyone else?"

"I just don't see who. Maybe it's something my accountant is doing. Business managers and accountants steal from people like me all the time. But he seems so respectable and serious, I can't see him doing this either. And why now? He's been doing my accounts for nearly twenty years. And that still doesn't explain Hunt cheating on me, if he is." She still hoped in her heart of hearts that Brigitte was wrong and it would turn out not to be true.

"Maybe your accountant is in some kind of financial trouble. People's circumstances change. You should have him checked out too."

"I will. But I want to know what's going on with Hunt and Brigitte first. I want to know who I can trust. And even if he's not stealing from me, Hunt could be cheating on me." They both knew that was true.

"I hope he isn't," Sam said unhappily. "I like him a lot. I always have." And he thought he was good for Tallie. Or had been until now.

"Yeah, me too," Tallie said glumly, and it was going to be really difficult to act as though nothing was happening now while she waited to find out. "Have you had dinner yet?" she asked her father with a look of concern, and he nodded.

"I want you to take care of yourself," he admonished her with a fatherly look. "This is very hard on you."

"No kidding." She smiled ruefully. "I feel like my whole life went down the tubes this week. I've been avoiding Max. I don't want to tell her about any of this yet. She loves Hunt too." And she had had so few male role models in her life that Tallie didn't want to spoil their relationship, at least not yet, until she knew if he was cheating on her or not. She hoped that the story Brigitte had told her wasn't true. Maybe he was just concerned about the girl in his office and had been kind to her, without it being an affair. For the moment, it was a slim hope, but she was clinging to it until she knew more.

Tallie and her father chatted for a little while, and then she went home. Hunt was out and had left her a note. He was having drinks with Mr. Nakamura's lawyers. They were getting the last details of the contract worked out, and he said he wouldn't be home late. He got home shortly after she did and was tired. Tallie looked exhausted and was lying on the bed.

"You look beat," he commented, as he took his jacket off and threw it on a chair.

"I am," she said without moving from their bed. "It's been a tough week."

"At least you'll be home from location soon. I miss you when you're gone," he said with a smile and sat down on the bed next to her. She didn't know whether to hit him or cry, or take him in her arms and hold on for dear life. She didn't want to lose him, but maybe she already had.

"Do you?" she asked, her voice small and muffled in his chest.

"Of course I do, silly. Do you want to go out to dinner?" She shook her head.

She was too tired and down to want to go out.

"Not really."

"I can rustle something up here." She nodded, wondering how many more nights like this she would have with him, how many home-cooked dinners and sharing the same bed. If Meg told her that he was involved with someone else, this was all going to be over, and she realized that it was possible their days were numbered. The very thought of it wore her out, and made her immeasurably sad. She already felt as though she had lost him. In her gut, she believed what Brigitte had said, and feared it might be true. It had happened to her before, though not after four years. This time she had thought she was safe and home free. Maybe not.

He went downstairs then and made an omelette and a salad for both of them. He opened a bottle of her favorite wine, and they sat quietly in the kitchen and ate dinner. Tallie was very quiet, and he put some music on. But she couldn't think of anything to say to him. He asked how the last two days of shooting had gone, and told her about his meetings with their investor's lawyers, and he said everything was going well. And after dinner, Tallie took a shower and went to bed. She had hardly said a word all night.

"Are you okay?" he asked, looking worried about her. She was painfully subdued.

"I think I might be coming down with something," she said vaguely. "I've been feeling weird since yesterday."

"Then get some sleep," he said, tucking her in, and he went downstairs to his office to look over some papers the lawyers had given him to read. And she pretended to be asleep when he came back upstairs. She felt like she was living a nightmare with him. It was a lonely feeling, and when he turned off the light, there were silent tears rolling slowly down her cheeks.

She went to the gym early the next morning, and called Max in New York afterward. She was out with friends for lunch in some noisy place, and Tallie was relieved. It was hard to talk and Max said she'd call her later, so she didn't hear the tone of despair in her mother's voice.

Hunt played tennis with friends that afternoon, while Tallie read new script changes and added to them, and he suggested they go to a movie that night. Tallie felt as though she were moving underwater and they were moving in slow motion. She wondered how long the investigation would take. It felt like an eternity and had only been a day, if that.

She realized that one of Meg's investigators must have followed them when they went to the movie, but she had no sense of it. Meg had assured her that they were good, and Tallie knew they must be. There was nothing to suggest that they were being followed or watched. When she looked around, she saw no one. And Hunt suspected nothing.

It felt like the longest weekend of Tallie's life. They took her father to lunch at the Ivy the next day, at Hunt's suggestion. It was a production taking him out, but Hunt had always been sweet about doing things like that, which made Tallie even sadder now. What if that was all over? She could see why people didn't confront a cheating spouse, as Meg had said. There was so much to lose. But she couldn't see living with him if she knew he was being unfaithful to her. She couldn't have done it, but losing her life with him would be hard if that was what happened in the end.

Lunch at the Ivy was busy and noisy and her father made an effort to appear normal, but she knew he was as disturbed as she was. They sat on the terrace and saw several people they knew. Tallie could barely get through the charade and was relieved when it was over.

Brigitte checked in with Tallie twice over the weekend, which was unusual for her, and she sounded uncomfortable too. She said that she was enjoying the spa in Palm Springs, but Tallie suspected that if she had been, she wouldn't have called. Brigitte was clearly worried. And so was Tallie. Only Hunt was oblivious to what was happening and thought she was sick. He made a gentle attempt to make love to her on Sunday night, but Tallie just couldn't. She wanted to wait for Meg's report now, and she told him she thought she had the flu. He brought her dinner on a tray and made her chicken soup, which nearly made her cry.

"You don't have to spoil me like that," she said sadly.

"I want to. I love you, Tallie," he said, and sounded so sincere. It made her wonder if Brigitte was wrong and had heard inaccurate office gossip. She didn't know what to believe. More than anything, she felt confused. And they chatted like old friends while she ate her soup. He tucked her into bed afterward, with a kiss, but she couldn't sleep. She'd had nightmares all night whenever she did.

She drove herself back to Palm Springs on Monday morning in the SUV she'd borrowed from the set, and she was in her trailer by six A.M. She tried to rouse herself to think about her work, but everything was hard right now and took ten times the effort it normally did to get her motor running and concentrate on the film.

She handed the script changes back

to the writers, and by eight the cameras were rolling and they were back to work. Brigitte had gone to L.A. for the day, to do some work, and she didn't come back to Palm Springs until Tuesday. Brigitte arrived in the Aston Martin, looking as sexy as ever. She put on a big show of being jolly and in good spirits. She had brought Tallie her mail from the city and had a number of things to show her. Tallie pretended to be interested but she wasn't. She didn't care about anything right now except what she was waiting to hear from Meg. It was Thursday when Meg finally called, six days after they had met. They had been the longest six days of Tallie's life.

"How are you?" Meg asked her politely. She sounded businesslike and cool, and Tallie wanted to scream at her to tell her everything immediately. She couldn't wait a minute longer, but that wasn't the way Meg worked. She was professional and precise.

"I've been going crazy waiting to hear from you," Tallie said honestly. She was in her room at the hotel, and hadn't gone back to L.A. all week. She told

Hunt she was still feeling sick, was too tired to drive back to L.A. at night, and didn't want to expose him to her flu.

"I'm sorry," Meg said quietly. "Sometimes it takes a few days to get the lay of the land. This is actually pretty quick for us, but I know it must seem long to you." It was the understatement of the year.

"Interminable," Tallie said grimly as she lay on her bed. "Can you tell me what's going on?"

"I'd rather we meet face-to-face. I can come out there if you like. When are you coming back to town?"

"Tomorrow night, or maybe in the late afternoon." Part of her wanted to press Meg to tell her now, and part of her didn't. She was afraid to hear the results of her investigation. What if she hated what she heard?

"I'm clear anytime tomorrow," Meg said crisply.

"Four o'clock?" Tallie suggested. "I'll try to get out of here after lunch." She could drive herself in again, and she was going home for the weekend. She had kept her dealings superficial with

Brigitte all week, or avoided her completely. She wasn't comfortable with her
at the moment. Tallie felt as though she
had been blindfolded and didn't know
where she was, or with whom, or who
to trust. Her confidence in the people
closest to her had been shaken, until
she talked to Meg. Only she could reassure her, and Tallie didn't know if she
would, or make it infinitely worse with
her report. She was dreading what
she'd hear.

"Four is fine," Meg confirmed. Tallie
didn't ask her if the report was good or
bad. She was too afraid to know, without the details. And she was awake all
night after they spoke.

The shoot the next day seemed endless and her nerves were on edge. She
had a meeting over lunch in her trailer
with the writers, and as soon as it was
finished, she took off, without saying
goodbye to Brigitte or anyone else. The
AD was taking over for her again and
seemed pleased. And Tallie kept her
foot on the gas all the way to L.A. She
was at Meg's office at four o'clock
sharp, with her heart pounding. She felt

her stomach tie in a knot as Meg's secretary showed her in.

Meg stood up with a warm smile as Tallie walked into her office, and she invited her to sit down across her desk. Tallie had never been as nervous about any meeting, or as frightened about what she was going to hear. Meg's face gave away nothing, she was a pro. But she looked sympathetic, which Tallie read as a bad sign.

"Well, I think we have what you wanted to know. Not all of it, after this brief an investigation, but enough to give you a general picture." Tallie noticed she had a thick file on her desk with a number code on it, which represented Tallie's case. She was discreet if nothing else.

"We've been following Hunter Lloyd since last week, and doing a superficial assessment of his financial situation. There are records we don't have access to, like his bank records, but we checked his credit, spoke to some people at his bank, and investigated as much as we could about how he spends his money. He has a big income, as you know. And his assets are solidly invested in a diversified portfolio. Everything we found tells us that he's financially sound. He's not afraid to spend money, as you probably also know. He drives a Bentley sports model that he owns, he has solid real estate holdings and investments. He's not irresponsible about his money, and it looks like just about all his purchases and transactions are done by credit card. There is absolutely nothing we turned up that suggests he's in financial trouble, needs money, or has a shady reputation. He has an A1 credit rating, and from what I was able to find out, he seems to make no purchases with cash. All the stores he deals with are paid by credit card. In fact, he seems to charge everything. There can always be something hidden we didn't find—this was really an initial investigation, not a forensic financial one—but he looks solid as a rock financially, and my gut tells me that he's not stealing cash from you. He has absolutely no reason to. Another three hundred thousand dollars a year would be nice, but he just

doesn't need your money." Tallie nodded as she listened. It was reassuring,
but if what Meg said was true, then Brigitte was lying, which was upsetting
too. But at least Hunt was clean about
the money. It was what she had thought
too. Why would Hunt steal from her?
There was just no reason to, he had a
lot more than she did, and he wasn't a
greedy person. He had always been
generous with her, and paid way more
than his share of their expenses. As far
as the money went, Brigitte's story
didn't hold water.

"The rest of what we found out about
Mr. Lloyd is more disturbing. Our
sources were consistent and told us
that he has been involved with this
young woman in his office for about a
year. It may have begun as a situation of
sympathy. She was in fact the victim of
domestic violence from her estranged
husband. She took him to court repeat-
edly over it, was hospitalized once, and
is currently waiting for her final decree
of dissolution, in about two months. Her
ex-husband was jailed twice for abusing her and their son. The boy is three

years old. And she does work for Mr. Lloyd. He sees her in the evening several times a week, meets her at the Chateau Marmont and Sunset Marquis, and spends the night with her frequently when you're out of town. He stayed with her three times this week. She leaves the child with a neighbor, and they usually go to a hotel. She may be afraid to have him stay at her house in case her ex-husband is watching or stalking her. They seem to spend a lot of time together." And with that, she took several blown-up photographs out of the file on her desk, and spread them in front of Tallie. He was kissing a beautiful dark-haired young woman in one of them, and in another he had an arm around her shoulders and was holding a little boy's hand, at the zoo. Meg pointed to the photograph and explained that it had been taken the previous Saturday. Tallie remembered that he had told her he was playing tennis with friends. Instead he had gone to the zoo with this woman and her son. The little boy looked very cute.

"Her name is Angela Morissey. She is

twenty-six years old. And he has told
several people he plans to marry her.
She believes that to be true too. And
she has told people that in confidence."

She showed Tallie several more pictures of them then, going to a movie,
coming out of a restaurant with the boy,
and getting out of his car at the Sunset
Marquis. He looked like he had a whole
life with her, and they both looked
happy whenever they were together.
Tallie suddenly wondered if she had let
him down in some way, if she complained too much, or wasn't as much
fun, or was too tired after working too
hard. Or was she too old since the girl
was so much younger? Why had he
done this to her? She had to fight back
tears as she looked at the photographs.
It nearly broke her heart to see them,
and he looked like he loved the little
boy.

"There is a previous history here as
well," Meg went on, looking slightly
apologetic. She could see how shaken
Tallie was, and had known she would
be. This was like being brought into the
doctor's office to be told you had can-

cer, instead of getting a phone call to say you had a clean test. There was nothing clean about this. Hunt had been cheating on her with this woman for a year. For an entire year, he had lied to her, and been sleeping with someone else. And in the photographs he looked happy and in love. And the girl was gorgeous and thirteen years younger than Tallie.

"In the course of our investigation, we were told that he had another involvement before this, with another woman. We have a full description of her, but no photographs. We can research it further if you like, but I don't think it's necessary. He also met her at the Chateau Marmont and Sunset Marquis several times a week during their involvement. He's been a regular in both places for several years. The woman before this one was mid to late thirties, blond, very beautiful, very sexy, looks like an actress. They were involved for approximately three years, and her first name is Brigitte."

As she said it, Tallie nearly threw up on the desk. She stared at Meg in disbelief and horror, as the investigator handed her a glass of water. Tallie took a sip and set it down on the desk, and looked at Meg blindly as she went on.

"It sounds like it was your assistant, from everything we heard about her." It also explained the credit card charges Brigitte had signed several times at the two hotels until a year ago. Either she had been careless, or maybe she'd gotten to the hotel first, and since Tallie never looked at the bills, she had never expected her to see them, until Victor's recent audit. And it had stopped a year ago when Hunt got involved with the other girl. And God only knew how many others there had been. "All our sources say that their affair stopped when he got involved with Miss Morissey, and supposedly Brigitte is very angry about it. In addition, although your assistant makes a great deal of money, she has a considerable amount of debt, her credit is not flawless, and you appear to be her only source of income. All of those records are not available to us since we're not a government agency, but we saw nothing to suggest she gets money from her family. And she spends a *lot*. And she is currently having an affair with a young man named Tommy Apple, who is a minor actor in the movie you're filming. She spent last weekend with him, and they've been together since filming started. It doesn't sound like a serious affair." She showed her several photographs of Brigitte with Tommy, which Tallie didn't care about. What she cared about was that Hunt and Brigitte had betrayed her. And his three years with her and one year with this new woman meant that Hunt had cheated on her for all four years they were together. For the entire time, he had been seeing someone else, and Brigitte, the person she had trusted most in the world, had had an affair with her boyfriend for three years. They had both betrayed her totally. And as hurt as she was by Hunt, she was even more so by Brigitte. He had turned out to be just another asshole who was lying to her and cheating, Brigitte had been her best and closest friend for seventeen years, since they were barely more than kids. It was a blow she hadn't expected and it hit her like a wrecking ball as she stared at Meg in disbelief.

"Are you sure?" Tallie said in a hoarse voice.

"I believe so. Our sources seemed very sure of what they were saying. The evidence seems to be pretty glaring." She looked deeply regretful to be reporting it to Tallie, and she felt sincerely sorry for her. It was a terrible shock for Tallie. And even if the report of Hunt's affair with Brigitte was wrong, which seemed unlikely, he was clearly involved with someone else now. She was thirteen years younger than Tallie, and he seemed to be deeply committed to her and her little boy. And all Tallie could think was that he was a cheater to the core, with no integrity or decency at all. And Brigitte was no better.

"I want to pursue another subject with you," Meg said quietly. "The disappearing cash. I think that's a very serious issue. I'd like to see you go to law enforcement with this. I think you need to pursue it before you lose more, and possibly you already have. We don't have the access that a law enforcement agency has to investigate bank records and financial matters. I don't think Hunter Lloyd is involved here, but you never know. It could be that several people are ripping you off, and not just one, or it could be a clever embezzler. You need to know. I'd like to see you investigate Hunter Lloyd further, just to be sure, your assistant Brigitte Parker, and your accountant Victor Carson. You just don't know what people are capable of. And you've already had a loss of close to a million dollars," Meg reminded her. "This is no small thing, and it could be a lot bigger than you already know." This had been a double hit, a triple. Her boyfriend had cheated on her for four years, her best friend had betrayed her with him, and someone was stealing money from her, in vast amounts. Tallie wanted to lie down on the floor and sob, but she maintained her composure and listened to what Meg had to say.

"Who would I go to?" Tallie asked her, feeling lost.

"I've spoken to one of my previous colleagues at the FBI, without telling him your name of course. I refer cases to him from time to time. I explained the situation to him, and he'd like to talk to you. It could be that this isn't a federal matter, there would have to be wire fraud involved, and bank fraud of some kind, but I suspect that's very likely with someone stealing in these amounts. Twenty-five thousand dollars a month is a lot of money. I think you should talk to the FBI, and have them investigate it, if they're willing. If not, you can go to the district attorney and the police, but I'd much rather see you in the hands of the FBI. I think they'll pay much closer attention and get to the bottom of it faster. If you'd like, my ex-associate said he'd be happy to meet you anytime this weekend. I strongly urge you to do that, whatever else you do about the other issues involved." She wrote down a name and cell phone number on a piece of paper and handed it to Tallie. "His name is Jim Kingston and he'll be expecting your call," she said gently. She could see how hard all of this had just been for Tallie. It was the worst she could have imagined, and not in a million years had she expected Brigitte to be involved with Hunt.

"What do I do now?"

"I would talk to Jim Kingston first, before you accuse your assistant. There may be some value in discretion and even stealth. He may want to do some investigation of her bank records before you alert her that she's been caught, or is under suspicion, if it's her. Ask for his advice. I think the matter is less sensitive and more awkward for you with Hunter Lloyd, given the situation. But in Brigitte's case, I would be cautious and line up all your ducks before you accuse her. You don't want to warn her and have her steal an even larger amount before she goes. And I wouldn't discuss the money issues with Hunter Lloyd either, or your accountant. I hope you call Jim."

"I will," Tallie promised her, and meant it as she put the piece of paper in her purse, and then she just sat and stared at Meg for a minute. "Thank you." She didn't know what else to say as she stood up. She felt completely disoriented and as though she were drowning.

"I'm sorry to give you such bad news." It was what she hated most about her job. Finding the puzzle pieces and fitting them together was fascinating, but doing what she had just done to Tallie and seeing the look in her eyes made her heart ache, and Tallie looked like a nice woman. Greg Thomas, her attorney, had said she was. Meg stood up to walk Tallie out of her office then, and told her to call if she could be of any further help. Tallie nodded, barely able to say anything as Meg handed her the file. "We have copies of all of this. You might want this for your records." Tallie clutched it to her with tears in her eyes. In it were the photographs of Hunt with the other woman, and the reports of their investigation and surveillance on him and Brigitte. Just having it was depressing. She wished she could throw it away and turn back the clock.

"Thank you very much," Tallie said softly. "I'll call the FBI man tonight."

"I hope you do," Meg encouraged her. "You really need to investigate this further." Tallie nodded again, and left the office. She almost stumbled as she walked back to the car. All she could think of were the things that Meg had said to her, about Hunt, about Brigitte, about the young woman with the little boy. She couldn't stop thinking of the photograph of him kissing her. She threw the file on the seat next to her, started the car, and drove away as she began to sob.

Chapter 8

Tallie was planning to call the FBI agent when she got back to her house, but she was crying too hard. Hunt was out, the house was dark, and she just sat in the living room, clutching the investigation folder to her chest, and cried. She hated everything in it, and everything Meg had told her. But she couldn't run away from it now. She opened the folder after a few minutes and looked at the photographs again as she continued to cry. She looked at the one of him kissing Angela Morissey and holding her little boy's hand at the zoo, only six days before. She felt as though her whole life had come down like a house of cards.

She was still sitting in the dark, when Hunt came home an hour later. He had a bag of groceries in his arms, and walked into the kitchen without noticing Tallie in the dark. She stood up and followed him into the kitchen like a ghost, and he gave a start when he saw her. She looked ravaged as she stood watching him. She still had the folder in her arms.

"Are you still sick? Poor baby, you look awful. You should be in bed. I'll make you some soup," he said. He was in good spirits, and she didn't even want to try to imagine why. God only knew what he'd been doing before he came home. She wondered why he even bothered if Angela was telling people they were getting married and he was spending every free night with her. She realized now that all the times he had told her he had been with their Japanese investor, it probably wasn't true. Their whole life together was a lie. He probably hadn't stolen her money, but he had broken her heart. "Are you okay?" The look on her face scared him. She looked as though she had drifted in from another world, like a ghost. She looked transparent she was so pale.

Without saying a word, she took one of the photographs out of the folder and held it up to him. He glanced at it, wondering what it was, and then his eyes widened, and he stopped dead in his tracks and stared at her. He looked as though he was about to faint, which was how Tallie felt too.

"Nice tennis game you had last weekend," she said softly, as his eyes met hers.

"Why did you do that?" he asked her, visibly near tears himself as she started to cry again. "You didn't have to do that. I would have told you if you'd asked me."

"I didn't know until I saw this. I had to have you followed to find out. She says you're getting married. Are you?" He didn't answer for a long moment.

"I don't know. I don't know what I'm doing. I never meant for it to happen. I

felt sorry for her. I tried to help her. She
wound up in the hospital when her husband beat her up. And then somehow I
got involved . . . Tallie, I love you both. I
love everything about our life together,
and our work . . . but she's a sweet girl
and she needs me." He sounded pathetic as she listened, and weak, as he
made excuses for what he'd done. It
was all so predictable, and so sad.

"I need you too," she said as she
cried.

He took a breath then and decided to
say it all. He had been putting the groceries away and the refrigerator was
still standing open as Hunt and Tallie
looked at each other.

"She just found out she's pregnant.
That complicates things even more." It
was so ridiculous, like a bad soap
opera, but it still didn't explain what
he'd done before with Brigitte.

"What about Brigitte? Did she need
you too?" Tallie's eyes grew hard as
they bored into his, and he gave a
groan.

"Oh my God. Did she tell you?"

"No. She lied too. You both did. For three years."

"You were on location. She was helping me get organized a few months after we started, before I moved in, when I was staying here one weekend. I thought it was very nice of her to help. We drank a lot of wine one night, and don't ask me how, but I wound up in bed with her, which was the dumbest thing I ever did. I talked to her about it the next day, and she wouldn't let me off the hook. She blackmailed me and said that if I tried to get out of it, she would tell you. I was in love with you, and I didn't want to lose you. For three miserable years I let her threaten me into meeting her twice a week. They were the worst three years of my life. I never loved her. I just didn't know how to get out of it without blowing my life apart. She kept threatening me that she'd tell you if I stopped. And then Angela came along, and somehow I got out of it with Brigitte, and I called her bluff. But I fell in love with Angela, and now I love you both. I don't blame you if you hate me, but honestly, Tallie, I love you and I don't know what to do." She had never seen anyone unravel as quickly as he did. But there was no excuse for what he'd done with Angela or Brigitte, even if what he said about her assistant was true. After all that she had learned that afternoon, anything was possible now. But if what he said was correct, he'd slept with Brigitte almost right from the beginning of his affair with Tallie.

"Will you give Angela up?" Tallie asked him in a strong, clear voice that surprised them both, and he stood there staring at her with a devastated expression, unable to answer.

"She wants to have our baby," he said in a strangled voice finally.

"And what do you want? Angela or me? You can't have us both. You've cheated on me for four years, Hunt, the whole time we've been together. I don't know if I could ever trust you again. Probably not." And then she surprised herself. "I might be willing to try, but you would have to swear to me to give her up."

Tears rolled down his cheeks as he

looked at Tallie, and they both knew the truth before he even answered. "I can't," he said softly. "I can't do that to her. Not now."

"And if she weren't having the baby?"

"I don't know. I love her and her little boy . . . and you. Christ, what a fucking disaster this is," he said as he sat down hard in one of the kitchen chairs and slammed the refrigerator door. "Why did you go to a detective?" He was angry at her, but more so at himself.

"Because of the money, and the hotel bills. You told Victor you went to those hotels with me, and it was a lie. Everything was a lie," she said, sobbing again. And all she wanted to do was turn the clock back. But she couldn't turn it back far enough. He had cheated on her the whole time, and if what he had said about Brigitte was true, it was yet another nightmare that she had to deal with too. She had lost two of the people she loved most.

"I'm not stealing your money," he said in a rough voice.

"I know, I believe you. But you lied about everything else. Our whole life together was a lie. You cheated on me the whole time."

"I didn't mean to," he said weakly.

"But you did anyway. And now you don't want to give this girl up. That tells me all I need to know. I'm not going to sit here, while you have an affair, and a baby, with someone else."

"I understand," he said in a dead voice. "What do you want me to do now?"

"If you won't agree to stop seeing her, I want you to move out." He nodded. What she really wanted was for him to love her and give up Angela, but she could see he wouldn't. He was hooked. You could see in the pictures the way he looked at her. He hadn't looked at Tallie that way in years. Or maybe ever.

"I never wanted it to be like this, and I didn't want you to find out this way," he said miserably.

"Then you should have told me."

"I didn't know how."

"The private investigator did it for you. And I guess one picture is worth a thousand words." She glanced at the photo of him kissing Angela and he winced.

"Tallie, I'm so sorry," he said as he walked across the kitchen to her and tried to put his arms around her, as she pulled away from him.

"Don't!" she said as she put a hand up to push him away. "Don't make it worse than it is. I think a year of Angela and nearly three of Brigitte is enough, and you could have gotten out of that if you'd wanted to."

"You don't know what she's really like. I didn't want her spoiling everything for us."

"You did anyway, and you went on sleeping with her for three years." It was all hard to believe. And all the while she had thought she was happy at last and he was the best man in the world, while he cheated on her. "I'm not going to make the next movie with you, Hunt," she added then, and he looked pained.

"Let's not try to solve everything in one night."

"There's nothing to solve. If you're staying with Angela, I'm done. And I'm not going to work with a man who did

this to me, and who's this dishonest."
He had proven that he had no integrity
at all. He didn't answer, he just sat looking at her with eyes full of embarrassment and despair. He had made a mess
of everything, right from the beginning,
and it had taken four years to come
home to roost but it finally had. "I want
you to move out now," Tallie said in a
choked voice. She didn't know what
else to do. She couldn't spend another
night with him, in their bedroom, in the
same bed, knowing that he was in love
with another woman and having a child
with her, even if he said he loved her
too.

"I'll get some things," he said quietly.
"I'll come back for the rest when you're
in Palm Springs."

"I'll send them to you," she said, as
he walked toward her. He tried to reach
out to her again, and she took a step
back. Her eyes burned holes into his,
and he could feel her pain searing
through him. It made him realize what
he'd done. He had Angela and their
baby, but he realized then that Tallie had
lost everything, and she looked bereft

as he walked by. He had done a terrible thing, and he knew it. Brigitte had been evil and cunning, but he had been weak. And he should never have gotten involved with Angela either. He had gone to the hospital to see her, just to be nice to her, and the next thing he knew he was in love with her and never wanted to leave her or her son. But now it meant leaving Tallie. Whatever he did, someone was going to get hurt, or all of them. And the last thing he had wanted to do was hurt Tallie, which was why he had put it off for so long. And now it had exploded, and they'd all been blown to bits, and his life with Tallie was destroyed. But he didn't want to stay with her either. He couldn't leave Angela now, particularly not with their baby. He had no other choice. And he knew it as he went upstairs to pack.

He came back downstairs ten minutes later with a small bag in his hand. He had some clothes at Angela's place anyway, and he could buy whatever he needed. He didn't know what to say to Tallie as he stood looking at her from the doorway. Without a word, he went to put his arms around her, and she let him and broke into a wracking sob. He held her as long as he could before he made promises he knew he couldn't keep, and then he gently let her go and walked out the door with tears running down his cheeks. He didn't look back at her as he closed the door softly behind him, and a moment later she heard his car drive away, and she looked around her empty house sobbing. She didn't know where to run from the pain or what to do. She just stood there crying, thinking about Hunt with Angela and their baby, and what Brigitte had done with him. She had been betrayed by them all.

Chapter 9

Tallie cried herself to sleep on Friday night, and she woke up on Saturday morning feeling as though she'd been on a two-week drunk. Every inch of her body ached, and her head hurt from crying. She could hardly get out of bed, and didn't even want to. She walked downstairs to the kitchen, thinking about what the rest of her life would be like without Hunt. She worried that she had been hasty in her decision or reaction, and as she sat huddled over a cup of tea, she realized again that she'd had no other choice. He wouldn't give up

Angela and their baby, and he had cheated on her for all four years they'd been together. She would never have trusted him again. There had never been a time when he was faithful or honest with her. It was just too much to forgive. There had been no choice except for him to leave. But the emptiness she felt around her sucked the air out of her like a vacuum. Her life felt like a wasteland, and she knew that she would miss him. No matter how dishonest he had been, he had always been so sweet to her, and to Max, and she had loved living and working with him. She thought they were so happy. She didn't have the heart to tell her daughter yet that he was gone, and when Max called her later that morning, Tallie didn't take the call. She knew she couldn't have talked to her without sobbing. She needed some time to absorb what had happened before she told Max. Tallie knew that she would be crushed too. She loved Hunt.

She remembered then the FBI agent that the investigator had wanted her to call. She didn't have the heart to talk to him either, but she knew it was important to call him. They needed to know now who was stealing money from her, and Meg had given her good advice. She looked for her big canvas tote bag, and found the piece of paper with the number on it. She saw the folder on the kitchen table with the photographs of Hunt in it, with Angela and her son, and she started to cry again.

She called the number for Jim Kingston, FBI special agent, and he didn't answer, so she left him a voicemail. All she said was her name and number and who had referred her. She didn't explain what it was about. And then she went upstairs and got back into bed. She couldn't think of a single reason to get up. She felt like her life was over as she sobbed into her pillow.

The baseball team of Hamilton High School was playing Fairfax High. A tall dark-haired boy was at bat. He was a sophomore, and he looked intent as he watched the pitcher and waited for the ball. The bases were loaded, and the

score was three to two, Fairfax was
winning, and when the batter hit the
ball, he sailed it right out of the ball
field, and everyone on base got home.
It was the last inning, and all the Hamilton parents in the stands were on their
feet and cheering. And a tall, good-
looking man in a baseball cap was grinning from ear to ear as he watched. He
went down on the field as fast as he
could get there and threw his arms
around his son. He gave him a high-
five, and the boy looked embarrassed.

"You did it!" his father said excitedly.

"We would have won anyway. Their
pitcher sucks," Bobby Kingston said to
his father.

"That's not true, and you know it.
You're a hero!" his father teased him.
Jim Kingston never missed a game if he
could help it. His older son, Josh, was
at Michigan State on a football scholar-
ship. Sports had always been a big part
of their lives, and Jim had gotten them
even more focused on athletics since
they lost their mother five years before.
He was a widowed single father, had
coached Little League for both boys,

and he loved spending time with them whenever he wasn't working. They were his whole life. That and his job at the FBI, as senior special agent. He had taken tamer assignments in recent years, since his wife died, and spent more time in the office. He had the boys to think about, although in two years, when Bobby left for college, he'd be alone again, but for the past five years, since Jeannie died of breast cancer, he had dedicated himself to them. The boys had been ten and fourteen when she died, and he had been mother and father ever since.

"Way to go, Bobby!" one of the fathers said as he walked by.

"You guys played a great game," Jim said proudly, as Bobby came out of the locker room a few minutes later and they left the field.

"Yeah, it was pretty good." Bobby grinned. He looked a lot like his father, with the same long, lanky, dark-haired appearance. And his brother did too, although Josh was broader and more powerful than his father or brother. Josh was the star quarterback at Michigan

State. Jim was very proud of both his boys, and Jeannie had been too.

It was a relief to Jim in some ways, once Jeannie died, that he only had sons, which was easier for him to manage and relate to than if he'd had girls. But now and then he wished that he had a daughter who looked like his late wife. She had been the most beautiful woman in the world, full of fire and life, always coming up with some new idea or project to keep them busy. She had been the light of his life, and then after two years of illness, remission, chemo, radiation, relapse, and a double mastectomy, it was all over, and she was gone. He still couldn't believe it, five years later. But thank God he had his boys. At forty-eight, he had been alone for five years, and still had no interest in dating. Some of the guys he worked with had tried to introduce him to other women, usually friends of their wives, and he just didn't care. He knew there was no one in the world like her, and no one could measure up. Jeannie had been enough for him for one lifetime. And now he could focus on his boys.

Josh came home to visit often, and he and Bobby went to see him play in all his big games. He had already been offered a contract by the NFL when he turned twenty-one, but Jim wanted him to wait and finish college, and so far Josh had agreed, although the offers he'd had to play pro football were very tempting.

Jim's cell phone rang as they were leaving the field, and he saw an unfamiliar number appear. He didn't answer, and figured he could call them back later, whoever it was.

He took Bobby out for a hamburger after the game, he was starving, and then he dropped him off at a friend's. He went to buy groceries and to pick up their dry cleaning, and then he went home to read some reports he'd brought from the office to work on over the weekend. He had a full caseload at the moment. He was dealing with mail fraud, credit card fraud, wire fraud, a bank robbery, and an embezzlement. It was more than enough to keep him busy. He checked his cell phone when he sat down at his desk, and then remembered the call he hadn't answered and listened to the message. The name sounded familiar to him, but he couldn't remember why. And then he checked the message before it, from Meg Simpson, and she explained that she had referred a client of hers called Tallie Jones, in a possible embezzlement case, and she'd appreciate it if he'd talk to her. Meg was an old friend, and before she left the Bureau they had worked together for two years. He had always liked her, and so had his wife.

He called Tallie's number, and it rang a few times before she answered. She sounded as though she'd been sleeping, which struck him as odd at five o'clock in the afternoon. He wondered if she was sick, and she seemed a little groggy. When he told her who he was, she woke up and was more alert.

"Thank you for calling me back," she said gratefully. Her voice was young, and she seemed a little scattered to him. "My accountant recently discovered that someone has been taking quite a bit of cash from me without my knowledge. I had Meg Simpson do an initial investigation. I didn't know if my boyfriend or assistant did it. And it looks like it might be my assistant, but I'm not sure. I don't know why she would, and she's worked for me for seventeen years. So maybe it's not her. This has never come up before. It's all very confusing at the moment. And Meg thought I should check out my accountant too." It was hard explaining it all to him as briefly as possible, without boring him with the details . . . *my boyfriend cheated on me . . . and before that he was sleeping with my assistant . . . and they both lied to me about the hotels they went to . . . and someone is stealing twenty-five thousand dollars a month.* She had no idea where to start and felt lost.

"How much money is involved?" he asked with interest. She gave him the impression that she was a little anxious. Meg had always referred good cases to him, and didn't waste his time, although he thought Tallie sounded disoriented.

"About twenty-five thousand dollars a month for the past three years, maybe longer. I don't really know." It was a siz-

able amount. "Close to a million dollars."

"And why the FBI instead of the police?"

"Because Meg said to call you. She
thought there could be bank or wire
fraud involved eventually, and she
thought we should check it out, that
is . . . if you think it's appropriate . . . I
don't really know. This is all very new to
me. I just found out and it's never happened to me before."

"How did you discover it?"

"My accountant found it, during an
audit I had to do for my business."

"And what business is that?"

"I'm a movie director," she said simply. Obviously her name hadn't rung a
bell for him. But as soon as she told him
what she did, he realized why it had
been familiar, and he felt foolish for not
having recognized it immediately. He
just didn't expect to have a major movie
director calling him at home. But he
should have known. Meg had some
very fancy clients and had made a good
name for herself. She had tried several
times to get him to come in with her, but

he still liked working for the FBI. It suited him and he liked the prestige that went with it. And eventually, the pension.

"Of course, I'm sorry," Jim said, still feeling silly for not knowing who she was immediately.

"It's fine." She didn't seem to care if he knew who she was or not.

"You suspect your assistant?" he confirmed. People usually had some idea of who it was, although often it was the person they suspected least and trusted most. That was common in embezzlements, and he saw it all the time. And Meg had done the initial groundwork.

"At first I thought it was my . . . the . . . uh . . . the man I was living with. He just moved out yesterday," she said, and he wondered if that was why she seemed confused. "Or my assistant. I can't even imagine that, though. She's the person I've trusted most in the world for seventeen years, but I also just discovered that she lied to me, and . . . uh . . . ah . . . she did some other things that have caused me to no longer trust her. I don't know what to think, but Meg says I should check it out."

"What kind of other things? Like theft?" He was being businesslike and thorough, like a doctor asking for her symptoms, and Tallie hesitated before she answered.

"No, of a more personal nature, but it makes me question everything now."

"I understand. Would you like me to come out and see you this week?" he offered, and she sounded flustered again.

"I would. I'm actually shooting on location, in Palm Springs right now, but I'll juggle my schedule and come in." He was the FBI after all. "Just tell me when and I'll work it out. I come home on most weekends anyway, and some nights. It's no problem to drive in." He felt sorry for her, she had a sad voice, and she was upset. He wondered what had happened, other than the money she'd lost. She sounded devastated.

"Are you in L.A. now?" he asked her.

"Yes, I am, till Monday morning. Or

maybe I can go in late on Monday, and see you then."

"Would it work for you if I come over tomorrow?" he offered, and she sounded relieved when she answered.

"That would be great, if you don't mind seeing me on a Sunday."

"That's fine." He knew Bobby had plans the next day, and he wouldn't be seeing him till dinner. "How about eleven A.M.?"

"That would be perfect," she said, sounding grateful again. "Really, thank you for seeing me on a Sunday . . . I'm sorry to bother you with this . . . maybe it's nothing . . . and it might not even be my assistant. Maybe it's all a big mistake." She was embarrassed to be calling the FBI, but Meg had said she should.

"We'll figure it out, and that's a lot of money, if you've lost twenty-five thousand a month for three years. Don't apologize. This is what we do." He was calm and reassuring and very professional.

"Thank you . . . I really appreciate it." Her noice was very small.

"Do you have any paperwork on it that I can look at?" he asked her, and she remembered the spreadsheet she had given her father. He still had it, and she could pick it up from him.

"Yes, I do. I have a spreadsheet, and my accountant has all the books. We just had an audit, for an investor." She had already told him that and forgotten. She was obviously distracted, but most people were if they thought they'd been embezzled. He couldn't know that she was also in a state of shock that her relationship with Hunt had ended. She gave him her address then, thanked him, and they hung up. And Jim called Meg Simpson after that. She was just about to go out with her husband and kids.

"Your client called me," Jim told her quickly, so as not to delay her unduly. He could hear her children in the background and her husband telling her to hurry up. "I just called her back."

"Tallie Jones?"

"Yeah. Moron that I am, I had no idea who she was until she told me she's a director. You and your Hollywood clients. Why didn't you warn me so I didn't make an ass of myself?" he teased her, and she laughed.

"How could I know you've become a shut-in and don't go to movies? What rock do you live under these days?"

"I'm busy with the boys, or with Bobby anyway. Josh is away in college."

"How depressing. I remember when they were born."

"Yeah, me too," he said, sounding wistful for a minute. He and Jeannie had been so happy then.

"She needs your help." She was talking about Tallie again. "She's pretty shaken up. I gave her a heavy dose of bad news. Her boyfriend is cheating on her, and apparently before that he slept with her assistant, whom she considers her best friend and who has worked for her for seventeen years. And she may be stealing money from her too. Nice people. People in her position are such targets for every kind of bad behavior, exploitation, and theft. I hated to tell her, but that's why she came to me. I think the money theft is serious, and you should give it a good look."

"You think it's the boyfriend?"

"I doubt it. He's rolling in dough. He doesn't need her money even if the guy is a shit."

"She said something about his moving out yesterday."

"That's new," Meg told him. "It must have happened after she left my office, with a folder full of photographs of him and his new girlfriend. As far as the money goes, I think it's the accountant or the assistant. Or God knows who else, other people may have access that I don't know about. She hired me mostly to check out the boyfriend, and figure out if her assistant had gone to a hotel and charged it to her. She did— with him."

"No wonder she sounded like she'd been hit over the head with a hammer. I don't know how you tell people stuff like that. All I do is tell them they're going to jail." It was more complicated than that, and they both knew it, but he did admire the work she did. Meg was smart and thorough, and worked fast.

He had really missed her when she left. And if he ever left the Bureau, which he had no intention of doing for the moment, he would go to work with her in a flash. She was still hoping he would one day.

"Are you seeing her?" Meg asked as her husband shouted again that they were late, and Jim could hear a child crying. It sounded like a normal family Saturday to him, and made him miss his wife even more.

"I'm going over to her house tomorrow."

"Good. I'm glad she called you. Be nice to her. She's having a tough time."

"I'm always nice," he laughed at Meg. "I'll let you know what happens."

"Fine. Take care." And then she rushed off the phone to go out with her husband and kids, and Jim sat thinking for a minute, about everything Meg had said about Tallie. It sounded to him like she had gotten a raw deal from the boyfriend and her assistant, and was being embezzled on top of it. Without even knowing her, he felt badly for her.

*   *   *

Tallie called her father after speaking to
the FBI agent. She wanted to get the
spreadsheet back from him that Victor
had prepared, and she told him that she
wanted to pick it up, which Sam said
was fine. She didn't say anything about
Hunt, but when he saw her that afternoon when she came by the house, he
was shocked. She looked awful and like
she'd been through the wars. She was
deathly pale and there were dark circles
under eyes.

"Are you okay?" He was genuinely
worried about her.

"I'm just tired."

"What's wrong?" He knew her better
than that, and before she could stop
herself, she was crying and told him
about Hunt. Sam was furious when he
heard. Hunt had cheated on her with
not just one woman but two? And what
was wrong with Brigitte? How could
she do a thing like that to her employer
and friend? He was disgusted with
them both, and sorry for Tallie. It was a
terrible blow. "Men are such fools

sometimes," he said as he hugged his daughter, and then handed her the spreadsheet she had come for. "What a stupid, rotten thing for him to do. And I always liked the guy. What a dishonest little shit." He was livid, and Tallie laughed through her tears.

"Yeah, that's pretty much what I think too."

"What are you doing about Brigitte?"

"I don't know yet. The investigator I used told me to call the FBI and have them check it out. An agent is coming over tomorrow, which is why I want the spreadsheet, to give to him. I don't know if Brigitte is taking the money or not, but she slept with Hunt for three years, so I guess that's grounds to fire her. I just haven't had the heart to deal with it yet. I'm still reeling over Hunt. He moved out last night."

"Does Max know?" He looked worried, and Tallie was too.

"I haven't told her yet. It's all a little fresh. I just found out at four o'clock yesterday afternoon. His girlfriend is pregnant on top of it, so I guess they're getting married. I asked him if he'd give

her up, and he wouldn't. So that's that."
She tried to sound blithe about it, and
failed abysmally. She looked and
sounded devastated, and she was. But
they both knew that Max had adored
him, and it would be a terrible shock to
her too.

"What are you going to do about your
next movie with him?" This touched on
so many areas of her life. Her father was
genuinely concerned.

"I won't do it. I told him that last
night. I couldn't work with him now. I'll
finish this one, and that's it. End of a
partnership and a romance."

"I'm sorry, baby," her father said,
touching her cheek with his gnarled
hand. "You two were good together, in a
lot of ways. You didn't deserve this to
happen. I guess he wasn't the man we
thought he was, if he cheated on you
for all four years. Maybe this is a blessing in disguise," he said, trying to cheer
her up, but she wasn't ready for that
yet.

"I'm a little tired of this kind of blessing, the ones in disguise. I like the ones

that sound like good news, not the ones that break your heart."

"I know, I know . . . someone else will come along," he said convincingly, although no one ever had for him. He had never had another serious woman in his life after Tallie's mother died. He always said she had been the love of his life. Hunt hadn't been that to her, but he had been very important to her. They had been comfortable and happy, and she had loved him a lot.

"That's the last thing I want, Dad," she said somberly, "for someone else to come along. This is it for me. I think I'm done. Three strikes, I'm out."

"At least you weren't married to him. There won't be a lot of legal complications. And you never bought any property together. That's always a disaster when things go sour, and you have to take it all apart." He had always told her not to, and she had listened to him. Her father gave good advice. Except when he had made her marry Max's father when she was twenty, but he had done that for Max, not for her, and maybe he was right about that too. At least she knew her parents had been married, if she cared. "I think you ought to fire Brigitte immediately," he added. He was furious with her. Tallie was less angry than deeply hurt. She was profoundly wounded by what Brigitte had done, her affair with Hunt and her lies for years.

"I'll deal with it on Monday," she said sadly. She couldn't imagine life without Brigitte either. They had worked together forever. Seventeen years. It was almost like a marriage. And they were best friends, as well as employer and employee. And Brigitte made her life run so smoothly. It was going to be chaos for a while. She didn't have the heart to look for a new assistant either. Tallie felt like her whole life was upside down and broken to bits, like her heart.

Her father asked her about the Academy Awards before she left. It was coming up soon, and he wondered if she was going. She said she didn't have the heart to now, and she didn't want to run into Hunt, and her father agreed. Particularly if the other woman was with him.

She left a little while after that, and when she went home, she looked in all the closets and looked at Hunt's things. He had a whole dressing room full of clothes, a kitchen full of equipment he had brought with him and added to in three years, two bookcases full of books, a home office full of his work, and odds and ends all over the house, tennis rackets, his rowing machine, a treadmill they had bought together. She didn't know where to start. She went to the supermarket that night and got some boxes, and little by little she started packing up, and the whole time she did, she cried. Normally, she would have asked Brigitte to help her with it, but she didn't want to do that now, not after what she'd done. She was going to pack it all herself, and then call a moving company to drop it off. She didn't want to see him again.

Her cell phone rang at midnight, and it was Hunt. She didn't know whether to answer it or not, but she missed him so much, she took the call.

"Are you okay?" he asked as soon as she picked it up. He sounded worried

about her and unhappy. Angela had
been thrilled when he showed up the
night before, particularly since she was
expecting his baby, but Hunt was sad.
Not sad enough to want to come back
and give up Angela, but sad anyway.
Angela was his future now, and Tallie
was his past. She had become ancient
history in his life overnight. It had all
happened so fast.

"No, I'm not okay," she said, deciding
to be honest about it. "I'm falling apart."
She started crying again as soon as she
said it. "How would you be if you found
out all those things about me?"

"Homicidal. Or suicidal. I'm not sure
which. But I don't think I'd be as decent
about it as you are. Tallie, I'm so sorry."

"You should be. It was such a rotten
thing to do to me, for the whole time we
were together," she sobbed, and he felt
like a total bastard.

"I don't know what happened. Things
got off on the wrong foot, when I got involved with Brig. I swear she did it on
purpose. She wants to *be* you, Tallie,
even if that meant sleeping with me. I
never knew what hit me after that first

time, and I couldn't get away from her.
She got me in her web." He portrayed
her as someone evil and himself as her
victim, and Tallie still couldn't see her
that way. Hunt was absolving himself
from all responsibility and blaming Brigitte. Tallie thought he should have had
more balls than that, and never gotten
involved with her in the first place. She
hadn't held a gun to his head after all.
And she said as much to him.

"No, but she threatened to tell you if I
stopped, and I didn't want her to do
that. I thought I'd lose you, and I did
anyway."

"That doesn't explain why you got involved with someone else after her. Did
Angela blackmail you too?"

"No, I was just a fool, and she's a
sweet girl. This isn't her fault, or Brig's,
I guess. It's mine. I did the wrong thing
all the way."

"Yes, you did," Tallie agreed.

"Did you tell your father?"

"Yes."

"He must hate me." He was embarrassed to have Sam know how badly
he'd behaved.

"He's pretty pissed." And he was right.

"Did you tell Max?"

"Not yet. She's going to be heartbroken. She loves you," Tallie said, crying. "So did I."

"I do too. I love you both . . . I told you that . . . I love you and Angela . . . and Max, and your father. This is such a fucking mess."

"Yes, it is," Tallie agreed. And he was having a baby, which added insult to injury. Tallie wanted to hate him, but she couldn't. She was just crushed, and he felt like a total heel. "I'll pack your stuff up and send it to you next week," she said sadly. It was the end of an era for both of them. He was embarrassed to tell her to send it all to Angela's, although he had just agreed to move in with her, because of the baby. And Tallie didn't want to ask, so she told him she'd send it to his office, and he said that was fine. There was nothing left to say except goodbye after that.

Tallie had never stopped crying during the entire conversation, and Hunt felt like a monster by the time he hung

up. He didn't know how he had expected it to end, but he realized now
that if you were involved with two people and lied to one of them, this was
what happened. He felt terrible about
what he'd done to Tallie, and now it
looked like he was jumping from one
woman to the next, which was in fact
what he was doing by moving in with
Angela right away. But he also wanted
to protect her from her ex-husband now
that she was carrying his baby. That
was a new concept for him too since he
had never had kids nor wanted them
before. And now he would have two almost immediately, since she was already four months pregnant. She had
waited to tell him until it was too late to
have an abortion, because she wanted
his baby so much. Hunt was feeling
overwhelmed too.

Tallie went on packing his things until
two o'clock in the morning. She had
cleared two closets and some of his
books by then. He had a mountain of
stuff. She wasn't even sure she could
pack it all before she left for Palm
Springs. And she went back to work on

it at nine in the morning on Sunday. She wanted to get it done, so she didn't just stand there and cry every time she opened a closet and saw his things. It took two boxes just to pack everything in his bathroom. She had never realized he had this much stuff.

She was working on his office when the doorbell rang and it was Senior Special Agent Jim Kingston from the FBI. She found herself looking up at a tall, dark-haired man with blue eyes and a pleasant face, wearing a shirt, tie, blazer, and gray slacks with loafers. He had come dressed for work since it was an official visit. He introduced himself immediately and she invited him in. There were boxes everywhere. She apologized, and he could guess what they were for, but he didn't comment.

She took him into the kitchen and offered him a cup of coffee or tea. He said he was fine, and didn't want either. They sat down at the kitchen table, and she handed him the spreadsheet she had retrieved from her father. He glanced at it for a minute and then found himself looking into her big green eyes. She looked sad, and he could see that she was in pain.

"Let's talk about the three possibilities here, about who might be taking your money," he said calmly. "What do you think? What does your gut say?"

"My gut says that I'm an idiot for not suspecting it before," she said, looking unhappy. "Apparently, a lot went on around here that I never suspected."

"People who embezzle money are very clever about it. They know just how far to go, how much they can take, when, and how to get away with it, under the radar. And if it makes you feel any better, in most cases it's the person you trust most, who has been there the longest time. If it were obvious, they'd get caught the first day. And usually schemes like this go on for a long, long time," he said to reassure her.

"Maybe it's my accountant. If it isn't, he should have figured it out."

"If he didn't do it, then whoever did knew how to get by him too. Believe me, this is the kind of thing we see every day. But I'll talk to your account-ant too, and we'll get you forensic accountants to look at your books and your general ledger. We'll do an investigation on the accountant and your assistant, and the man you were living with." Tallie nodded. They were the only three people who could have been ripping her off, and she really didn't think it was Hunt. She said as much to Jim.

"Meg Simpson said that too. Your assistant actually fits the profile of the most likely suspect," he said calmly.

"Why?" Tallie was puzzled by what he said.

"Because you trust her implicitly. That gives someone a lot of leeway if they're dishonest, and she's already lied to you once that you know of." They both knew about what, and didn't need to go into detail, much to Tallie's relief.

"I'm going to fire her tomorrow," Tallie said sadly. She had thought about it all night, and decided when she got up that morning. She couldn't keep her after what she'd done.

"I'd rather you didn't," Jim said quietly, and Tallie was surprised. She thought the FBI would expect her to move quickly, although Meg had told her to be cautious too.

"Why not?"

"Because if she's a serious suspect, I'd rather she not realize that we're suspicious of her, and see what she does. Have you confronted her about the money yet?"

"No. I asked her, and she told me it was Hunt, and I believed her."

"Have you spoken to her since you got the report from Meg?"

"No, she doesn't know about that. And I just got it Friday."

"If you think you can pull it off, I'd rather you not tell her anything you heard from Meg. Your assistant told you about your boyfriend's other woman. You could tell her that you broke up over that, without telling her you know the rest. And you can tell her you're suspicious of him and your accountant about the money. If you can deal with it, I'd like to give her some room, and see what she does, although she can't blame the ex-boyfriend for money that disappears now, so she might be more careful for a while. But it gives us a big advantage if she doesn't know we suspect her. She'll relax. If we find strong evidence that it's her, you can fire her then. Right now we're not sure, and what we need is time."

"How much time?" Tallie didn't look enthused about his plan. It also meant that she couldn't confront her over Hunt. As far as Brigitte knew right now, Tallie was upset that she hadn't exposed Hunt's crimes earlier, but Tallie had never suspected her of taking the money, she had only asked, not accused her of it, and Brigitte had no idea at all that Tallie knew about her and Hunt, and their affair of three years. All of that was new.

"It could take us a month or two to get what we need, or longer. I actually think we might know in a month. We can reassess the situation then. But until then I'd like you to give her the impression that you've forgiven her, and let's give her enough rope to hang herself, while we conduct the investigation. We can keep an eye on her, and your money going in and out, and we can interview your accountant and Mr. Lloyd

to see if they are viable suspects or not.
I'd like to save the most likely one for
last, if you agree." Tallie nodded her
head slowly. What he was asking of her
sounded difficult and uncomfortable,
and it would be unpleasant to keep an
enemy close to her for that much
longer. But it made perfect sense too.
"Do you think you can pull it off?" he
asked with a look of concern, and she
smiled ruefully.

"Yes. I was an actress before I was a
director. I can do it. It just sounds unpleasant to have to act like everything is
fine."

"It might give us the best results in
the long run. And I don't want you to tell
her you've contacted the FBI about the
money nor went to a PI." He warned her
then that they might have to turn it over
to the police in the end, if there was no
wire fraud or bank fraud committed and
no federal offenses, but they could assess that later on. He sounded infinitely
professional and interested in her case.
She was glad that he'd come to talk to
her, and so was he. Tallie felt somewhat
reassured that she was in good hands,

and he thought the case was worth pursuing. She had been betrayed by two people she loved and trusted, and he wanted to figure out who was stealing money from her.

"Thank you, Special Agent Kingston," she said with a look of relief. She felt safe with him handling the case. He had a very sympathetic, comforting style about him, which put her at ease.

"Jim. Please. If you're patient with us, we'll solve the problem. Sometimes these things move slower than the victim likes." She winced at the word.

"I hate to think of myself as a 'victim.' It sounds so awful."

"It is awful. But you've been the victim of a crime, and sadly often people in your position are a very appealing target."

"Yeah, I've always relied on her so much. And after all this time, I don't question what she does. I trust her totally."

"And she, or someone else, has taken full advantage of that. If this goes to trial and she's convicted, her sentence will be increased because of the abuse of trust. Judges take a dim view of that in situations like this. Abuse of trust is a serious offense." She thought wistfully that that applied to Hunt too, and he hadn't committed a crime. Just breach of promise, and trust, and all her faith in him. "I'll get the investigation started tomorrow." She gave him Hunt's and Victor's contact information, and he was planning to ask for interviews with both of them. He was going to leave Brigitte alone for a while, to see what she did, and if Tallie lost money at the same rate. She'd have to be more careful now that Hunt was gone, and she could no longer blame him. She'd have to be even more cunning, if it was her. If it was Hunt, it would stop entirely now that he was gone. And if it was Victor, it might continue at the same rate, though in different ways.

Jim Kingston stayed for an hour and a half, and then he stood up, and she thanked him again for coming.

"I'm sorry to eat into your Sunday," she said apologetically, and he smiled.

"It's fine. I had nothing else to do. I spend Sundays with my fifteen-year-old

son, and he had better things to do today than hang out with his dad. That
seems to be happening a lot these
days." He smiled ruefully as he said it.

"My daughter's eighteen, in college in
New York, and it's pretty much that way
with her now too. When she's home,
she'd rather be out with her friends."
Tallie smiled as they chatted about their
kids. It established a friendly link between them, which was his style.

"I have a son at Michigan State too,"
he added. "Once they're gone, they
don't belong to us anymore. I'm hanging on to my fifteen-year-old for dear
life," he confessed, and they both
laughed. She wondered if he was divorced. He somehow made it sound
like he didn't have a wife, just his kids,
or maybe she was wrong. He seemed
like a pleasant man to her. He was
wholesome, intelligent, and clean-cut.
She felt like her case was in good
hands. He seemed mildly impressed
with her Hollywood status, but not
overly so. He referred to it but didn't
have stars in his eyes. And he apolo-

gized again for not knowing who she was when she called.

"I don't mind at all," she assured him. "It's a lot better that way." She looked as though she meant it, which he found refreshing. There was nothing pretentious or Hollywood about her despite how famous she was.

"I'll give you a call this week if I have any other questions or if something comes up that you should know," he said as they walked to the door. And after they shook hands and he left, she watched him as he drove away. She was glad she'd called, although she wasn't thrilled about not being able to fire Brigitte yet. It was going to be uncomfortable playing a game for the next month or two. That sounded like a very long time. He had also explained to her that it would take them a while to get bank records that would allow them to assess the suspect's financial activity. He promised that they would move as fast as they could, but banks moved slowly, and everything took time.

Her father called an hour later when

she was in the midst of packing Hunt's things again.

"How did it go with the FBI?" Sam asked, anxious to hear what they'd said.

"They said they're going to check it out, and I can't fire Brigitte yet. They want me to buy time, and not let on that we suspect. They want to see what she does."

"Clever tactic, though hard on you, given what she did with Hunt."

"She doesn't know that I know that, Dad. I can just tell her that Hunt confessed about his current girlfriend. She doesn't need to know that he admitted about her too. And she sounds a little nuts from what Hunt told me. Anyway, we'll see how crazy she really is. I can pretend to have forgiven her for not telling me sooner what Hunt was up to, and then we can go about our business, while the FBI keeps an eye on her."

"Sounds like a good plan to me. But tough on you."

"I guess I'll have to live with it. He says it's the best way. So I can't even fire the bitch tomorrow," Tallie said, sounding angry, and Sam nodded, thinking unhappily about what an evil person Brigitte had turned out to be. He was furious on his daughter's behalf, but there was nothing he could do. All they could do now was wait and trust the FBI. It was all hard to believe.

Chapter 10

In order to satisfy Jim Kingston's request to appear normal, Tallie let Brigitte drive her to Palm Springs on Monday morning. And after their usual stop at Starbucks, Tallie fell silent for a while. She wasn't sure what to say, and then she knew what she had to do, to throw Brigitte off the scent.

"How was your weekend?" Brigitte asked casually as they drove along.

"Not so great," Tallie said, staring out the window sadly. "Hunt and I broke up. He moved out on Friday night."

"Oh my God, how did that happen?

Did you confront him about what I told you?" Tallie nodded without looking at her. She was as genuinely sad as she appeared, but not only for the reasons Brigitte had told her.

"Yes, I did," Tallie said, turning her gaze toward her, and Brigitte could see how devastated she was. "He said it was true, about the girl in his office. I asked him if he would give her up, and he said he wouldn't. And then he admitted she's pregnant." Brigitte caught her breath sharply at that, and she didn't look happy about it either.

"Is he going to marry her?" she asked, looking astounded. It was pretty shocking news and had been for Tallie too.

"I think so. In any case, he says he's in love with her and he wouldn't leave her, so I told him to move out." There was a long moment of silence in the car as Brigitte absorbed it. Tallie knew her well enough to see that she was distressed at the news of his marriage and a baby.

"Did you ask him about the money?"

Tallie nodded in answer. "What did he say?"

"He lied, of course. He denied it. But that problem is solved. He won't be asking you for money now." They rode along in silence for a while, and then Brigitte looked over at her sympathetically.

"I'm sorry, Tallie." She could see that Tallie had believed her that it had been Hunt taking the money, and was heartbroken over the girl. "Why didn't you call me?" Brigitte said, trying to get close to her again, as they had been before.

"I was too upset. I stayed in bed all weekend and cried. I don't know, maybe I told him to move out too fast, but if he wasn't going to give her up, what was the point of being the pathetic one in a triangle? And if she's pregnant, I didn't have a chance."

"I thought he didn't want kids." Brigitte frowned.

"So did I. But apparently he wants this one, and he's crazy about her little boy." And it didn't help that she was thirteen years younger than Tallie. That point hadn't been lost on her either.

And then Brigitte asked in a soft voice, "Are you mad at me for telling you about the girl in his office and the money?"

Tallie shook her head. "No. Someone had to tell me, and I'd rather it was you." She almost retched as she said it. What Brigitte hadn't told her was that she had slept with him herself for three years. Tallie had learned a lot about both of them in the past few days. Both of them had betrayed her and lied to her, he had cheated on her during their entire relationship, and one of them was stealing her money. They were a disgusting pair, both of them. And she knew she would never feel the same way about Brigitte again. It had killed any feelings she had for Brigitte when she had lied about the hotel bills and Meg Simpson had told her that she and Hunt had had an affair for three years. *Three years!* And all the while Brigitte had looked her in the eye every day, and pretended to be her best friend. They had both lied to her. It didn't get

lower than what they did, and she expected better from Brigitte if not from
Hunt. It was a double loss for her. "I
wish you'd told me sooner, that's all,"
Tallie said softly. She didn't seem angry
at all, just sad, which was an act.

"I was afraid you were still mad at
me," Brigitte said, looking relieved. Tallie had given her the impression that all
the blame had been put on Hunt, and it
was all over, and she and Tallie could go
back to the way things were before. "I
agonized over whether or not to tell
you."

"I'm sure you did," Tallie said with a
sigh, and didn't pursue the conversation any further. All she could hope was
that the FBI would move quickly and
complete their investigation. She didn't
want to live this charade with Brigitte
for many months. The two months Jim
Kingston had said it might take
sounded like a nightmare to her, and
every time she looked at Brigitte now
she would remember that she had lied
to her, while sleeping with Hunt and
meeting him in hotel rooms. She felt
sick whenever she thought about it. It

was painful, and she wanted Brigitte out of her life now, whether or not she was stealing money. She was a liar and a cheat anyway. It was like discovering that your best friend had been sleeping with your husband. She hadn't been married to Hunt, but she had lived with him and she loved him.

"Are you going to investigate further about the money?" Brigitte asked Tallie, who shook her head.

"I'll never get it back anyway. What's the point?" she said to throw Brigitte off the scent and reassure her. Brigitte nodded and they drove on in silence.

Working on the set that morning kept Tallie busy, and she was grateful for her work now. It forced her to think of something else besides Hunt and his cheating on her, and Brigitte, and their betrayals. It was a hard one to swallow, and when she got back to her trailer at lunchtime, she called her attorney, Greg Thomas.

"How did things work out with Meg Simpson?" he asked her.

"That depends how you look at it. She found out what I wanted to know, even if it wasn't what I wanted to hear. It turns out that Hunt has been cheating on me for the whole four years we've been together, for three years of it with my best friend. And I found out some other things that were equally unpleasant." She sounded tense and unhappy.

"I'm sorry, Tallie. Was he taking the money too?"

"I don't know. Maybe not. To be honest, I don't think so. I'm keeping it quiet for now, but Meg called an FBI agent she used to work with, and I met with him over the weekend. He's doing an investigation. There are some other possibilities as far as the money goes. It's in the hands of the FBI."

"I'm relieved to know that. They'll get to the bottom of it. What can I do to help you?"

"I want you to send official notification to Hunt that I won't be doing our next picture with him. I'm out. I told him that on Friday night before he moved out, but I'm not sure he believed me. I haven't signed a contract for it yet, as you know. And I want to make it official. I won't be part of the project. He needs to know for his investor, before he signs their contract."

"Are you sure?" Their first film had made a lot of money, and giving up another one was a big sacrifice for her. But there was no question in her mind now. She had made movies before Hunt, and there would be successful films after him. She didn't need Hunter Lloyd to make a movie, and if she wanted to produce, she could do it on her own. A movie directed by Tallie Jones was a sure box-office hit.

"I'm positive," she said without hesitating. "I wouldn't work with him again no matter how much we make on the back end. Besides, he's a liar, and that's not the kind of person I want to work with." Tallie was a principled person, and her ethics were more important to her than money. "Just send him a letter."

"I'll take care of it today," he said quietly. He could tell that she meant it. She hadn't wavered for an instant.

"Thanks, Greg."

"I'll send his attorney an e-mail and give him a heads-up."

Tallie knew Greg had notified them, when Hunt started frantically calling her at four o'clock. She didn't take his calls, so he texted her about her withdrawal and begged her to call him. Reluctantly, she finally did at six o'clock when they finished shooting and she left the set. She had decided to drive back to L.A. for the night. She drove alone in one of the SUVs, and told Brigitte she needed some time to herself. She called Hunt from the car and put it on speaker, since there was no one in the car with her.

"Tallie, you can't be serious. That's crazy. This is about our career, not our love life."

"That's right," she said coldly, "and both are over. I don't work with cheaters and liars." She sounded bitter, but she was tired after a long day, and still hurting over what he'd done. She knew she would hurt for a long time over this one. The agony had only just begun. She'd been there with her second husband ten years before.

"Do you realize what you're going to cost us both? And Mr. Nakamura will pull out of the picture without you. I just spoke to his attorney."

"That's too bad, Hunt. Maybe you should have thought of that before you slept with my assistant for three years and the girl in your office for the last one. You didn't really expect me to work with you again, did you?"

"Can't we separate the two parts of our lives? We do such great work together. You can't just wipe that out."

"No, you did. Let's be very clear about this. I won't work with you again. I'm done."

"Can we talk about it sometime?"

"No."

"What am I supposed to tell Mr. Nakamura?" He sounded nervous when he asked.

"Tell him you screwed my assistant and some girl in your office and you lost your partner. I'm sure he'll understand." She was getting angry at him now, and it felt better than being sad.

"Look, I'm sorry, I know it was terrible. I was wrong. You didn't deserve that, Tallie. But do we have to fuck over our careers to prove a point?"

"I'm not proving a point, Hunt. I'm not going to work with you again. I don't want to. I'll finish this picture and that's it." He suddenly panicked that she might walk out on that, but he knew that she was too professional to do that, but he also knew how principled she was, and how fair. And how stubborn if she thought she'd been wronged. And he knew she had been. There was no moving her off her position now, although he hoped she might reconsider it later, but he doubted she would. And then he thought of something else.

"Did you fire Brigitte?"

"No," she said flatly.

"Why not?"

"That's none of your business."

"Why? You can forgive her, but not me? That's ridiculous."

"I didn't say I forgave her," she said quietly. She couldn't tell him that she had kept her because the FBI had told her to. And he was under investigation too, so she couldn't say anything to him. "That's my business, Hunt, not yours. I gave you the option to stick around. You said you wouldn't stop seeing Angela, it was your choice. My choice was not to live with a man who wants to sleep with two women, and lie to one, or both."

"I still love you, Tallie, even if I screwed up."

"So do I, Hunt. That's unfortunate for both of us. We'll get over it. But I won't work with you again. That's all I have to say about it. And one other thing. Please don't say anything to Max about us. She'll be very upset, and I want to tell her myself, in person, not on the phone. I'll go there when I can. Thanks for your call. Take care." And with that, the phone went dead in his hand. They were supposed to sign the contracts with Nakamura in the next few days, and now he had to tell him this. He knew it was the price to pay for what he'd done. And he knew he'd been rotten with her, and dishonest. He didn't blame her, but he wished she'd at least work with him. They were going to lose the biggest investor they'd ever had, and without Tallie directing he had much less to sell. He needed her. But

he needed Angela too, and he didn't
want to give her up. And he couldn't
leave her pregnant with his baby and go
back to Tallie now. His whole life was
falling apart, and he thought it was all
Brigitte's fault for telling Tallie and causing her to investigate further. He hated
Brigitte for what she'd done. But even
more than Brigitte, he hated himself for
what he'd done to Tallie. He couldn't
hide from that.

Tallie called her father on the way
home from Palm Springs that night, to
tell him about her notifying Hunt that
she wouldn't work on his next film with
him.

"How did he take it?"

"He tried to talk me into doing it so he
doesn't lose his big investor."

"And?"

"I told him to take a flying leap." She
laughed.

"That's my girl. I have to say one
thing, you've got guts."

"Thank you, Dad. I couldn't imagine
working with him again after this."

"How do you feel?"

"Lousy. Like I'm crawling out of my

skin. Between him and Brigitte, I wish I were a million miles from here. We'll be through on location next week, I think. We get a break before we start shooting again in L.A. I think I'm going to spend a few days with Max in New York."

"It'll do you good to get away. I wish I could go with you," he said sadly. He hadn't been able to travel in the last ten years, and he missed it.

"I wish you could too," Tallie answered. They talked for a few more minutes, and then they hung up, and Tallie drove the rest of the way in silence, thinking about everything that had happened, and how badly she'd been betrayed by Brigitte and Hunt. Brigitte called her just before she got home, and she didn't take the call. Gone were the days when she wanted to talk and laugh with her best friend. Brigitte was no longer her friend, never had been, and never would be again. She knew that now. It was a double loss for her.

The house was dark and silent when she got home. There was no one waiting for her at home. No lights. No romantic meal set out on the table with her favorite wine. Hunt was doing that for Angela now. The thought of it hit her like a bomb. She walked into the kitchen, opened the fridge, and decided there was nothing she wanted to eat. She went upstairs, and took a bath, and Jim Kingston called when she was getting out of the tub.

"I just wanted to check in," he said in a friendly tone when she sounded surprised to hear him. "How did it go with Brigitte? Did she say anything? Did you?"

"Yeah, I told her that Hunt moved out this weekend. She asked if it was because of the information she gave me about the girl in his office, and I said yes. I didn't tell her that I had found out about Hunt and her. Then she asked if he admitted to taking the money, and I said no, he hadn't, he lied, but I knew he did. She seemed perfectly comfortable with that, and I think she relaxed when I told her I wasn't going to investigate it or pursue it any further. She thinks we're best friends again, and I told her I wasn't mad. My nose grew about four feet when I said it, and you can call me Pinocchio from now on," she said, and he laughed. She sounded better to him than she had on Sunday. She still had a sense of humor despite what she'd discovered about both her boyfriend and her best friend. He wasn't sure he could have handled it as well, and doubted he could. "Anything new at your end?"

"I filed an initial report and opened the case today. I have to get approval from one of the deputy U.S. attorneys here to proceed with it, but that's more of a formality. If I tell them that I think it's a good case, they'll let me go forward with it to check it out. All I have to do now is get enough evidence so they feel they can prosecute it. And hopefully I will. We're just starting, but I think it's a valid case." He sounded optimistic about it.

"How long do these things usually take to get to court?" Tallie asked him, and there was a short pause at the other end.

"You won't like my answer," he warned her. "Nine months to a year. The wheels of justice grind slowly, but we get there in the end."

"At what point would you arrest her, if you get the evidence?" She had become convinced that Brigitte was stealing from her, and no one else. Even if she didn't need the money, she had the access and the opportunity, and she had proven herself to be a liar, so maybe she was a thief too. And Jim Kingston agreed with her. His gut told him it was Brigitte too. All he had to do now was prove it, and he hoped he could, for Tallie's sake.

"We arrest her when the prosecutor thinks we have enough evidence for an airtight case, beyond a reasonable doubt. That's the clincher for us. We don't try them if we think we could lose. Most of our cases don't go to trial. We get so much solid evidence that suspects usually plead guilty instead, which saves us all a lot of trouble."

"That sounds like a tall order," Tallie said, sounding discouraged.

"Trust me. That's my job. If the evidence is there, we'll find it." He didn't tell her he was meeting with Victor Carson the next day. He had called him that morning. Jim was moving fast. If nothing else, he wanted to rule Carson out. And he had already lined up a forensic accountant to check his books. Jim had asked Tallie's permission to use him, since she had to pay for it, and she said of course it was fine. And he was hoping to meet with Hunter Lloyd later that week. Jim was curious to meet him now, after what he'd heard from Meg and Tallie. He didn't sound like a great guy to him. "I'll call you later this week," Jim told her, "if I have questions about some of the interviews I have. Will you be available?"

"I'll arrange to be, and I'm coming back to the city every night." She thought it would be too depressing now to stay in a hotel room in Palm Springs. Even if it was dark and empty, she wanted to crawl home to her own nest, and sleep in her own bed. She felt too miserable and sad to be far from home, and he could hear it in her voice.

"I'll call you if I get anything, Tallie. Try not to get too worked up about it. To be honest, it's always a long haul. Just leave the worrying to me." He made it sound so simple, but it wasn't. All she could think about was what Brigitte and Hunt had done, how trusting she had been, how she had believed them, and how they had betrayed her. But the wounds were still fresh and raw. In time, it would settle down, and all she'd have left were the scars. She couldn't imagine it yet. She felt as though she were bleeding from every pore. "I'll be in touch," he promised. He had wanted to give her a ray of hope. He just hoped he could get the evidence they needed about the money, but he had to figure out who the suspect was first.

Tallie lay in her bed, thinking about it again that night. She was sure now that it had been Brigitte who'd been stealing the money from her. After everything else she'd done, that was the icing on the cake. And as she had for the past three days, Tallie lay awake, thinking about all of it, for the rest of the night. It was dawn before she fell asleep, and her alarm went off minutes after she closed her eyes.

Chapter 11

Jim Kingston was led into Victor Carson's private office by his secretary. She was young, wore a short skirt, and had masses of blond hair piled up on her head. And Jim couldn't help noticing that her sweater was too tight. He was wondering if Carson was sleeping with her, when Victor walked into the room. He was wearing a white shirt, a dark gray suit, and an expensive tie. He looked like a banker or a lawyer. Jim knew the firm had many important clients, and they sometimes took a percentage of their clients' revenues, but in

Tallie's case she paid a retainer and hourly fees. Her income was too big for her to agree to a percentage, and Victor had told him on the phone that Tallie was one of his biggest clients. He had been shocked to get a call from the FBI, and Jim had confirmed that it was about her missing cash.

"I had no idea that Ms. Jones had reported it to the FBI," Victor commented, looking nervous. He appeared uncomfortable as Jim looked around his office, and as though he might have something to hide. But he had been quick to invite Jim and the forensic accountant to look over his books and Tallie's. Jim wanted to see both, and to see what kind of financial shape Victor and his firm were in.

Jim spent a few minutes looking over Tallie's spreadsheet again, the same one that had been given to their Japanese investors, and that Tallie had given him on Sunday morning at her house. Victor showed Jim her electronic general ledger then, from which most of the information on the spreadsheet had been taken, and then Jim told Victor that he wanted to look at his books too.

"What does that have to do with Ms. Jones's accounts?" Victor asked with a protective look.

"We like to look at everything," Jim said quietly. "How long have you known Ms. Jones's assistant, Brigitte Parker, by the way?"

"For as long as we've done Ms. Jones's accounting, for the past fifteen years."

"Would you say she's usually accurate in the information she reports to you?"

"I've always thought so," Victor said thoughtfully. "She's very efficient. Or at least she seemed to be, until I noticed the cash that was unaccounted for in the audit. I thought maybe they were paying some of Ms. Jones's bills in cash, and I didn't want to lose the deductions, so I mentioned it. And Ms. Jones informed me that they don't pay any of the bills in cash."

"Did you ask Ms. Parker about it?"

"Only superficially. She said they spend that amount in cash every month and Ms. Jones spends more than she thinks."

"Or Ms. Parker spends more than Ms. Jones thinks," Jim Kingston said cryptically. "Where do you think the cash is going, Mr. Carson?" Jim asked him with a pointed look.

"I have no idea. Restaurants, clothes, gifts. It's hard to guess what people spend it on. Ms. Jones doesn't spend a lot of money on frivolous things, although she lives well. And it was hard figuring out who was paying for what while Mr. Lloyd was living there. He spends quite a lot of money too."

"And you do his books as well?" Jim noticed that Victor was perspiring increasingly, as Jim asked him the questions. He looked like a very nervous man.

"Yes, I do. And I prepare Ms. Parker's taxes, I have for several years."

"So you work for all three of them?" Victor nodded. "And how would you say your firm is doing? Has it been a good year?"

"Not as good as some earlier years,"

he admitted. "Things are tight for everyone right now. Even in my business."

"And would you say that you spend a
lot of money, personally?" Victor hadn't
expected the question and started
sweating profusely when Jim asked. He
had no idea why he would want to
know that, and Victor hesitated before
he answered.

"Yes, I have considerable expenses . . ." He glanced around ner-
vously and then back at Jim. "I have a
very young wife. She expects a lot, and
things aren't quite as . . . as flush as
they were when I married her three
years ago. She wanted to be an actress, and it hasn't worked out as well
as she'd hoped." He was babbling, and
Jim said nothing as he watched. "She's
been . . . she's been . . . she's been ne-
gotiating a postnuptial agreement with
me."

"Really?" Jim looked fascinated as
Victor burbled on. "And how much does
she want?"

"Five million. I told her that's impossible. Then she asked for three, but that's
impossible too. I gave her seven hun-

dred thousand three years ago when we got married, but I couldn't do that again either right now. I thought that initial gift would keep her happy, but now she wants more." He looked panicked as he explained it to Jim.

"And if you won't pay her what she wants now?"

"She says she'll divorce me." He looked as though he was near tears. "She's a beautiful girl. And she's twenty-nine years old. It's hard for a man my age to satisfy someone with ambitions like that. I've been divorced twice before, and paid alimony and settlements. I have children . . . she doesn't understand. And she's had quite a lot of plastic surgery, for her movie career, and that's expensive too. She doesn't realize what it takes to amass a fortune in today's world. I have a sizable income, but not enough to be giving away several million dollars in a lump sum. I'm not sure I could afford a divorce either right now, or the kind of alimony she wants." He sounded like a desperate man, but it was all out front, he was waving his problems at Jim like a red flag at a bull. There was nothing hidden about him, and Jim had already figured that he was married to a young gold digger who was taking him for a ride, and twenty-five thousand in cash was probably nothing to her. A girl like that wanted more, and he didn't think Victor Carson was dumb enough to be stealing small amounts from his clients to satisfy a greedy young wife. He may have been foolish and gullible, but Jim sensed that he was ethical too. They would take a serious look at his books, and he was sure that he would find in Victor's own balance sheet a man mortgaged to the hilt, trying to squeeze out every penny he could of his own money, so his wife didn't divorce him. He was willing to ruin himself for her, but probably not steal from his clients and go to prison. He might end up in the poorhouse, thanks to her, but not behind bars. Carson struck Jim as the kind of man who was scrupulously honest, paid all his taxes, and did everything by the book, for both himself and his clients. He was too nervous not to, and his obvious desperation made him an unlikely suspect.

The person who was stealing from Tallie was more likely to be far more hidden, more clandestine, and much smoother. Victor looked so guilty, he probably wasn't, and Jim felt sorry for him as he listened to another hour of his woes. He wanted to tell him to divorce his wife before she destroyed him, but he didn't say anything, he just listened. If he had to guess, Jim would have said that he wasn't the culprit. He was just a sad old man being used by a young woman who had seen him as an easy mark and was going to get everything out of it she could before she dumped him. And it sounded like it was going to be soon.

"Why don't we have a look at your books, then?" Jim suggested, and they went into the conference room where the forensic accountant was working, and Jim's partner Jack sat quietly by. The accountant had several ledgers spread out in front of him, and a computer with Tallie's general ledger on the screen, and everything seemed to be in order, to the extent that it was on the spreadsheet Jim had already seen. There was twenty-five thousand taken out in cash every month, but other than that, it was all accounted for.

And that afternoon they looked at the ledgers of the firm itself, and Victor's own spreadsheet. By five o'clock Jim said they were through for now, would let him know if they had further questions and thanked Victor for his cooperation. Victor was mopping his brow with a white handkerchief when they left, and he looked exhausted. For a moment, he had thought they were going to arrest him and accuse him of stealing Tallie's cash. Jim wished it could have been that simple, but there was no question in his mind, Victor Carson wasn't it. Far from it. And he felt genuinely sorry for him.

"That poor old guy is going broke for some bimbo," Jack Sprague said, after talking to the forensic accountant. "She spent two hundred thousand on plastic surgery last year alone, not to mention four hundred thousand on clothes. She must be something."

"Probably not," Jim said, grinning. "But he thinks she is. That's the problem. It's sad when women sucker in guys like that. What do you think of his books?"

"They look clean to me and the forensic guys," Jack confirmed.

"They did to me too. I think we're wasting our time if we go after him. He's not cooking his books. He's too busy trying to keep his head above water to keep his beauty queen happy."

"She must be a real bitch," Jack commented as they got back to their car in the garage underneath Victor's building.

"She's trying to hit him up for five million dollars," Jim told him.

"He doesn't have it," Jack said emphatically.

"I know. He told me. Twenty-five thousand a month wouldn't keep her happy for ten minutes. He knows it too, and it wouldn't be worth the risk to him. He needs millions."

"She spends more than twenty-five thousand on shoes," Jack said, shaking his head as Jim started the car. They paid for the parking and drove away.

"Next," Jim said with a smile. It had been an interesting day, but had gotten them nowhere, and they were going to have to go back to Victor Carson's office to see his books another day. But he hadn't really expected Victor Carson to be their embezzler. It would have been too simple and too sweet. And it never worked that way.

Their next meeting was with Hunter Lloyd the following week. Jim wanted to interview him. Hunt hadn't been able to see them till then, he was too busy. His secretary said he was meeting with investors. Hunt looked concerned when Jim and Jack walked in. He thought they looked the way FBI men did in movies. They were perfect for the part, and just what he would have expected. He said so to them, and Jim laughed.

"Maybe we should audition for a movie," Jim said with a broad smile, but he was taking the measure of the man as he observed Hunt. He already didn't like him from what he knew about him. "Looking for new investors?" he asked Hunt casually, and he nodded.

"Yes, we've just had a problem with a deal that fell apart for our next picture," Hunt said, looking distressed.

"And why is that?" Jim asked innocently. There were days when he loved being FBI and could ask any question he wanted, no matter how uncomfortable it made the subject. He could see Hunt didn't like the question.

"Some of the elements fell out of bed on our next movie. We lost our director."

"And who was that?"

"Tallie Jones," Hunt said through pursed lips and then relaxed. "Maybe you knew that already?" Jim shook his head.

"You're making a film with her right now, aren't you?" Jim asked with interest.

"Yes, I am. But there have been some changes in our circumstances," he said, and Jim raised an eyebrow. He was all ears and curious about how Hunt would explain it. "We were living together. I just moved out. You know how women are about those things. They get vengeful." He tried to brush it off, and Jim nodded as though he understood completely. Jack had said nothing so far. He was watching the exchange and Hunt's expression. He didn't know the history as well as Jim did, but he knew enough to let Jim take the lead. Interrogation had always been Jim's strong suit.

"How long were you together?" Jim asked him, pretending not to know. He was convincing.

"Four years."

"That's a long time. Sorry it didn't work out."

"So am I," Hunt said, looking uncomfortable. "It's complicated. We're both busy, travel a lot. Sometimes it's hard to keep things on track and heading in the right direction." Jim nodded sympathetically and wanted to add "especially if you cheat and sleep with her best friend," but didn't.

"Understandable," Jim said vaguely. "During the time you lived with her, did you ever get the feeling that anyone was taking advantage of her and stealing from her?"

"Not really," Hunt said with a thoughtful look.

"Is she careless with money? Lose track of what she spends?"

"No, she's not careless. But she's busy, and she trusts other people to handle those things for her, and maybe she shouldn't."

"Like whom?"

"Her accountant, her assistant. Tallie gets so busy with her work that she forgets everything else. She likes having other people handle the details in her life, and she assumes they're honest and will do it correctly." Jim suspected that was an accurate description.

"Do you think her accountant is honest?" Jim asked then.

"Of course. He does my financial work too. I think he's completely trustworthy. A little too conservative but good."

"And her assistant?"

There was a long pause before Hunt answered. "I don't know," he said slowly. "She and Tallie work very closely. They seem to have their own systems. I never interfered or asked much about what they did."

"After four years?" Jim looked surprised.

"We weren't married, and I didn't think her finances were any of my business. She never asked for my advice."

"Did you get the feeling, though, that her assistant was honest? Does she strike you as an honorable person?" It was a trick question, and Hunt couldn't answer it, because he hadn't been honest or honorable either, and he wondered if Jim knew it.

"I think Tallie thought so. They've worked together for seventeen years, and Tallie trusted her implicitly for that entire time."

"And now?"

"There was some question about cash when I left. I think her assistant said something about my taking it. I never did. I don't need Tallie's money and never used it, for anything. And I do all my business by credit card. I assume

that's why you're here, about the missing cash."

"In part. And whatever else turns up
along the way." Jim smiled expansively
at him. "Anything else about the assistant that you noticed or concerned
you?" Hunt thought about it for a long
minute, and Jim wondered what he was
thinking.

"I think she wants to be Tallie. I always thought that," Hunt said quietly.
"That happens a lot in our business,
with celebrities or stars. The people
who work for them are starstruck, and
then slowly they get sucked into wanting to be them. You hear about it all the
time. They get a sense of entitlement by
association, and confused about who
they are and what their role is. Some of
them are far grander than the stars
themselves. Like in Tallie's case, she's a
very modest person and very unpretentious and down to earth. Brigitte is a lot
more glamorous than she is. I've always
thought that she's confused. She's a
classic Hollywood wannabe. She drives
around in a fancy car, wears expensive
clothes and a lot of jewelry. Tallie looks

like she dresses at Goodwill, and will
drive anything on wheels no matter how
battered. Brigitte is a lot more con-
scious of her own image. And that's expensive to maintain, although I'm sure
Tallie pays her well and she gets a lot of
perks with her job."

"Like what?" Jim looked interested
by what he was saying.

"Free clothes, free jewelry, free trips,
a good deal on fancy cars."

"And did you see a lot of those free
gifts come in while you lived with Ms.
Jones?"

"No, I didn't," he admitted, "but I
heard a lot about them, and I know it's
common practice."

"Did you hear about them from Tallie?"

"No, from Brigitte. I don't think Tallie
cared or even thought about them. It's
not her thing."

"Do you think the gifts went to her assistant's house?"

"I have no idea." He looked uncomfortable to be asked.

"Did you ever go to her house?"

"No, I didn't."

"Did you meet her anywhere else outside of work?" Hunt glared at him when
Jim asked the question, and he didn't
want to lie to the FBI. He didn't know
what they'd heard.

"It's not important, but yes, I did meet
her outside of work occasionally."

"Did Ms. Jones know?"

"No, not at the time. She does now."

"Did you tell her?"

"No."

"Did Brigitte?"

"I'm not sure. I think a private detective did. Maybe Brigitte told her too by
now. I don't know." Hunt looked excru-
ciatingly uncomfortable as he answered, and then he gave up more than
he had originally intended. "I had an affair with her, which was extremely stupid of me. It went on for almost three
years. She blackmailed me into it. And
it's part of why Ms. Jones and I sepa-
rated recently."

"Do you still see Brigitte now?" Jim
asked him quietly.

"Hell, no. She's a troublemaker of the
worst kind. I was seeing someone else,
and I believe Brigitte told her, as re-

venge because I finally ended our affair. So she told Tallie about the other woman. I guess you could say that I was a fool twice. I'm not proud of it, and Ms. Jones is very upset about it. It all came to light very recently. I'm living with the other woman now. We're having a baby." He figured they'd find out anyway, so he wanted to put it all on the table.

"Congratulations," Jim said about the baby, and Hunt literally squirmed in his seat.

"Well . . . yes . . . thank you. It's all a little complicated and difficult."

"Did you ever take money from Tallie—Ms. Jones while you lived with her?"

"No. I don't need to. We kept everything separate, and I paid some of the expenses to make up for living at her house." Jim nodded. "It all worked very well for a long time." He sounded almost sad as he said it.

"Except that you had affairs with two other women and fathered a baby, while living with her. That does sound complicated," Jim said with a rueful smile, and

Hunt looked away. It sounded terrible when someone else said it, even to him. Jim wondered if he was a decent guy who had behaved like an asshole, or if he was just an asshole. Sometimes it was hard to tell the difference. It made him think of Victor Carson, who was ruining himself over a young girl and making a fool of himself. Hunt wasn't much better, although he had more style. But Victor was probably faithful to his gold digger. And Hunt had cheated for four years on a decent woman who loved him. It made you wonder sometimes what people had in their heads, or if it was all in their pants.

"Anything else you'd like to tell me about Brigitte?"

"No, except that maybe I think she's conniving. And she's no friend to Tallie if she was sleeping with me. She tricked me into it, and I think she planned it, while Tallie was away, right in the beginning when we were dating. She wanted what Tallie had, that wannabe thing again. She threatened to tell Tallie if I didn't keep seeing her. It was a miserable situation."

"Did Brigitte ever ask you for money?" Hunt shook his head. "Or blackmail you for money?"

"Just with exposure. But she obviously doesn't have Tallie's best interests at heart, although she pretends to. She wants to *be* Tallie, not work for her or be her friend. And Tallie has no concept of how big a star she is. Envy is a terrible thing, and very dangerous. Tallie just goes along, with her immense talent, doing her work and leading her quiet life, oblivious to all of it," he said wistfully, and Jim thought he was still in love with her and regretted what he had done. But it was too late now. And he was living with another woman and having a baby, so loving Tallie would do him no good.

"I think we've covered it for now, Mr. Lloyd," Jim said as he stood up. "We'll let you know if we have any other questions, as things develop."

"Do you know who took the money?" Hunt asked with interest.

"We're getting there." Jim smiled at him. "Thank you for your time." The three men shook hands, and Hunt looked troubled as they left his office. He hoped the prime suspect wasn't him.

Jim and Jack didn't speak as they left Hunt's office, and not until they were in the car.

"He seems like a pretty honest guy," Jack commented. "He acted like a jerk to her, but other than that he seems like a decent guy." Jim didn't agree with him, but he didn't get into it. A man who had cheated on the woman he lived with, for four years, was not a decent guy in his book, nor an honest one. Although Jim believed that he had told the truth to them. And to Jim, honesty was not something you took on and off, like a hat.

"He's not our suspect," Jim said firmly.

"I agree with you, but what makes you say that?" He always liked comparing notes with Jim. He was a smart guy.

"He was honest with us. He's not afraid to look bad. He's not covering up. I knew the answers to some of those questions, and he told the truth. And he doesn't need the money."

"I agree on all points. And I think he's still in love with her."

"Probably," Jim said coolly. He didn't think much of him, but he didn't believe he'd been stealing money from Tallie. He was certain of that. That left Brigitte, but he wasn't ready to see her yet. He wanted to line up all his ducks before he did.

Chapter 12

Once Tallie finished the location shoot in Palm Springs, making full use of the desert, she was busier than ever when they moved back to L.A. The house was lonely and quiet without Hunt, but she was getting used to it, and to coming home to an empty house. The sense of shock she had had in the beginning was still there, but she was slowly adjusting to life without him. She had no social life at the moment, she was too busy with work to even think about it. And Hunt was still having his lawyers call Greg Thomas and beg her to work on the next film with him. She wouldn't consider it, hadn't talked to Hunt in many weeks and didn't want to. His betrayal weighed on her like a concrete suit. And she still hadn't told Max about it, and didn't intend to until they met in person in New York. Conveniently, Max had been invited to Florida by friends over spring break and Tallie had agreed to let her go. Max knew her mother was busy trying to finish the film, and Tallie was relieved not to have to tell her about Hunt moving out. Max always asked about him when she called, and Tallie said he was fine. She wasn't ready to deal with Max's reaction yet, so Florida seemed like a good idea, and she was planning to go to New York to see her shortly after.

They'd been shooting in L.A. for two weeks after they got back from Palm Springs, and she'd heard nothing from Jim Kingston. He had said he would call her when he had something to report, and she had her hands full at work now anyway. She was trying to stay on schedule, before they took a hiatus and gave the cast a week's break, while they got ready to move the shooting to a new location in L.A., under the freeway. They were still waiting for street permits, which also gave them time to build some additional sets they needed. Tallie was keeping her eye on all of it, along with her leading lady's belly. She had announced to them halfway through the film that she was pregnant, and now they had to use a body double for her in a lot of the shots. It was one more thing to worry about. But her work was always a welcome distraction from misery of any kind. And Tallie managed to call her father almost every night when she came home from work, except if they shot too late. Sam had mentioned several times how disappointed he was not to have heard from Hunt himself. After a warm relationship between them for four years, it seemed disrespectful of Hunt not to call him. Tallie had a simple explanation for it: Hunt was a coward with her father, just as he had been with her. And her father didn't disagree. Hunt wasn't the man he had thought him.

She had spoken to Victor Carson

several times about her monthly disappearing cash, and interestingly, it had
stopped when Hunt moved out, which
meant either that he'd been taking it, or
that the person who was wanted her to
think so, and no longer had the cover of
Hunt's presence to blame it on, so they
were being cautious. And Tallie was
convinced now it was Brigitte. She
didn't trust her anymore, after all these
years, and she had adopted a seemingly easy way with her, but none of it
was real. Being around her now was
stressful for Tallie and a constant strain.
She tried to keep things light, but Brigitte's betrayal weighed heavily on her
too. Nothing was easy right now, and
hadn't been in well over a month, nearly
two, since Hunt moved out.

She had seen a photograph of him
with Angela on the front page of the
tabloids when she bought groceries
one weekend. And Angela's pregnant
belly was in full evidence. Hunt had
been laughing and looking happy with
his arm around her in the picture. And
Tallie was so shaken by it that she left
her groceries in the cart at the checkout

stand and walked out. She wasn't eating much now anyway. She was living on salads that she picked up from the deli on her way home.

There had been another photo of him in the tabloids with Angela at the Academy Awards, and Tallie was relieved she hadn't gone. She told Max she was too busy when Max questioned her mother about it. She would have hated running into Hunt, and she was amazed that Max hadn't seen the photo herself, and grateful that she hadn't. She was either studying for exams, or busy with her friends. She paid no attention to the tabloids, she had better things to do.

The only good news in Tallie's life was that she was planning to spend a week with Max in New York while they were on hiatus, after Max came back from Florida with her friends. Tallie could hardly wait to see her, it had been too long, but Max sounded happy at NYU. She had a new boyfriend and was making lots of friends. And Tallie still wanted to tell her about Hunt in person, not over the phone. This was going to be a major change for her as well. And Tallie's father was urging her to tell her daughter soon, before she found out some other way. He was afraid she would be angry at her mother for keeping it from her. Sam was relieved to know that Tallie was planning to go to New York.

Jim Kingston called Brigitte for an appointment with her during their last week of shooting before their hiatus, and at first she tried to tell him that she was too busy to see him. She seemed unimpressed when he told her he was from the FBI. Tallie had vaguely mentioned to her that she had talked to them about Hunt taking the money. She made it sound like more of a routine formality, or something she had done to scare him, so Brigitte hadn't been concerned about it, nor interested in making time for him in her schedule. Tallie hadn't said it was a priority. She had said very little about it.

"I have a very busy week," Brigitte told Jim officiously. "I have to be on the set with Ms. Jones."

"Next week then," Jim said easily. He had a casual way about him that put people at ease, took them off guard, and usually made them open up to him.

"I'm sorry, I'll be away," she said brusquely. "We're on hiatus next week. Maybe when we get back." He almost laughed when she said it. Most people didn't have the guts to say "maybe" to the FBI. He was used to getting a more cooperative response than that. Brigitte appeared unconcerned.

"Actually, this isn't a 'maybe,'" he said with laughter in his voice. "We need your help about the lost or stolen money. Since you'll be away, let's make it tomorrow, shall we?" This time it was a rhetorical question and there was no option in his voice. "Or today, if you prefer. I'm sure Ms. Jones will be very happy to have you meet with us. I can call her myself if you like."

There was a split-second pause. "No, that's fine." Brigitte sounded casual and made it clear that she had better things to do with her time.

"Noon tomorrow then?" Jim said

pleasantly. "On the set? Or at your place afterward?"

"My place at seven," she said, pleased to call the shots and set the venue. She wasn't going to meet with the FBI on the set. What if someone thought it was about her? Jim was delighted with her suggestion. It fit perfectly with his plans. She had walked right into it with ease.

The next day he arrived at her house on Mulholland Drive promptly at seven. It was a beautiful old home that had been remodeled, with a handsome garden and a big pool. Her Aston Martin was in the driveway. Jack Sprague was with him when he rang the bell. Jim had worn a suit, which he often did for work, and a tie, which was rare in L.A. His son Bobby said it made him look like a cop, but it was a good suit. After all, as he told Bobby, he was FBI. It was a standing joke with them.

Brigitte answered the door wearing a short Balenciaga dress. He wouldn't have recognized the label, but he knew it was expensive and looked great on her. She had a heavy gold cuff on one arm, with small diamonds sparkling in it, and the diamond studs on her ears that she often wore. She had just had her long blond hair blown out, and it looked fabulous, and she had a fresh manicure and pedicure. Her makeup was subtle and flawless as always, her hips slim, her bust generous, and she looked like she'd just stepped off the cover of *Vogue*. She was an enticing sight to any man, and no one would have believed she was thirty-nine—she didn't look a minute past twenty-four. Jim Kingston was impressed, and Jack nearly drooled.

Brigitte was cautious as she opened the door. Jim introduced both of them, and walked into the entrance hall as she stepped aside. Beautiful old cathedral ceilings and an antique crystal chandelier met his gaze. There was a smattering of antique furniture, a round modern carpet, and a large modern painting above the stairs. She led them into a living room that overlooked the pool. It was quite a place. It didn't have the comfort and ease of Tallie's house, but in some ways it was similar, and looked like what Tallie's house could have, if she'd made as much effort with it as Brigitte, or spent as much on the art and antiques. Jim looked at Tallie's assistant carefully, as she sat down on an elegant white couch. She was actually much less beautiful than the woman she worked for, but she had maximized and enhanced all her assets, surgically or with flattering clothes, hairstyle, and makeup, and wound up looking far more impressive than her boss. But it was Tallie who was the real beauty, in spite of her ragbag style, no makeup, and disheveled hair. Brigitte just knew how to work it all better, and looked like, and apparently lived like, a star.

Her house was spectacular, and seemed as though a decorating magazine was about to arrive to shoot it. It was exquisite, impeccable, and elegant, and the garden looked like a corner of Versailles.

"Wow! This is quite a place," Jim said with obvious admiration as he glanced outside. "How long have you had it?" It sounded like a conversation, not an interrogation, which was a sign of his considerable skill. Jack admired his style. Brigitte blossomed like a flower as he chatted casually and admired her home, and Jack just stared at her. As their kids would have said, she was "hot"!

"I've been here for seven years now," she said proudly. "I was in Santa Monica before, on the beach, but the house was too small. I came into some money, so I upgraded to here. It's a work in progress. I'm always working on it. I just redid the upstairs, and remodeled my bathroom, and put all new trees in the garden."

"I'd love to see what you've done," Jim said, smiling at her. "I'm remodeling right now too. It's driving me nuts. I can't get anything finished." They were talking about contractors and what a headache they were as she led him upstairs. Her bedroom looked as though it had been designed for Marie Antoinette, in contrast to Tallie's very stark bedroom he had seen at her home, whose main features were a large flat screen and an unmade bed. Brigitte's bedroom was totally perfect, and she had a large antique four-poster bed, covered in miles of pale yellow silk.

"An heirloom?" he asked, pointing to the bed, and she nodded.

"It was my great-grandmother's. I've had it in storage for years. Thank God my evil stepmother didn't take it." She talked about her a lot, the evil step-mother who had caused her to flee San Francisco and move to L.A. eighteen years before. She had been there ever since, although she went home from time to time, but the stories she told about her stepmother were legion.

She showed him three handsome guest bedrooms on the second floor, all with antique beds, although less grand than her own, and the remodeled bath-room that he gazed at with envy and awe.

"That would take my contractor two years to produce," he said, admiring an enormous round tub with a Jacuzzi in the middle of the room, and a fabulous shower built for two. Everything in the bathroom was pink and white marble, including the walls and floor. And it had a view over the garden. You could see the layout of the beautiful garden even better from here.

"It took my contractor a year," she admitted, "and I had to beat him up every day, but he did a good job. And he came in at a good price." She was obviously very proud of her home. Tallie enjoyed hers, but you could tell she didn't really care. All her creativity went into her work. Clearly, this was Brigitte's realm of expertise and pride and joy. She had no children, so she could afford to spoil herself. She didn't have to worry about kids in college. All she had was herself.

They walked back downstairs afterward as they chatted, and she offered them both a drink, and they declined. Jim asked for a glass of water instead, and they walked into her kitchen, which was state-of-the-art, with every piece of fancy culinary equipment imaginable. Everything was done in black granite, even the kitchen table.

"This really is quite a house," he said in awe, and she beamed. "You must love it here." He looked envious, which thrilled her and flattered her ego.

"I do. I work hard, and it's a joy to come home at the end of a day or a trip. Especially if we're in a hut somewhere in Africa while we shoot, with snakes all over the place."

"You must be happy to be back from Palm Springs," Jim commented, taking the glass of water from her.

"Yes, I am. 'There's no place like home!'" she quoted from *The Wizard of Oz.*

They went back into the living room again then and sat down.

"So tell me," Jim said with a sigh, nursing his glass of water in the Baccarat glass she had handed him. "I gather Hunter Lloyd was taking Ms. Jones's money from you."

"Yes, he was," Brigitte said with a disapproving look. "I was very upset about it, and I should have told her, but I was afraid to screw up their romance if I exposed him." Jim nodded as though he understood completely and admired her for her silence.

"I gather he had a romance with you too," Jim said, and Brigitte looked as though she were about to fall off the couch.

"Not really," she said, recovering quickly, "not at all. What we had was a blackmail situation. He got me drunk one night, and I ended up in bed with him, he forced me to have sex with him, and from then on he blackmailed me, and said that if I didn't continue sleeping with him, he'd tell Tallie we had an affair. I did it to save our friendship and my job."

"That's a nasty position to be in," he said sympathetically. "It must have been rough for you."

"It was."

"How long did that go on?"

"Three years," she said with a martyred look.

"Why did it stop?"

"He got involved with someone else."

"That must have been a relief for you," Jim said, and took another sip of water as Brigitte watched him.

"It was. Does Tallie know about this?" Brigitte tried to look relaxed as she asked. "I never told her."

"No," he said conspiratorially, "I got it

from another source, but I assumed I could discuss it with you."

"Of course. Actually, it's a relief not to have to keep it a secret. I would never tell Tallie, though. I think it would break her heart."

"It probably would. She seems pretty upset about the other girl, the one he left her for, Angela Morissey, the one who's pregnant."

"It was a rotten thing for him to do to Tallie."

"Do you know who told her?"

"I did. I thought she should know. It came out when she asked about the money. I finally had to tell her about that too. Hunt got away with it for four years. And she's such a good person, she doesn't deserve it," Brigitte said with her bright blue eyes. "We've been friends now for seventeen years, ever since we went to film school together."

"I think she started out as an actress, didn't she?" Jim asked with interest. He looked fascinated by every word she said. And as always, Jack sat in a chair nearby, looking bored and half asleep, but he was listening too.

"Yes, she was in a big movie, as a supporting actress. She was very good. She hated it, though. All she ever wanted to do was direct after that. She had some offers, but acting was never her thing. She made an indie movie and the rest is history."

"What about you?" Jim asked, and Brigitte laughed, showing rows of perfect white teeth. She had a fabulous smile, and he had to admit she was pretty enough to be an actress; she just wasn't quite as distinctive looking as her boss. "Were you ever in movies? You should have been."

"A few minor ones. I kind of went to film school for fun. I was never really interested in making movies, like Tallie. I did some modeling when I was in college, and then I helped Tallie make her first movie, and I had more fun working with her after that. I never had the kind of drive about it that she did." She implied without saying it that she didn't need to. "And let's face it," she said modestly, "I don't have her talent." At least she gave her that, Jim thought. "She's going to be one of the legendary filmmakers of our time. I'm sure she's going to win an Oscar one of these days. She deserves it. And she doesn't need Hunt to make her career. She's done it all on her own." Brigitte sounded proud of her longtime friend, and they exchanged a smile.

"What do you think Hunt did with her money that he was taking from you?" He went back to that again, and Brigitte shrugged.

"I have no idea, spend it on other women, maybe."

"He doesn't seem to need the money," Jim said practically.

"Who knows? That's like all the Beverly Hills housewives who get arrested for shoplifting. Some people just get a thrill out of stealing other people's stuff."

"Did he ever give you anything, expensive gifts when you were involved with him?"

"We weren't *involved*," Brigitte corrected him. "I was being blackmailed."

"Well, did he ever give you anything?"

She shrugged again. "Some nice din-

ners, a couple of weekends at good hotels. We went to Hawaii once, and to
New York a couple of times, when Tallie
was on location without me." Jim didn't
comment.

"Was he generous with Tallie . . . Ms.
Jones . . . ?"

"He paid some of the bills, maid, util-
ities, groceries, a few things they
bought for the house together."

"And then he'd steal her money to
pay for it? What a sleazy trick," Jim said
innocently, and Brigitte didn't comment.
She had said enough. "Did she ever
cheat on him?"

"Not that I know of. She's not that
kind of woman. She's really a very quiet
person, and a straight shooter." *In contrast to her assistant,* Jim wanted to add
but didn't. He didn't like this woman,
but nothing he was thinking about her
showed. He had led her down the garden path very nicely, to all the places he
had wanted to visit along the way. She
was reveling in the attention, and what
appeared to be their common interests
and shared points of view about life.
Jim had made interrogation an art.

"Can you think of anyone else who might be taking cash from Tallie?" Jim asked with a thoughtful look.

"Victor Carson maybe. He's kind of a fusty old guy, and he has an expensive-looking younger wife."

"Yeah, that'll do it." Jim laughed at her comment. "We've already spoken to him and Hunter Lloyd." She looked surprised when he said that, and then he flattered her, and she looked pleased. He implied that he was flirting with her, and she clearly liked that too. "We saved the best for last."

"It all stopped anyway when he left, didn't it?" she asked with a flirtatious smile.

"It appears that way. But if it's someone else doing it, or several people, it'll start up again. Be sure to let us know if that happens. Right away."

"Absolutely. I had no idea he was taking as much as he did. He took it in relatively small amounts, and it slipped right through my fingers. I never really kept track."

"And Ms. Jones never pays her own bills or checks her accounts?"

"She doesn't have time, especially when she's on location, or even in town."

"She doesn't sign her own checks, does she?"

"No, she doesn't," Brigitte said primly.

"Does she ever look at her bank statements?"

"She never has. That's why she has me. I keep it all in good order, and then send it all to Victor Carson."

"That's a lot for you to keep track of too," Jim said sympathetically.

"I love doing whatever I can to help her. We've had a wonderful time together for all these years."

"She told me how much she counts on you. She said she has complete and total faith in you," he assured Brigitte, and she looked pleased. "She's lucky to have you," he complimented her again.

"I'm just as lucky to have her," Brigitte said as Jim stood up, and Jack appeared to wake up and followed them from the living room back to the main hallway.

"Thanks for the tour of the house," he

said warmly. "It really was a treat. Great house you have here, and you've done a terrific job. You can always become a decorator if the director's assistant market dries up," he said with a warm smile.

"I hope it never will," she said happily, and opened the front door.

They were gone a minute later, and Brigitte bounded up the stairs to the bedroom and took off her clothes. Tommy was coming by that night, and she wanted to get ready before he did. The FBI had taken forever, they had been there for two hours. The questions were all run-of-the-mill, but she thought it had gone well. She hoped it was the last of it, especially since there had been no outflow of Tallie's cash since Hunt had left. There was nothing further to pursue. The mystery had been solved. And the FBI could go back to whatever else they did.

She slipped into a perfumed bath then, just as her cell phone rang. It was Tommy, telling her he would be late, but he promised to be there in an hour.

"Perfect. That's all the time I need to

get ready for you," she said with a sultry smile that would have melted steel. He could sense her good humor even over the phone. He could hardly wait to get there. Their nights together were fantastic, and he was going to Mexico with her over the hiatus. To the Palmilla in Cabo San Lucas, one of the most luxurious hotels in the world. She had invited him. She was quite a woman, and he had never had so much fun or wild sex in his life.

"So what do you think?" Jack asked Jim as they drove down the hill after their visit to Brigitte. The whole setup was impressive, and she was a beautiful woman in a gorgeous house. Jack couldn't figure out why she needed to steal and lie. She had everything going for her, and a fabulous life.

"You know what I think," Jim said quietly with a serious expression. He particularly liked the part where she had been taken by force and blackmailed for three years thereafter by Hunter Lloyd, which had included expensive dinners, fancy hotels, and vacations. It didn't sound like a hardship for Brigitte to go along with it.

"Are you ready to go to one of the deputies on this?" Jack asked him. "We've been doing interviews for weeks." They had interviewed Tallie's maid and gardener too, who had testified that Hunt had always given them tips and was a very generous man. They had interviewed Brigitte's employees too, who said they never saw her, but commented on the variety of young men who went in and out of the place. When they showed them a photograph of Hunt, none of them had ever seen him at the house, but the employees of the Chateau Marmont and the Sunset Marquis had, and remembered them well. They had been regular guests for several years, and always seemed to be having a great time. They drank a lot of champagne, ordered room service, and never left the room. And sometimes they spent the night. It was clear they were both enjoying themselves and their stays at the hotels had been frequent and regular.

"I want to wait for the report from San Francisco," Jim said seriously. "It's coming in tomorrow. Let's see what that says first."

"Probably nothing earth-shattering," Jack said.

"I want to go to the stores of the designers she wears too, and some jewelers. Tallie gave me some names, although she didn't think we'd come up with anything. Everything she wears is a gift, given to her by designers and stores so she will get Tallie to wear their things." He had been meaning to do it for weeks, but he'd been too busy. They had other cases to deal with, some of them more pressing than this. "After that, we're through. I'm ready to make a recommendation. All we have right now is circumstantial evidence and our instincts. But it's the best we can do. That and the fact that the victim lost close to a million dollars in cash in the past three years. That ought to do it."

Jim was itching to make an arrest, and he knew that Tallie wanted that too. She had also been waiting for Jim to tell her that she could fire Brigitte, and it was getting more and more difficult to have her around. And Jim felt that she could do that now. They almost had enough, and it was probably all they would get. He had seen Brigitte's bank accounts, obtained through the bank with a confidential agreement, which precluded them from telling her that they had released her accounts to the FBI, and she had made many large deposits in the last few years, always in cash. And the money had gone out as fast as it went in. There was no way to tell what she had done with it. But what he hoped was that, confronted with the accusation and an arrest, she would cave, confess, and agree to make a guilty plea. It would be the cleanest scenario for them all, and he was sure she wouldn't want the embarrassment and expense of going to trial, although she looked as though she could afford it. She made a hefty salary, and there was a fair amount of money in her bank accounts.

Jim dropped Jack off at the FBI office and went home. Bobby was there, eating a pizza and watching TV with a couple of friends.

"No homework?" Jim asked, raising an eyebrow.

"All done." Making sure the boys did their homework had been Jeannie's department, but for five years now it had been his. Breakfast, dinner, homework, laundry, housekeeping, Little League, carpool, getting the boys to all their sports games, field trips, taking care of them when they were sick, going to doctors, back-to-school clothes and supplies, teachers' conferences, decorating the house and tree at Christmas, Christmas cards, taking their black Lab to the vet. He was a one-man band, and there were times when he missed her so much it nearly killed him. Not for what she did, but for who she was. He had loved her since high school. He had loved her for twenty-seven years, and he still couldn't believe she was gone. It still took his breath away sometimes.

The boys had their feet on the coffee table, watching TV, still in their sports clothes, and were laughing loudly. The pizza box had just fallen on the carpet facedown, and they had open Coke cans on the table that were about to spill, and often had before.

"Hey, you guys!" Jim reminded them. "Could we not destroy the house, please?"

"Sorry, Dad," Bobby said with a penitent look, and then they began shoving each other and rough-housing on the couch. It was hopeless, but he loved having them around. He rolled his eyes and went upstairs to work on his computer. He was thinking about Brigitte Parker's house when he did, with all its glamour and glory. It was so different from the house where he had seen Tallie Jones, which was so much warmer and more real. But there was no denying that Brigitte's home was beautiful. And he knew how much she made. Tallie paid her a whopping salary every year, with perks, benefits, bonuses, and numerous gifts. And she had still slept with Tallie's boyfriend. That had to hurt. No wonder Tallie had looked so ravaged the first time he met her, it had been the night after she saw Meg, and why she wanted to fire Brigitte now, whether or not she had been stealing money from her. The betrayal had been just too much to forgive. And Brigitte still thought she didn't know. Tallie had played her part well. Brigitte was right. Tallie was a damn good actress as well as director.

Bobby's friends went home at eleven o'clock, and he stopped in his father's room when he came upstairs.

"Still working, Dad?"

"Yeah." Jim swiveled in his desk chair with a smile to look at his youngest son. He dreaded his leaving for school in two years and was glad he was still at home.

"You work too hard, Dad," Bobby said kindly, and came over to rub his shoulders. It was the only human contact Jim had now. The only hugs and touches he got now were from his sons. He had never been able to bring himself to date after Jeannie, and still didn't want to. The guys in the FBI office had razzed him about it for a while and wanted to introduce him to their wives' friends, but now they finally left him alone. They got it. He wasn't ready, and maybe never would be. The memories he had of their years together were enough, and he had the boys. "Working on any interesting cases, Dad?" Bobby asked him as he flopped down on the bed.

"Some." Jim never talked about them at home until they were resolved, but the boys always loved to ask, hoping to hear tales of blood, gore, and excitement, and the occasional shootout, although those were rare. Jim shied away from those cases. He always carried a gun, but very seldom had occasion to use it. He was better known now for his success with white-collar crime than with the more violent ones. He liked solving his cases, not just shooting his way through them, and he didn't like the physically dangerous stuff since he had lost Jeannie. If something happened to him, there would be no one to take care of his kids.

"What are you working on right now?" Bobby asked him, staring at the ceiling as he lay on the California king-size bed that was too big for Jim now.

"A very interesting credit card fraud

case that covers thirteen states, an industrial espionage ring, and two embezzlements, one of them for nearly a million dollars," Jim said as he smiled at him. He was such a good boy, as was Josh, and he loved them both. He missed Josh a lot and talked to him as often as Josh was willing. He was enjoying college.

"Sounds boring," Bobby said with a blasé look as he got up. "I guess you're not going to shoot anyone this week."

"I hope not," Jim laughed, and went to get undressed as Bobby headed to his room to put on his pajamas. He was sure the boys had left a mess downstairs, but he could clean it up in the morning before he left for work. He always did. They had a woman come in to do the heavy cleaning once a week, and he and Bobby did the rest.

He went in to say goodnight to Bobby, who was watching TV from his bed, and then he went back to his own room. He reminded himself that he wanted to hit the stores on Rodeo Drive in the morning. Tallie had given him a long list of stores that sent Brigitte expensive gifts. That was an assignment that would really have disgusted his son, and he was thinking about it as he went to bed, and smiled nostalgically. Jeannie would have loved a morning on Rodeo Drive. Everything he did and thought about always led him back to her.

Chapter 13

Jim started with the stores on Rodeo Drive, and walked from one end to the other. Gucci, Fendi, Prada, Jimmy Choo, Dolce and Gabbana, Roberto Cavalli, and there were several jewelry stores whose names Tallie had given him too: Cartier, Van Cleef, and Harry Winston. He was mildly embarrassed not to have checked the stores sooner, but he just hadn't had time. His priority had been interviewing the suspects and reviewing the evidence gathered by the forensic accountants. If they went to trial, they needed proof "beyond a reasonable doubt."

In each store he walked into, he asked for the general manager, and inquired about the free gifts given to Brigitte Parker, Tallie Jones's assistant. Tallie had assured him that Brigitte got free merchandise everywhere, for some very high-end items, everything from jewelry to furs to luggage. Tallie said Brigitte always bragged to her about it, but Jim just wanted to check it out for himself. It was a phenomenon he wasn't familiar with, to that degree, and he wanted to know how it worked.

And in each case, he got the same answer. Some claimed that once a year they sent out a gift, like a scarf, a nightgown, or a sweater, a decorative glass, a pen, a crystal table object, in thanks to their best customers, usually at Christmas. In some cases they offered VIP discounts, for which Brigitte didn't qualify. They all assured him that Brigitte was one of their best customers, and she paid for everything she bought, and only occasionally with a small courtesy discount. And they confirmed that

the items she purchased were expensive. Several fur coats, in a rainbow of
colors, including a fifty-thousand-dollar
golden sable jacket at Dior, four-thou-
sand-dollar handbags, a diamond
necklace, and a vast number of sweat-
ers, shoes, and dresses. But in every in-
stance, they assured him that Brigitte
paid for her purchases herself, and
none of them had been gifts from the
store, contrary to what she told Tallie.
Once again, Brigitte had lied.

He asked if she paid by check, credit
card, or cash, and their records showed
that she always paid cash, except for
the sable, which she had paid for by
cashier's check. Jim asked the manager then if it was possible that his
sales force actually gave her the items
as gifts without his knowledge. The
manager of Prada laughed when Jim
asked him. "Not if they intend to stay
employed here. That would be theft, as
far as we're concerned. I'm sure Ms.
Parker has had gifts from us at Christmas over the years, but that would be a
key chain, a wallet, or a scarf. Nothing
larger. We're running a business here,

not a charity drive. We make our share of charitable donations, but not to our clients." Jim looked faintly embarrassed to have asked the question. But the picture of Brigitte's shopping habits had become clear to him in two hours on Rodeo Drive. She spent a fortune, always in cash, and none of the expensive items that she wore were gifts, contrary to what she claimed and Tallie believed. She was one of the best customers at every store, some more than others, and she had never used a credit card in any store, just cash. Her employer's cash, most likely.

The jewelers told him the same story, and from what he could tell, her expenditures on jewelry and clothes far exceeded her income, not to mention the expensive decorations and antiques he had seen in her house the day before. He could have kicked himself for not making this little exploration sooner. It was all the evidence they needed. She had even bought herself a diamond ring the year before for nearly a hundred thousand dollars. And unless her family was sending her money he knew nothing about, that hadn't shown up in her bank accounts, Brigitte Parker was getting all this cash from somewhere. She had stopped taking it when Hunt left Tallie's house, but at the rate she spent money, Brigitte wouldn't be able to stop for long. And it was going to be easy to get her shopping records from all the stores Jim had just been to and several others. He had been to ten stores on Rodeo Drive and three jewelers, and he was beaming when he walked into his office.

"Do I want to know what happened to you on the way to work this morning?" Jack asked him as he walked into the room where Jim was sitting at his desk with a beatific expression. He had everything he needed for the assistant U.S. attorney he had spoken to initially to pursue the case and issue a warrant for her arrest.

"I got lucky." Jim grinned at him.

"You look it." Jack leered.

"I've been on Rodeo Drive all morning, and thank your stars you're not married to Brigitte Parker. The woman spends a fortune."

"I thought it was all courtesy gifts because of her employer."

"Not a one. She must have spent
more than a million in the last three
years. We're going to have to check Tallie Jones's books again. She's pulling
out more than we think. And she pays
for everything she buys in cold, hard
U.S. currency, cash." He was grinning
from ear to ear, as Jack dropped a
printout on his desk.

"This must be your lucky day then."
Jack's smile matched Jim's as he
pointed to it. "That's a present to you
from the San Francisco bureau. They
talked to her father, her stepmother, and
her sister. The story about the stepmother is true—they hate each other.
But other than that, nothing she told her
boss is true. She has no trust fund.
They have no money. Her father is retired and worked for the phone company. Her mother died when she was a
kid, and the stepmother says she's a
pathological liar and always has been,
even as a child. She has ripped them all
off for money on various occasions.
She slept with her sister's husband,

borrowed money from him, blackmailed him, threatening to expose their affair to her sister, and pretty well wiped out their savings. It sounded a little like her threats to Hunt. She never goes back to San Francisco, and if she does, she never calls them, and they don't want her to. Barney in the SF office says the father is a nice old guy and cries when he talks about her, says he doesn't know what's wrong with her. She spent about a year in a psychiatric hospital after her mother died, and got picked up regularly for shoplifting as a kid. There was something about credit card fraud, on a small scale, but it was never prosecuted. None of them have seen her in about fifteen years and hope they never do again. Oh," he remembered and then added, "and she was never a debutante, if anybody cares."

"Hollyyyyy shit," Jim said with an even bigger grin. "Bingo!" And then his face clouded over. "Do you think the family will warn her that we're on to her?"

"According to the boys in SF, they never talk to her and don't want to. Her sister says she hopes she goes to jail where she belongs. And with a little luck, and the help of the U.S. attorney's office, we may just be able to make her dreams come true. I don't think you need to worry about them tipping her off. It's all yours, maestro. It's all in the report," he said, pointing to the papers on his desk.

"You'd better get out of here, or I'm going to kiss you!" Jim warned him, and Jack pretended to run to the door.

"Don't you dare!" The two men were laughing as Jack left and went back to his own office. Jim read through the report carefully, and now he had everything he needed. The only question he knew the deputy U.S. attorney would ask him would be if it qualified for the FBI, or if they had to turn it over to the police, but Jim thought he had a good case for keeping it with them. They had discovered that she had used Tallie's free air miles several times without her permission, which was a federal felony, and Victor had pointed out that she had made several improper transfers from Tallie's bank online, which was federal

wire fraud, so they were clean. Jim
didn't want to give up the case. He
wanted to do Tallie Jones the favor of
prosecuting this woman, and getting
back whatever they could for her, the
merchandise if nothing else, so Tallie
could sell it. And maybe her house, furniture, art, and antiques. It looked as
though she spent the cash she took
very quickly. And now he wanted to investigate how she had paid for her
house, since it was obvious she hadn't
inherited the money, as she said, nor
paid for it with her trust fund, which
she'd never had. Brigitte was a liar from
beginning to end, and poor Tallie had
trusted her and fallen for it hook, line,
and sinker. He wondered how long Brigitte had been stealing from her, and
suspected that she had for many, many
years, possibly the entire time, ever
since Tallie started making money, and
really serious money from her work. The
only thing that had hidden what Brigitte
had done was the fact that Tallie made
such huge amounts from her films, and
that she trusted Brigitte so completely,
she never checked her accounts, or Bri-

gitte's handling of her money. Her assistant had had free rein for all those years. It had been foolish of Tallie to trust her to that extent, but Brigitte had carefully cultivated their friendship, and developed Tallie's total trust in her, and being trusting and believing in people you thought you knew well wasn't a crime and didn't deserve to be met by a criminal response and wholesale exploitation. Jim wanted to do everything he could to help.

He put the most recent printout in the folder and went to the U.S. attorney's office across the street, to see one of the deputies he worked with most frequently. Henry Loo was at his desk when Jim walked into the room, and the two men smiled at each other. Jim liked him because Henry was tough, but also reasonable to work with. They had had a lot of successful cases together.

"You look like a happy camper," Henry commented, pointing to the chair across his desk. "Whatcha got?"

"A nice one for you. All gift-wrapped and tied up in ribbons." Jim knew that pursuing stolen cash was always more

difficult to prove than credit cards or
checks out of a victim's account, or the
perpetrator's, but the stream of cash
was so direct, the expenditures so far
beyond her means, and the lies so perfectly executed that Jim had no doubts
about his case. And by the time he finished explaining it to Henry, and
handed him the file across his desk,
Henry was pleased too. Jim said, "I've
been working on this for two months,"
which was pretty quick for them. And
he realized now that it might have been
less than that if he had gone to Rodeo
Drive sooner. But now everything had
fallen into place, particularly with the report from the San Francisco FBI office.
And he also explained to Henry why it
should stay with them and not go to the
police, and Henry agreed. They were
clear. "She tried blaming the victim's
ex-boyfriend at first, whom she slept
with by the way. But the guy makes a
fortune and seems to be honest in his
financial dealings. So is the accountant,
we checked him out too, although the
poor guy is a wreck, with a younger wife
who's pumping him for money. But this

is a good case. We've got what we need here. I'm sure we can convict."

"Sounds like it," the young deputy said, looking pleased. "Think she'll plead?"

"Hard to say. Depends how tight we make the noose around her neck, and how smart her attorney is. I don't think she's going to love going to prison, but given the amounts, she has no choice there. They're not going to let her off as a first-time offender, because it's aggravated by repeated theft on a continuing basis, and you have a serious case of abuse of trust here," which they both knew would increase her prison sentence. "The victim trusted her completely."

"The victim doesn't have a problem with it? She's not going to beg for mercy for her best friend?"

"Not a chance. The assistant slept with her boyfriend for three years."

"Has she fired her?"

"Not yet. I asked her to hold off until we were sure what we had from the investigation. I didn't want our suspect to disappear on us. She's waiting to hear when she can let her go. I think it's okay now."

"Did you interview the assistant?" The deputy U.S. attorney wanted to make sure they had all the loose ends tied up before he went to the grand jury and asked a federal judge for a warrant for her arrest if the grand jury cleared it. Jim was sure they would and so was Henry.

"I interviewed her yesterday," Jim said confidently.

"What'd you get?"

"Lies from beginning to end, all the same bullshit about her trust fund and her inheritance. And I got a very nice house tour. It's a spectacular house in the hills, and was probably purchased by the victim without her knowledge, using her cash. I'll look into that now too. It would be good if we can get it for her as restitution. A least she can sell it."

"You'll have to talk to the judge and the IRS about that." They both knew that Brigitte wouldn't have paid income taxes on the stolen money, which absurdly was the law, so she would be liable for tax evasion now too, and the IRS would want their quart of blood. They always did. There was always a battle between the victim and the IRS for property that had been purchased with stolen funds, and it would have to be negotiated, but that was far, far down the road. Jim wanted to get restitution for Tallie, and the U.S. attorney could help, but ultimately it would be up to the judge when Brigitte either pleaded guilty or was convicted, and she hadn't even been arrested yet or indicted.

"How fast can you get me a warrant for her arrest?" Jim asked with a gleam in his eye. He wanted to move forward now, and he knew it would be a relief to Tallie. It was some kind of vindication for what she'd been through, and the betrayal she'd experienced at Brigitte's hands, not to mention the loss of an enormous amount of cash.

"Give me a chance," Henry said, holding up his hands. "I've got to get it to the grand jury and get an indictment. I'll do that as soon as I can, and then I'll

go to the judge for a warrant. I need
your summary report."

"I'll have it for you tomorrow, two
days latest," Jim said and Henry nodded.

"And our judges are swamped. But I
promise you that as soon as you get me
the report, and the grand jury gives us
the go-ahead, I'll walk it over."

"Good enough." He knew it would
take about a week after that to get the
warrant, as the judge went through the
stacks of requests for warrants on his
desk, and Brigitte wasn't a physical
danger to anyone, so others would
come first, who were. And once Jim
had the warrant, he could make the arrest. He could notify her attorney, if she
had one, and spare her the embarrassment of being taken out of her home or
place of work in handcuffs. But as far as
Jim knew, she didn't have an attorney
yet, since she had no idea she was a
suspect.

"Some of that cash may be hard to
trace," Henry reminded him.

"Yeah, but the spending pattern isn't.
I think she took it straight to Rodeo

Drive and her jewelers, and then she
pretended to her employer that it was
all gifts. She's pretty smooth, and the
story was entirely believable, particularly if she had family money supposedly, so no one suspected for all these
years. It showed up in an unexpected
audit, so she blamed the boyfriend. In
fact, he and Tallie Jones broke up over
it, that and the affair he had with the assistant for three years."

"Maybe they can get back together
now," Henry said facetiously, with a
smile. He was happy with the case, and
so was Jim. The case looked solid to
both of them.

But Jim shook his head. "Actually,
the boyfriend is having a baby now with
someone else, another woman he was
cheating on her with." Henry looked up
at him and laughed.

"You lead a much more exotic life
than I do. Where do you come up with
these people?"

"Hollywood." Jim grinned. "Although
the victim is a very nice, seemingly normal woman, who isn't involved in all the
bullshit and bling, which is why I think

all this went right over her head. She spends all her time working, while the assistant spends her money. As my mother-in-law used to say, 'Nice work if you can get it.'" They both laughed, and a few minutes later, Jim left Henry's office and went back to his own. They were on their way.

He called Tallie as soon as he got back to his desk. She sounded distracted and was on the set.

"I'd like to speak to you later, if you have time," he said to Tallie.

"I'm working late. Something wrong?"

"No, on the contrary. Extremely good. You can let her go now. We got everything we wanted, to get started anyway. We're ready to roll. I have to write my report, and then the deputy district attorney will go to the grand jury for an indictment, and then he'll ask a judge for a warrant. I just came from the U.S. attorney's office. You can fire her whenever you want." Tallie looked suddenly amazed. She had come to think this day would never happen, and she hadn't heard from Jim in weeks. She was beginning to think he'd forgotten or lost interest. It all moved so slowly, although he assured her this was fast for them. And the fact that she was an important celebrity had helped. It had created interest in the case, and they didn't want to just ignore her. She had lost a huge amount of money.

"When do you think it will happen?" she asked cryptically, but he knew what she meant.

"I'll probably get the warrant next week or the week after. I'll move on it then."

"I'll be in New York with my daughter." She sounded disappointed.

He chuckled. "I wasn't expecting you to be there for the arrest. I think I can manage it myself. Trust me, I've done it before." She suddenly laughed and felt relieved. Jim had done everything he said he would. And now she had to figure out when to fire Brigitte, and how. That would be a relief too. She wanted to get Brigitte away from her now. Any vestige of their friendship and trust had been destroyed, and in spite of that she'd had to fake it for two months.

Now all she wanted to do was get it all behind her and never see Brigitte again. She didn't allow herself to think of the friend she had lost, or what she had done to her. "Do you want me to come by and talk to you about all of it after work?" She thought about it for a minute. She still had questions and didn't want to discuss them at work, and she was leaving in the morning to see Max.

"I have to wrap up here, and I want to see my father tonight after work . . . and pack . . . Is nine o'clock too late for you?"

"I can manage it," he said quietly. He could have dinner with Bobby before he met her. He had a real life too. "That's fine," he confirmed.

"See you then . . . and thank you!" she said, and then hung up. Brigitte was just walking by when she ended the call.

"Who was that?" She was curious about everything these days, or maybe she always had been. But Tallie was more sensitive to it now.

"Greg Thomas. I promised my father

I'd help him get some of his papers in order. You know how old people are." Her father was old but sharp as a tack, and Brigitte didn't question her excuse.

"How's he feeling?"

"Not so great," Tallie said sadly. That much was true. He seemed to be failing slowly, like a candle being slowly snuffed out. She did everything she could to keep him engaged and alive, but some days he was just too tired to care or get up.

Tallie and Brigitte went back to the office together to take care of some last-minute details before she left for New York. Tallie wondered if she'd ever see her again. Maybe at the trial, if there was one, unless she pleaded guilty before that.

"Do you need anything?" Brigitte asked her with a smile, as they got to their cars parked next to each other.

"No, I'm fine. I've got to see my father, and pack. I can't wait to see Max." She was excited too. And she had so much to tell her. She knew nothing about Hunt or Brigitte, or any of what had happened. They would have a lot to talk about during their week together.

"Do you want help packing?" Brigitte offered. The perfect assistant, who had stolen her blind, and slept with Hunt. She could forgive her none of it now, and wanted her gone as soon as possible. She couldn't even imagine what it would be like to be arrested, and what her life would be like now. Jim said she would go to prison for sure because of the amount she had stolen, and there was probably more. "I can bring over dinner if you want."

"I'm just going to pack and go to bed. I hate that early flight," Tallie said, smiling back at her. And every time she did now, it felt false. She was used to getting up early to be on the set, so even that was a lie. Everything was now. Everything Tallie said to her felt wrong, and everything Brigitte had done had been worse.

Brigitte gave her a hug as they left each other, and Tallie hugged her back, feeling her insides cringe when she did. "Give Max my love."

"Have fun in Mexico!" Tallie called out

as she left. Brigitte had said she was going to Palmilla, but she hadn't said with whom, and Tallie didn't care. It made Tallie wonder, as she walked to her car, when and how she was going to fire her. She called Greg Thomas from the car. She wanted to discuss it with him, and she told him everything that had been happening, and that the FBI were going to make the arrest in the next week.

"I've been waiting to fire her until they told me I could. The special agent in charge of the case called me today and told me. He's coming by tonight. So what do I do about her?"

"I'd like to notify her by letter and e-mail," Greg said quietly. "I don't want you doing it face-to-face. This could get nasty, or even dangerous for you. Do you think she could get violent?" He was worried about Tallie, especially since she was alone at the house now that Hunt was gone.

"I don't think so. I hope not." Tallie hadn't really thought about it. They had been so busy getting evidence and building the case that she had forgotten

what it might be like once she fired Brigitte, and she got arrested. "I think
she'll have bigger problems on her
hands once they arrest her. What are
you going to say to her in the letter?" It
felt strange now thinking about it, as
she drove toward her father's house.
She wanted to talk to him about it too.
But she didn't want him worrying about
her. Every day was a struggle for him.

"I think it should be very businesslike
and clear. Irregularities have come up in
your books that have shaken your confidence in her ability to handle your affairs, and circumstances have come to
light that no longer make it desirable for
her to be your assistant. Best wishes,
good luck, and get lost. How does that
sound?" He laughed.

"Fine, except for the last line." It was
a strange feeling after seventeen years,
which was most of their adult life. But it
was all true. She had no idea what Brigitte's reaction would be, if she would
be angry or crushed. She would probably call Tallie in tears, and deny everything. All Brigitte ever did was lie, as it
turned out.

"Don't worry. I'll clean it up. I'll do it for my signature, not yours. I want you out of the front lines on this. You can always blame it on me. I want to discuss something else with you too. Once she's arrested, we need to file a civil suit against her to try and get some of your money back, as much as we can. She has a house, possessions, jewelry, a car, probably some money in the bank. My guess is it's all yours. I'll start the ball rolling on that while you're away." Tallie realized then that Brigitte's life was about to come down like a house of cards. She had done it to herself. "I'm going to call the bank for you in the morning. We've got to take her off all your accounts and change the codes. And I want the locks changed on your house too. I want all of that taken care of before she gets the termination letter. Do you have anyone who can meet a locksmith at your place tomorrow?" Tallie sighed as she thought about it. Brigitte had done everything for her, until now.

"No, I don't and I'll be in New York all

week," Tallie reminded him. "You can reach me there."

"I hope I won't have to. Enjoy your daughter. I'll take care of everything here. I can send my secretary over to your house to meet the locksmith. And I'll handle the bank for you. Leave all the details to me," he reassured her. She had already given him a set of her keys.

"Thanks, Greg. Brigitte will be away too."

"She'll get the letter by e-mail. And I'll send a hard copy to her home address."

"I guess they'll arrest her when she gets back."

"Let the FBI worry about that. I'll take care of the civil suit and everything else. Go have fun in New York."

"Thank you, Greg." She felt well taken care of, and less alone now without Hunt than she did at first. This had been hard.

She had lost a lot in a short time, and she hated the perception of herself as a victim, but she had been, both Hunt's and Brigitte's. They had both played her for a fool and double-crossed her, in so many ways. It was a terrible feeling, though she was less shocked than she'd been at first. She was beginning to feel like herself again. And she had a few weeks of shooting to do when she got back, and then they would go into post-production, and she'd be finished with the film. She wanted to take a break after that. She had earned it. This had turned into the most stressful year of her life, so far anyway, and she suspected it wouldn't be over for a while, although according to what Jim Kingston had told her, it would take a long time to come to trial, maybe as long as a year, or nine months.

Tallie spent an hour with her father and told him what was going on. He was satisfied with how things were moving and what she could tell him, although he was still shocked about Brigitte. She had fooled them all. She was a total sociopath.

After she sat with her father for a while, Tallie went home. She turned all the downstairs lights on for Jim's visit, dug in the fridge for something to eat while she waited, and came up with half a melon and a piece of cheese. She hadn't eaten a decent meal in two months. She didn't have time to cook, and she didn't care, and she had lost weight as a result. Her torn jeans were hanging off her.

The doorbell rang just as she finished the melon, and she let Jim into the house and thanked him for coming. He had brought a copy of the report from the San Francisco bureau with him, and he handed it to her as they sat down in the kitchen.

"I can offer you soda water, half a lime, a Diet Coke, and a PowerBar, which might be stale. I just checked. What would you like?" she offered with a grin, and he laughed.

"Wow, that's a tough choice. Do you want to share the Diet Coke?"

"I'm fine with water," she said, as she got up to pour the Coke for him.

"You keep a well-stocked kitchen," he complimented her. "Mine would look like that too, if it weren't for my fifteen-year-old son. He eats a pepperoni pizza every two hours. I try to make some-thing decent for him on the weekends."

She hadn't before, but she couldn't resist asking him a personal question then.

"You're not married?"

"My wife died five years ago, of breast cancer. I live with my two boys, one of whom is in college in Michigan. The younger one is still at home."

"I'm sorry about your wife," she said kindly, and meant it.

"Me too. These things happen. I'm lucky I've got great boys. I'd have been lost without them for all these years. We manage pretty well now, but it was tough at first. Very tough. She was a wonderful woman." Tallie nodded, watching his face as he told her. He looked sad, and like he still missed her a lot.

"I brought my daughter up alone too. Her father and I were divorced when she was a baby. It's a terrible thing to say, but sometimes it's easier that way, when you're divorced. Not to have to wrestle with someone about a child. He disappeared out of her life for a long time, and mine."

"Does she see her dad now?" Tallie shook her head and laughed ruefully.

"Not really. She's seen him four times in her life for about half an hour each time. He's a cowboy from Montana on the rodeo circuit. I fell in love with him in college, and Max happened—that's my daughter. My father thought we should get married. It was never a marriage. We were kids. He went back to Montana when she was six months old, and that was that. She's eighteen now, and a truly great kid." She was a year younger than his son Josh.

"I was married one other time for eleven months," she volunteered. "Simon Harleigh." He was an actor the entire world knew. "He cheated on me with the leading lady in his next movie. It was all over the tabloids and that was that. Hunt is the only other man I've ever lived with, and it lasted longer than either of my marriages." She smiled at him while he thought to himself that Hunt had cheated on her too. She hadn't had great luck with men, or made good choices perhaps. And yet she seemed like an extremely kind, decent woman and down-to-earth person. But she lived in a complicated world full of untrustworthy people, dishonesty, and superficial values. He felt bad about how vulnerable she was to people like that. It was hard for some people to resist taking advantage, like Brigitte. And he knew it couldn't be easy for Tallie.

She read the San Francisco report he handed her, and she looked up at Jim afterward in amazement. "She lied about everything. Absolutely nothing she ever said was true, except that her mother had died. The rest was all lies." It was utterly amazing. "It doesn't sound like her family likes her much," she commented.

"It sounds like they have good reason not to. She lied to them too, and ripped them all off. She doesn't seem like it, but she's a sick woman. She looks like anything but that." He told her all about the stores on Rodeo Drive then. It was an incredible story and harder still for Tallie to believe that it had happened to her. She didn't feel like a victim, and she didn't want to be.

"When are you going to arrest her?" She told him about Brigitte's trip to Mexico the following week.

"We'll get her as soon as she gets back," he said dryly.

"Then what happens?"

"She gets arrested, we take her into custody. She gets arraigned a couple of days later and is bound over to trial. The judge sets bail at the arraignment, or lets her out on her own recognizance, they take her passport away, and then we wait to go to trial."

"That's it?" Tallie looked startled. "She walks around for a year like nothing ever happened?"

"Yeah, that's how it works, except in crimes of violence. Otherwise, in white-collar crime like this, she goes on with her normal life until she goes to trial or pleads guilty. Then she gets sentenced, and hopefully she's gone, to prison for several years."

"What if she runs away?"

"We catch her and bring her back. If they set bail, then she posts a bond, or gives up the deed to her house or some similar piece of property to guarantee she won't run away. If she's on her own recognizance, she's pretty much free till the trial. But they won't do that if she's a flight risk. Do you think she is?" Jim asked her, looking concerned. He didn't think Brigitte was. She had a home she obviously cared a lot about. She wouldn't just walk away from that.

"I have no idea," Tallie said honestly. "I don't even know the woman. I thought I did, but I surely don't," she said, waving at the report. "I have no idea what she'd do in a circumstance like this."

"Most people stick around and go to trial or plead. Very few ever run away. I've only had one do it in twenty-six years with the Bureau, and we brought him back. We had to extradite him from England on a big embezzlement case, and that was a long time ago. It'll happen, Tallie, this will be over. It just takes time. And by the time it is over, you'll feel like it took forever. These things move very slowly. But sooner or later, they get resolved. The main thing for you to concentrate on now is getting restitution, and getting back as much as you can, which won't be much. Or it won't be everything you lost. In this case, it sounds like she spends it all, other than her house. Nice house by the way," Jim commented, and Tallie laughed.

"I call it Palazzo Parker. I guess it turns out to be Palazzo Jones. It's a lovely house."

"You may find yourself the proud owner of it when this is all over. My guess is that you paid for it."

"She told me she paid for it with her trust fund, or her inheritance, I can't remember which, and of course I believed her." It was all lies. All of it.

Jim Kingston stood up then and wished her a good trip, and told her he'd see her when she got back. She hoped that Brigitte would be arrested by then, but Jim couldn't be sure. He had to wait for the grand jury, the judge, and the warrant, and then they'd be off and running. But they were almost there. Brigitte's journey into the criminal justice system, and to prison eventually, was about to begin. Tallie felt guilty for

thinking it, but after everything Brigitte
had done to her, she could hardly wait
for it to start, and for Brigitte to pay the
price for the crimes she committed.

Chapter 14

The night that Tallie was packing for New York was a busy one at Victor and Brianna's house too. The war between them had been raging for weeks, and Victor had finally accepted defeat. Brianna had never relented on the postnup or the money she wanted, and Victor's not getting them invited to the Academy Awards nearly two months before, or any of the parties afterward, was the last straw for her.

"You know how badly I wanted to go!" she railed at him. "You promised!" She was half-whining and half-shouting. All she had done was accuse him of things for the past months.

"I didn't promise, Brianna," he said reasonably, looking unhappy. He looked even older than he had before. "I'm not a member of the Academy. I don't get invited to the Oscars. I never told you I could pull that off."

"You didn't even get us invited to the after parties," she accused him with a fearsome pout.

"I would have had to ask one of my clients, like Tallie Jones, and I didn't want to impose. Besides, she has much bigger problems to deal with right now, than getting us invited to the after parties of the Academy Awards." *Vanity Fair* always gave the best one, but he had no access there either.

"So do I." Brianna looked surly as she threw her clothes into Vuitton suitcases she had spread out on the bed and floor. "I have a husband who doesn't give a damn about me, who doesn't want me to feel financially secure, and who broke every promise he ever made about helping me with my career."

"I did everything I could," he said un-

happily, as she emptied racks of platform shoes into a suitcase, and the bed
was piled high with her furs. This was
more than just a statement to impress
him. It was the end, as far as she was
concerned. "Where are you going, Brianna?" he asked with a worried look.

"I reserved a suite at the Beverly
Wilshire." Her announcement filled him
with terror for what it would cost him,
and even more so for the location. It
was across the street from all her favorite stores on Rodeo Drive, which
was why she had reserved there. The
expense for Victor didn't bother her at
all. She turned toward him with an angry look then and confirmed what he
had known was coming at him ever
since she brought up the postnup, and
he no longer believed it had been suggested by her lawyer. The concept was
typical of her.

"Victor, I'm getting a divorce. You're
not the man I thought you were." He felt
her words like a physical blow, but he
was no longer surprised. He knew that
there was no way he could keep her,
and he hadn't been able to afford her

for many months, or even the past two years. What frightened him now was what kind of settlement she would want, and how much alimony she would demand. Even with a prenup, he knew that the divorce was going to cost him a fortune. Brianna had been a disaster in his life. He quietly left the room while she was packing, and went to sit in his study alone. All he could do now, he knew, was let her leave, and hope that he would survive the aftermath of the war.

Brianna packed all night, and when Victor woke up in the big leather chair in his office in the morning, she was gone. It was over. He felt a thousand years old, and numb. She had left no note, no message. Leaving financial chaos in her wake, and closetsful of empty hangers, Brianna had moved on.

The early flight from L.A. touched down at JFK in New York at three in the afternoon. With the time difference, Tallie lost most of the day getting there. And after she got her bags off the carousel,

and took a cab into the city, she was at
her New York apartment at five o'clock.
Max had said she'd be back from class
at six. And the apartment was dark and
empty when she let herself in. It was a
spacious, sunny apartment in a high-
end modern building in the West Village
with a doorman and security. Tallie liked
the fact that she felt Max was protected
there, and she had agreed to let her
stay at the apartment instead of the
dorms. It wasn't showy, but it was a
nice building, and the neighborhood
was safer than most. And the apartment was bright and sunny, and simply
decorated.

There was the usual student debris
lying around, clothes in her bedroom,
books spread out on the table, full ash-
trays, some empty Coke cans, and a
pizza box from the night before. Tallie ti-
died up while she waited for Max to
come home. She threw the garbage
away, made Max's bed, and ran a bath
for herself. She was wearing a cozy
pink terrycloth bathrobe and lying on
her bed when Max walked in, gave a
squeal of delight when she saw Tallie,

and took a flying leap at the bed and lay laughing next to her mother in tattered jeans, a red sweatshirt, and flip-flops. She looked no different than she did in L.A., or than Tallie did anywhere. They almost looked like clones.

"I missed you so much!" Max said as she clung to her mother. They had big plans for the week ahead. Dinner out, meeting Max's new friends, all the places, shops, and restaurants Max had discovered since living there, and Tallie was dying to see at least one Broadway play.

"I missed you too," Tallie said, holding her in her arms. She suddenly felt as though she had come home. Being with Max was like sinking into a big cozy feather bed. For the first time as she lay there, she realized just how brutal the past few months had been, and what a toll they had taken on her. Max could see it too. She thought her mother looked tired, although she didn't say it to her.

"You've been working too hard, Mom," her daughter scolded her. "I'm so glad you came!" And then a minute later, the question Tallie had been dreading. "How's Hunt?"

"I guess he's okay," Tallie said, sounding vague.

"What do you mean you 'guess' he's okay?" Max sat up on the bed and looked down at her mother. "What's that supposed to mean? Is he away?" Tallie didn't answer for a minute, searching for the right words.

"Kind of." And then she took a breath and plunged in. "I didn't want to tell you till I saw you," but she had hoped this question wouldn't come this soon in her stay, "Hunt moved out."

"When?" Max looked shocked.

"About three months ago," she said gently.

"And you didn't tell me? How could you do that?" She was suddenly angry at her mother, for keeping a secret from her, especially something as major as this. She had lived with Hunt since she was fifteen, and he was the closest thing to a father she'd ever had, even if he had arrived late.

"It was complicated. It's really been kind of a difficult time," Tallie admitted, and there were tears in her eyes. She didn't want Max to be angry at her too. The rest was bad enough.

"Complicated how?" Max wanted to decide for herself.

"Well, a lot of stuff has come up in the last few months that I didn't know about. It made it impossible for me to go on living with him."

"Like what? Stop being so mysterious about it. I'm not a child. I'm eighteen." It sounded like childhood to Tallie, but she could still remember how grown-up she had felt at Max's age. She'd had a baby two years later. But Max was nowhere near that, and had no intention of getting married and having a baby at twenty in whatever order.

"To be honest, I don't know where to start. It's a long story, but we had a new Japanese investor for our next movie, which I'm not doing with Hunt, by the way, since you want to know everything. The investor wanted an audit, so we did one, and our accountant discovered that I had quite a lot of missing money, as in close to a million dollars. Someone had been stealing about

twenty-five thousand dollars in cash
from me every month for several years.
So that was the beginning. My accountant was worried. I couldn't understand
it. I asked Brigitte about it, she said she
didn't know anything, although she
should have since she took care of all
my bills. And finally, a couple of days
later, she told me that Hunt had been
stealing money from me, or having Brig
get it for him, and swearing her to se-
crecy—" Max interrupted her before
she could go on, and looked irate.

"Mom, that's bullshit! And you know
it. Hunt would never take any money
from you, or anything else. He's always
giving me money. Hunt would never
steal anything from you. Was Brigitte
crazy or what?"

"Actually, that turned out to be the
case. Brigitte is crazy, and Hunt wasn't
stealing money from me, but someone
was, and I didn't know who. Brigitte
really did convince me it was Hunt, for a
while."

"That's shitty of you," Max said, looking annoyed, as she lay down next to
her mother on the bed again, and

listened to what had happened. It sounded like a long story, and totally insane to her.

"Anyway, aside from the money, Brigitte gave me more bad news." She took a breath before she continued. "She said that Hunt was involved with another woman." With that, Max rolled her eyes and shook her head.

"That's bullshit too. Hunt would never do that to you, Mom. What's wrong with Brigitte? Why is she saying all this stupid stuff about Hunt? Is she mad at him or something?" Max had always loved Brigitte, but the whole story sounded ridiculous to her, and mean to Hunt.

"Yes, she is mad at him. But it turns out she was right. He was seeing someone else, he had been for the last year. I didn't believe her either, so I went to a private investigator, and she showed me pictures of them. To cut the story short, he was involved with this other woman, he's in love with her, and they're having a baby, so that's not such great news," Tallie said with a lump in her throat as Max sat up again and stared at her mother.

"You're lying," she said, wanting that to be true, but it wasn't.

"No, I'm not, sweetheart. I'm sorry, I know you love him, and I do too, or I did . . . but he lied to me. He admitted it about the other woman, though. I asked if he'd stop seeing her and he wouldn't. He loves her. So he moved out." She made it sound matter-of-fact, but it was an ugly story, and that wasn't lost on Max, who was crying by then, as her mother put her arms around her. It was a huge disappointment to them both. "I don't know what happened to him. He just kind of went off the deep end, I guess. But it was very dishonest of him. And as much as it hurt, I'm glad Brig told me."

"How did she know?" Max asked, cuddled up next to her mother like a child. She was badly hurt by what she'd just heard.

"Someone told her. Anyway, the story's not over." Not by a long shot. "When I went to the private investigator, she also told me that Hunt had had an affair with Brig for three years before that. He cut it off when he started seeing this other woman, so you're right. She's pissed at him. Meanwhile, if you add up his three years with her, and the year with this other woman, that means Hunt cheated on me for all four years we were together. Brig claims he forced her into it, he says she did, but you don't force anyone to do something they don't want to do for three years. They were having an affair behind my back. Hunt's a very sweet guy, but he's a cheater and he lied to me. And even if you love him, I couldn't stay with him."

"Of course not, Mom. I understand," Max said, wiping her eyes and hugging her mother. "That's so sad. How could he do such a terrible thing to you? And how could Brig? You're always so good to them, and she's been your friend forever."

"Yeah, I know. I felt pretty bad for a while, a little better now. And there's more. The money. Since they both lied to me, I didn't know who to believe, so the private investigator sent me to the FBI. They investigated the whole thing. Brig has been embezzling from me, maybe for a few years, maybe longer. It turns out that nothing she ever told me about her history is true, she's a liar, and a thief. She's been ripping me off." Max looked totally shocked.

"Oh my God! Mom! How awful!"

"Yes, it is," Tallie said quietly.

"Is she going to give it back?" To Max, it was all so simple. If she took it, she should give it back. Tallie wished she would, but Jim Kingston said that wasn't likely to happen, or not in full anyway, probably only a fraction of what she lost, if that.

"I don't know yet," Tallie said with a sigh. Telling the story to Max, even in a simplified version, made her realize again how truly awful it was. "They're going to arrest her next week. There will be a trial in about a year, and I'm going to sue her to try and get some money back, or her house or something. And she'll probably go to prison." Max was shocked into silence. The man who had been her hero and father figure had cheated on her mother for the whole four years and lied to them both, and the woman who was like an aunt to her was an embezzler, a cheat, a liar, and was going to prison.

"Did you fire her?" Max asked in a hushed voice.

"My lawyer is doing it this week." Tallie made it all sound so straightforward, but it wasn't that easy. "And you know all those gifts she always claims she gets, all the jewelry and furs and Prada bags and stuff? It turns out she was buying them with my money. So that, my love, is what's been happening at home. Other than that, Mrs. Lincoln, how was the performance?" She tried to put a note of levity into it, but Max looked as shaken as Tallie had been herself, for months.

"Shit, Mom. How did you get through all that? It must have been so awful for you, with Hunt and Brig and everything." She looked appropriately and profoundly shocked, about all of it.

"It was pretty bad," Tallie admitted. She wondered herself now how she'd gotten through it. And it wasn't over yet.

"Why didn't you tell me? It must have been terrible for you to go through all that alone." Max looked sympathetic and hugged her closer.

"It was too much to tell you on the phone. I wanted to wait till I saw you. So there it is. Not a pretty story."

"Will Brig really go to prison?" Max couldn't imagine it, and neither could Tallie. It seemed unthinkable, but Brigitte had done it to herself. More important, how could she have stolen money from Tallie day after day, and year after year, and look her in the eye, not to mention sleeping with Hunt?

"The FBI says she will."

"I'll bet Brig is really shocked when she gets arrested. Does she know she's in trouble?"

"Not yet. I think it's all going to happen pretty quickly in the next couple of weeks." But nothing had gone quickly so far. Everything had seemed to move in slow motion to Tallie. And it would be a long time before she got any money back, if she did.

"Do you still talk to Hunt?" Max asked her quietly. She was very sad about him and she could see that her mother was too.

"Not really. I try not to talk to him. Our lawyers communicate about business issues. That's all. There's nothing left to say."

"Can I talk to him?"

"If you want to." Tallie didn't want to just cut her off from him. If nothing else, she needed some kind of closure, or maybe she needed to keep contact with him. If so, Tallie wasn't going to stop her. She was eighteen, and had a right to do what she wanted about him, as long as she didn't bring him to the house. He was a weak man who had taken the easiest course of action, and the most painful for her. "It's up to you. If you see him, don't bring him home."

"I wouldn't do that to you, Mom," she said solemnly.

"I just want to tell him what I think of what he did to you. It's disgusting. He's a huge liar. And Brig too. What they did is as bad as the money." There were times when Tallie thought so too. The money was dishonest but impersonal. But what they had done together was a knife in her heart. She couldn't bear thinking of either of them anymore. It was the definition of betrayal.

"I think so too. Anyway, it's wonderful to be here, and I'm happy to be with you. I'm sorry to start it off with an awful, sordid story."

"I don't know what to say to you, Mom. It's so terrible. Do you think you'll ever date anyone again?" Max couldn't imagine her trying again, or trusting anyone after this, neither woman nor man, since she had been exploited by both, and sorely abused.

"Not at the moment," Tallie said firmly. "That's the last thing on my mind, and the last thing I'd want to do."

"Does Grampa know?"

"Yes. As always, he gave me good advice."

"How is he?"

"So-so, kind of weak right now. But he gets that way sometimes, and then he perks up. I hope he will."

"I'll be home in a few weeks, and I can keep him company. I'm coming home before summer school." Unlike most of her peers, who wanted to drag their college education out for five or six years now, Max wanted to finish in less than four, and go straight to law school, if they'd let her. She had signed up for summer school that summer, and Tallie was proud of her and so was her grand-father, with good reason. She was an outstanding and dedicated student, and always had been. "When do you finish the picture, Mom?"

"A few weeks after I go back. Then I've got post-production, and then I'm done. We can go somewhere when you come home after summer session. I'm taking some time off after this movie. I need it." And since she wouldn't be working with Hunt on the next one, she wanted some time to find a new project that appealed to her. She loved the movies that Hunt produced, but there were plenty of other good ones out there. She was determined to find one of them.

They lay cuddling on the bed for a while then, while Max tried to absorb all that her mother had told her. It was so enormous that it was hard to get her mind around it. It was huge!

"What a dick Hunt is," Max said sadly. She had lost all respect for him after hearing the story. "And Brig is a total crook."

"You're right on both counts. No morals, no principles, no honesty, no integrity. They're rotten people."

"Are you glad she's going to prison?" Max was curious.

"Yes, I am. It's not very forgiving of me, but I think she should pay for what she did, and pay me back as much as she can."

"Will she?"

"I don't know. Supposedly you lose money on these deals and you don't get much back."

"Let's hope it will be different for you. I'll say a prayer for you, Mom." When she said it, Tallie nearly cried. She had all the correct instincts about right and wrong.

"What do you want to do for dinner tonight?" Tallie asked her. Max wanted to go to a small neighborhood restaurant with her mother. It sounded good to Tallie too. After all her hard work and misery in L.A., she wanted to get out, and she loved being with her daughter.

Tallie loved Max's favorite restaurant too. They had burgers and French fries, and they walked home afterward in the balmy spring air. New York was beautiful that time of year, and when they went back to the apartment, Max got in her mother's bed, and they watched TV and relaxed. Max's head was still spinning with all the news.

Chapter 15

The next morning Max and Tallie got up and went out to breakfast. They ate at Café Cluny nearby. Tallie had eggs Benedict, and Max scrambled eggs. And they took their time and talked a lot. Tallie loved catching up with Max's doings and news. The boyfriend had already faded out, and she was working hard at school and having fun hanging out with her friends, and she wanted to introduce her mother to some of them that night. Tallie had agreed to take four of them to dinner. They went to Da Silvano, which was one of Tallie's favorite restaurants, with delicious Italian food. And they sat at a table outside on the sidewalk, where they could watch people wander by.

And for the rest of the week, they walked through SoHo and Chelsea, went to galleries, shopped, went uptown to MoMA, walked through Central Park and listened to a steel band. They went to a Broadway play one night, and did all the things they both loved doing in New York. For the entire week, Tallie kept checking her cell phone to see if there was a message from Jim Kingston, telling her that Brigitte had been arrested. But she knew it was too soon since they had to get the indictment from the grand jury and the warrant from the judge, and Brigitte was probably still in Mexico anyway, but Tallie checked her phone several times a day. She would have preferred it to happen while she was away, but suspected it probably wouldn't.

The week went by too fast, and Tallie was getting ready to fly back to L.A. on Sunday night. She'd had almost a week there, and she and Max had had a ball.

And now she had to finish the movie, starting on Monday.

When she left Max at the apartment, Tallie held her tight and thanked her for her understanding about everything that had happened.

"Of course. Next time the shit hits the fan, don't wait to tell me," Max admonished. She had written an e-mail to Hunt, and shown it to her mother, telling him how disappointing and dishonest he was, and she felt better after she wrote it. Tallie was touched by what she'd said. Max was totally let down by him. And she had nothing to say to Brigitte. At least Hunt hadn't stolen anything from her mom, except her time and trust. But Max thought what he had done was terrible too, he had turned out to be a liar and a cheat and she'd told him that she never wanted to see him again, so it was a loss for her too. And she wanted nothing to do with his new girlfriend and the baby. He was fired. And she told him what he'd done to her mother was unforgivable. And in a strange way, the losses they shared had brought them closer to each other in the past week. And Max was coming home soon.

Tallie didn't hear anything from Jim for the first few days she was back in L.A. She was working hard on the set, trying to bring the film in on time, and she was almost there. They had a heat wave, and everyone complained about the long hours she was insisting they work. And much to her surprise, she heard nothing from Brigitte after she got Greg Thomas's e-mail, letting her go. She sent nothing to Tallie, not a text or an e-mail or a letter, no apology, no regrets, no remorse, no sadness over the friendship they had lost and the seventeen years that had gone up in smoke. Just silence. Tallie's father said he wasn't surprised.

"I'm not sure people like that ever feel remorse," he said when Tallie dropped by one night on the way home. It was late, it was ten o'clock, and she had been on the set since six that morning. "I think the kind of flawed character that allows someone to lie and steal like that has no empathy for the people they hurt. They just turn the page and go on," her father said wisely. He looked better again when she got back from New York, and he seemed to have more energy than he'd had in a while, and Tallie was relieved.

"I think you're right, Dad," she said sadly. She had expected to hear something from her. She also told him all about the time she'd spent with Max in New York, and he loved to hear about it. Max called him once a week, but occasionally she forgot when she was busy, and he called her. He was excited about Max coming home before summer school, and so was Tallie.

It was another week before she had a message from Jim Kingston on her phone, and she called him back as soon as she saw it.

"Anything new?" she asked anxiously, and he sounded very calm when he answered.

"Yes. Jack and I arrested her this afternoon. She's in custody tonight, and she's being arraigned tomorrow." After waiting months for this, her heart fluttered when she heard it. She felt ghoulish being excited about it, but she was. She wanted closure, but that was still a long way away. This was just the beginning of all the official procedures.

"How did it go? Was she freaked out?"

"No, not at all. She was very calm and extremely pissed." He didn't sound surprised, but Tallie was. That wasn't the reaction she'd expected. She thought Brigitte would be scared when she was finally caught, maybe hysterical and crying.

"Do you think she expected it?"

"No. I think she thought she had gotten away with it. I think she thinks she still will. She thinks she's very clever. Now she has to get an attorney and defend herself," he said matter-of-factly.

"Do you think the judge will keep her in jail?" Tallie asked hopefully.

"No. She'll be out on bail or her own recognizance tomorrow, after she pleads at the arraignment." She was going to plead not guilty, of course. Even if she pleaded guilty later in some kind of deal with the U.S. attorney to reduce her sentence, no one ever pleaded guilty at the arraignment. "How was your trip to New York?" He hadn't spoken to her since.

"Nice. I had a great time with my daughter." She sounded happy when she said it.

"How did she take all this news?"

"She was shocked, and very disappointed in both of them. She loved them both, and she's known Brig since she was a baby. At first she couldn't believe it." But neither could Tallie, he knew. "Then we got our minds off it and had a lot of fun."

"I'm glad. You deserve it. I'll let you know when she gets out after the arraignment." But there was nothing more for Tallie to do. Now the U.S. attorney assigned to it had to build their case over the next many months and go to trial, and Tallie would be a witness, as the victim. That was her official role in the whole sordid affair.

Jim called her again the following afternoon, and told her that Brigitte had given the deed to her house as a bond in lieu of bail, and she had been re-

leased. So she hadn't gotten off scot-
free, but she was out of jail.

"Be a little bit careful," he told Tallie.
"You don't have to be paranoid, just be
alert. She probably wouldn't do it, but
you don't want a confrontation with her
at this point."

"No, I don't. How was she in court?"

"Cool, arrogant, and rude," he said,
which stunned Tallie, but not him. "Nature of the beast. She acted like the
whole thing was an imposition, and she
talked down to the judge."

"Did he react to it?" Tallie asked in
fascination.

"No, he's used to it. It probably hasn't
sunk in yet that she's not getting out of
this. She thinks she's still in control, and
she kept saying 'Do you know who I
am?'" It was what Jim had suspected
about her from the beginning. She
thought she was the celebrity and the
star. She thought she was Tallie, or
who Tallie would be if she chose to act
like a star, which she didn't. Brigitte's
sense of entitlement oozed from her
pores, and was offensive. "She's being
charged with four counts of embezzle-

ment, fraud and wire fraud, and tax evasion, as I suspected. She's in deep shit
now, but she hasn't accepted that yet.
She'll be a lot less grand when she's in
prison cleaning toilets." The image he
conjured up made Tallie shudder. It was
all too real, and she couldn't imagine
Brigitte there for a minute. "It'll probably
wind up in the press fairly soon," Jim
warned her, "because you're listed as
the victim. When the reporters see that,
they're going to be calling you."

"I have nothing to say," she said
calmly.

"That won't stop them." They both
knew that was true.

"I'm glad Max isn't here." Tallie called
her that night, though, and told her. She
wasn't keeping secrets from her anymore now that she knew the story. And
they talked about it for a while. It was
still so shocking to both of them and
nearly impossible to believe.

The next morning, Tallie realized that
that would be the last she'd hear about
it for the next many months. It wouldn't
go to trial until the following year. The
wheels would move slowly, the govern-

ment would build their case, and in a
long, long time it would be over. It
seemed to take an eternity for criminal
cases to be put to rest. And she talked
to Greg Thomas about it the day after.
He was preparing their civil suit, which
would also take about a year before it
went to court. It was frustrating and like
watching paint dry it was so slow. She
complained to her father about how
slow the process was, and he reminded
her that that was the way the law
worked, and Tallie wasn't going to
change that, no matter how frustrated
or impatient she was.

Tallie hadn't hired a new assistant.
After everything that had happened
with Brigitte, she didn't want to, at least
not yet. It made more work for her, but
she was more comfortable doing it herself.

She was sitting in her kitchen, paying
a stack of bills, when her cell phone
rang on Saturday, and she answered it
without looking at who it was, and her
heart nearly stopped when she heard a
familiar voice. It was Brigitte. She
sounded matter-of-fact and ice cold.

"I want to pick up some things I left at your house," she said to Tallie without preamble. Her voice was cold, without apology or explanation of what she'd done.

"There's nothing of yours here," Tallie said calmly, but her heart was pounding. She wondered if Brigitte was going to say anything about getting arrested. But she knew Brigitte couldn't get in. Greg Thomas had had her locks changed when she was in New York, and she was glad he had.

"I left a briefcase with some papers in it, in the downstairs hall closet," Brigitte said in a determined tone.

"I'll send it to you," Tallie said, sounding firm.

"I want it now," Brigitte said, and her tone was degenerating rapidly to a high pitch.

"I'm not home," Tallie lied, beginning to feel uncomfortable about the call, and she remembered Jim's warning to be alert and cautious.

"Yes, you are. I'm standing outside your front door," Brigitte said, and the word that came instantly to Tallie's mind was *evil*.

"It won't do you any good. I'm not letting you in. And I'm not alone here." She had added that for good measure, and Brigitte just laughed.

"What bullshit. You're always alone, and you're going to be forever. You're pathetic. He didn't love you. You know that, don't you? He loved me. That's why he stayed with me for three years. He was just using you for his movies. He told me that many times." Her words cut through Tallie like a knife, which was what Brigitte had intended. She wanted to get even because she'd been caught.

"He didn't love either of us," Tallie said quietly. "He loves the girl who's having his baby. He told me that too, that he loves her."

"No, he doesn't." Brigitte sounded furious at what she'd said, and Tallie wondered if she really was outside, but she didn't want to look. "She trapped him. She's a clever little whore, and she screwed both of us over and stole him from us, and got pregnant to do it. She's a lot smarter than we are."

"Maybe so." And then Tallie couldn't keep herself from asking. "How could you do that to me, Brig? After all those years, how could you do that with him, with the money, all of it. How could you look me in the eye every day, or yourself when you looked in the mirror?"

"Oh please, don't make me laugh. Don't give me all that morality crap. You bumble around looking like a homeless person. He didn't want you. What man wants someone who looks like that? I carried you around for all those years, while you were making 'great' movies. You had his money backing you, and his name, and me keeping your head on straight and driving you around like a cripple. Without the two of us you're nothing. And without your name, no one is going to invest in his movies. If it hadn't been for me, no one would even know who you are. Half the time people think I am you. The only reason they even know who you are in this town is because I was out there doing PR for you, looking like a star. Tallie, you're nothing. Hunt used to say it to me all the time. We used to laugh at you when we were in bed." She was vicious and angry, and her voice was rising in pitch, and Tallie didn't want to hear another word of what she was saying. She knew it wasn't true, but what Brigitte said was sick, the product of a disturbed mind. And Tallie was shaking from what she'd heard so far.

"Stop it, Brig."

"You realize this is his fault, don't you," Brigitte said in a trembling voice. "If he hadn't gone off with that little whore, we'd still be together, and you wouldn't know the difference, you'd be happy. And if he hadn't confessed to you about me, I'd still be with you." *Yes, and stealing my money,* came instantly to Tallie's mind.

"He didn't tell me," Tallie said firmly.

"Yes, he did, he must have. No one else knew."

"Someone else told me. You weren't as discreet as you thought."

"I don't believe you."

"Well, it's true. Let it go, Brig. It doesn't matter now, and it won't change anything, for any of us. It's all over."

"It's all his fault," she repeated. Tallie could tell she wanted her to be angry at Hunt too. She was, but more than that, she was hurt. And she wasn't going to ruin the rest of her life over him and Brigitte. She wanted to put this behind her now. She was only sorry it couldn't happen sooner, and Brigitte couldn't go to prison tomorrow, instead of in a year, after the trial. But there was no doubt in her mind that Brigitte would wind up behind bars, and belonged there. "He thinks he's going to testify against me, doesn't he?" Brigitte said in a voice of utter fury. "If he hadn't gotten involved with that girl, you wouldn't have known about any of this."

"Yes, I would. I found out about the money because of the audit for the Japanese investor. You were up shit creek from then on, and it would have come out eventually anyway. Someone would have figured it out, even Victor."

"It's all Hunt's fault." It was her fault, as well as Hunt's, but Tallie didn't want to talk to her any longer.

"I'll send you the briefcase."

"I don't want it, throw it away." It hurt Tallie that she made no mention of how she had betrayed her and didn't seem to care. Her dishonesty mattered nothing to her. And with that, she hung up without saying another word. Tallie sat looking at her cell phone and shaking. Brigitte's call had given her the creeps. She thought about calling Jim, but she didn't want to bother him on the weekend. She thought of calling Hunt too and warning him that Brig was on a rampage, but there seemed to be no point to that either. He was a big boy, he had gotten involved with her, and he could deal with her now. It wasn't her job to protect him. The phone rang again as she sat there, and it was Max. Tallie answered immediately in a shaking voice.

"What's wrong? You sound awful." Max heard the tremor in her voice.

"I just had a weird, very creepy call from Brigitte. She sounds crazy. She said she was outside, but she probably isn't. I'm going to stay home this afternoon anyway. I have work to do. It's go-

ing to be a long year till this gets to
trial," she said glumly, but she sounded
calmer again by the time they hung up,
and Max reminded her to be careful.

Tallie went to look for the briefcase in
the downstairs closet then, and found it
where Brigitte had said it was. There
were a few papers in it, some decorating articles, a bill from her doctor, and a
couple of magazines. It was nothing
she needed, and Tallie realized she had
just wanted to get into the house and
berate her, or maybe attack her. Tallie
wasn't taking any chances and made
sure that all the doors were locked. But
when she glanced out the windows, she
couldn't see anyone outside. She
hadn't heard a car arrive or drive away.
Maybe she had never even been there
and had called from somewhere else
and just wanted to scare her. Tallie was
sorry she hadn't stayed in jail.

She took her stack of bills upstairs
and locked herself in her bedroom and
turned on the alarm, and she spent the
afternoon in bed paying all her bills. She
had just finished paying the last one,

when Jim Kingston called her, and he sounded tense.

"Are you okay?"

"I'm fine. Why? I had a weird, very unpleasant call from Brigitte today. She sounded hysterical, and she wanted to come in. I'm in my bedroom with the door locked and the alarm on, but she didn't call me again. I hope she isn't going to stalk me for the next year until the trial."

"She won't," he said firmly. "I'm coming over," he added quietly.

"Why?"

"I'm already in my car. I'll be there in five minutes." He didn't explain further, and she thought it was nice of him to come. The doorbell rang five minutes later. She unlocked her bedroom door and turned off the alarm, and hurried down the stairs to open the front door to him. But the look on his face told her that something terrible had happened, and she was frightened as she waited to hear what it was. What if Brigitte had gone to her father's house and done something to him? It was the only thing she could think of.

Jim didn't waste time waiting to share what had happened. He told her as they stood in the doorway.

"Brigitte just killed Hunt. She showed up at Angela Morissey's apartment, and fired at him, right in the chest. She told him he would never testify against her, and then she shot him."

Tallie looked shocked, and her face went deathly pale as the room reeled around her, and she grabbed Jim's arm to steady herself. "And Angela and the boy?"

"They're fine." But Hunt was dead. Hunt, who had lied to her and betrayed her, whom Brigitte said had never loved her. And who was having a baby with someone else. It didn't matter now. It was over. He was dead. She realized too how lucky she was that Brigitte hadn't shot her. Maybe their years of friendship had meant something to her after all and saved Tallie. Or maybe she was just angrier at Hunt, because of Angela. Tallie was grateful she hadn't let her in that morning. She might have shot her.

"Where's Brigitte?" she asked in a

wan voice as he led her into the living room, and they sat down.

"She's in custody. She went back to her house and was packing a suitcase when they got there. She's in jail. She'll be there till the trial." But now she was going to be tried for murder as well. Her life really was over. Tallie couldn't imagine it, and she suddenly realized she had to call Max before she saw it on the news. She was panicked and ran upstairs to find her phone. He followed her up the stairs and she sat down on her bed to call Max, while Jim stood by to offer support. Max answered immediately and she could tell something had happened by the shaking tone of her mother's voice.

"Are you okay, Mom?"

"I'm fine. But I wanted to tell you before you heard. Brig just killed Hunt. She shot him. She came here first, and I didn't let her in."

"Oh my God, Mom!" Max burst into tears immediately. "What if she'd shot you?"

"She didn't. And it's all over now. She's in jail. She's not going to hurt anyone else, but poor Hunt. He's dead. He was an asshole, but he didn't deserve this."

"Did she shoot anyone else?"

"Just him." And as she said it, Tallie picked up the remote control and turned on her TV. Hunt's face was huge on the screen, and then it went to the scene at the apartment where he'd been living with Angela. Tallie could see her in the background with her enormous belly. She was crying, and there were police cars all around. And then they flashed a picture of Brigitte on the screen in an evening gown. It was an old picture from some Hollywood event and she looked fabulous. And then Tallie heard them mention her name. She talked to Max for a few more minutes about what had happened and then they hung up and Tallie called her father, who had just seen it on TV, and was as shocked as they all were. She promised to call him back when Jim left.

"What now?" Tallie said as she turned to look at Jim, after she ended the call to Sam.

"She'll have to cop a plea, or claim temporary insanity, but either way she's done. They'll probably get her to plead to everything now. She's going away for a long, long time. She's crazier than I thought she was. She seemed sane when I talked to her at her house." As he said it, his cell phone rang. It was Jack Sprague.

"Yeah, I know," Jim said. "I'm watching it on the news. They called me as soon as it happened. I'm at Tallie Jones's. She came over here first, but Tallie didn't let her in. Yeah. Yeah. I know. I'll call you later," he said, and hung up. "How do you feel?" he asked Tallie as he looked at her.

"I don't know." She seemed disoriented. "Scared. Sick. Numb. I was going to call and warn him that she was furious with him, but I figured it was none of my business, so I didn't." Her eyes filled with tears as she looked at Jim. "I guess I should have. Maybe he'd still be alive if I had."

"I don't think so. She was out to get him, and she would have eventually."

"She didn't want him to testify against her. That's what she said."

"Did she tell you she was going to get him, or kill him, or anything like that?" He had slipped into FBI mode without even realizing it, and she shook her head.

"No, she didn't. She was very wound up. She kept repeating that he wasn't going to testify against her."

"But she seemed sane?" As sane as anyone was who went out and shot someone.

"More or less. She was very angry at me too. I wasn't even sure if she was really outside, or just saying she was to scare me."

"What did she want?"

"She wanted to come in for her briefcase, and I said I'd send it to her. And after she insulted me for a while, she hung up and went away, I guess."

They went back downstairs again to her kitchen, and Jim made her a cup of tea. He looked in the fridge for milk, and then he smiled at her.

"Do you ever buy groceries?" he asked.

"Not lately." She smiled back at him. "I'm not big on domestic skills. It's not my thing."

"Apparently. Do you ever eat?"

"Yeah. Sometimes. Well actually, no. Not often. I haven't been doing that much lately either." He could tell. She was very thin. "I can't believe Hunt is dead. It just doesn't seem possible. I wish I'd called him." She looked sad as she said it, and he was stern.

"Stop it. If she wanted to kill him, she was going to, no matter what you did. You couldn't change that." She nodded, trying to believe him, but she didn't, and she started to cry. The whole thing had been such a nightmare for the past few months. But it was over, Jim knew, more than Tallie realized or was able to understand right now. Brigitte was gone forever, or for a very, very long time.

Jim sat with her for an hour, and talked to her in her kitchen, and then he got up to leave. He knew she was no longer in any danger, and when he opened the front door, he saw news trucks outside. There were four of them, and a flock of photographers on foot.

The press had arrived to lay siege. He closed the door again and spoke to her.

"The press are outside. Keep the door closed. Close the curtains. Don't go out. Don't talk to them, unless you want to." She looked horrified and shook her head. "I'll bring you something to eat later, or you'll starve to death." He smiled at her. "It'll be all right. Can you stay somewhere else for a few days?"

"At my dad's, but I'd rather be here."

"Then just stay here, and stay out of sight." Her phone started ringing then in the house. He disconnected it, sure that it was the press. Anyone close to her would call on her cell phone. "It will all be over soon." She nodded and wanted to believe him. He stepped outside then and walked toward the cluster of press with a determined look. He held his FBI badge up so they could see it.

"Ms. Jones has no statement to make. She knows about what happened. She is deeply sorry and extends her sympathy to the family. She's not going to speak to you so it's pointless staying out here. If she has anything to say, we'll contact you." They looked disappointed, but they didn't move. And with that, Jim walked past them, got in his car, and drove away.

In the house, Tallie saw a TV news flash of Jim outside her house making his statement to the press. They were still out there, and they weren't leaving. Her father called her on her cell phone then, and she told him again that she was fine. She watched the news all night, and at nine o'clock Jim came back, with a bag full of hamburgers and Mexican food. She let him in, and they went back to the kitchen. A full fleet of press was still outside, hoping for a glimpse of her. They had announced several times on the news that night that she had lived with Hunter Lloyd for a number of years until recently. And then they showed shots of Angela crying with her huge pregnant belly. And they explained that she was having his baby. And they had shown footage of Brigitte as she was led into the jail with her head down. It didn't even look like her. The glamorous still shot of her in the evening gown did. That was the Brigitte Parker everyone knew. The one who looked like a star. And Tallie laughed when they ran a still shot of her that they'd taken on some movie set somewhere. She looked like she'd been shipwrecked for a year.

"Which one is the star?" she said, as Jim unpacked the food, and she got out plates. He had even brought a six-pack of Cokes and another one of beer.

"You're the star. That's what she hated about you. She wanted to be you. But it didn't matter what she stole from you—she still couldn't be you. She didn't have your talent or your looks or all the things that make you you. It takes more than evening gowns and furs and jewelry to make someone a star," he said, smiling at her, and she was touched by how kind he was. She had become a prisoner in her own home, and she was actually starving.

"I guess it wouldn't hurt if I combed my hair once in a while," she said sheepishly, and he laughed.

"No one would recognize you if you did. It might be a pretty good disguise though. You could go out looking like that, and people wouldn't know it was you." They both laughed, and sat down to the dinner he had brought her. His son called as they were eating and he said he'd be home soon.

"I'm sorry to screw up your Saturday night," Tallie said apologetically, haunted by the fact that Hunt was dead. It just didn't seem possible. And it was so wrong despite how dishonest he'd been to her. And she felt sorry for Angela now. Her baby would have no father. By ten o'clock they said that the interment would be private and later that week. Tallie knew when she heard it that she wasn't going. It would have been hypocritical of her. He belonged to Angela now, and their baby. She had no place in his life or at his graveside, and she didn't want to be there. She'd rather remember the good times, for what they were worth. Not much, after the way he'd behaved. Their whole relationship had turned out to be a lie.

She ate a cheeseburger and a taco and downed two Cokes. And she looked gratefully at Jim. "Thank you. That was delicious." She had needed it

more than she knew and felt better after
she'd eaten.

"I enjoyed it too, and you're not
screwing up my Saturday night by the
way. The alternative was pizza and root
beer with a bunch of fifteen-year-old
boys. Besides, I wanted to be here." He
had brought her some pastry for the
morning too. "Are you going to be okay
here tonight?" She nodded. There was
no danger. Brigitte was in jail, and the
press were locked outside. The only
problem would be if she decided to go
somewhere eventually. She could tell
that they were camped out for the duration, probably till after his funeral. She
wouldn't go, but she also realized suddenly that she was currently working on
the last Hunter Lloyd film that would
ever be made. It was a strange feeling.
She wanted to make it as good as she
could as a suitable last tribute to Hunt.
It was all she could do for him now.

She and Jim talked for a while about
everything that had happened, and then
he left again, and said he'd be back in
the morning. She was a hostage in her
own house. She thanked Jim again for

dinner before he left, locked the door behind him, and left the TV on in her bedroom all night. There were bulletins and news flashes and commentaries about Hunt. And occasional mentions of her, Angela, and Brigitte. An unidentified source at the Sunset Marquis had volunteered that Hunt had been involved with Brigitte for several years, and a reporter questioned if the fatal shooting had been the result of a lovers' quarrel, or a love triangle with the woman carrying his child. Tallie was awake for most of the night.

She was up and dressed when Jim came back the next morning, and she was wearing jeans without holes in them for a change. Her hair was pulled back, and her face was clean and fresh. She looked wholesome and young and more relaxed. He had brought her an egg sandwich from McDonald's, and they ate the pastry he'd brought her the night before.

"It's going to be a long week," she said, referring to the press still camped outside.

"They'll give up eventually. Someone

will shoot someone else, and they'll move on."

"That's a cheering thought." At least it wasn't going to be her, and she realized more than ever that she had narrowly escaped it, and it might have been her if she had let Brigitte in. But she had known not to. Brigitte had sounded so crazy on the phone.

Jim stayed until he had to pick up his son for a ball game, and then he left her for the afternoon. He came back that night with more food, but he couldn't stay. He said he had to go somewhere with his son, but he was worried about her alone in the house, ruminating over Hunt's death.

"I had no idea that the FBI provided catering service too," she teased him with a tired smile.

"Absolutely. I'll have to make dinner for you sometime. We take culinary classes during our training." He was smiling, and he had made the weekend more bearable for her, in the face of a bad situation.

"Thank you, Jim. It would have been a terrible weekend without you." He had eased the pain of Hunt's death, her guilt over not calling him, and her regrets about how his life and their relationship had ended.

By Monday morning, she felt sad but at peace with it, and the press had finally given up and left.

They came back again the day of Hunt's funeral, but she hid out at her father's for the day, and they talked about him. It felt better being with her father than standing at Hunt's grave, and they talked to Max several times. Tallie went back to her own house late that night. The next day in the mail, she had a letter from Angela Morissey. She had meant to write to her, but hadn't done it yet.

"Dear Ms. Jones," it said politely, "I know that I caused a great deal of unhappiness in your life, and Hunt did too. But he truly loved you. He got caught in a difficult situation, and he didn't handle it well, but he always told me how wonderful you are and how much he loved you. I'll miss him so much, and I know you will too. I'm sorry for any pain we caused you. I hope everything comes out all right for you. Respectfully, Angela Morissey." It was a sweet gesture, and Tallie appreciated it. It put balm on the wound Brigitte had tried to make worse when she told her Hunt had never loved her. He was a foolish man, Tallie knew, and a weak one, but also in some ways a good one, despite the mistakes he had made. She folded the letter and put it away, and silently wished Angela well too, and hoped that Hunt's soul had found peace.

Chapter 16

Max came home for vacation before summer school, as planned, and her mother and grandfather were thrilled to see her. She went over to visit her grandfather almost every day, and when Tallie finished work, she took them both out for ice cream, and Sam had a root beer float, which he said had been his favorite when he was a boy. And in the afternoons, Max would take him out for walks in his wheelchair, which he used more now than the walker. He was less steady on his feet, but his mind was as sharp as ever. Sam loved having his granddaughter around and hearing her views of the world. And they were all still trying to recover from the shock of Hunt's death and his betrayal before that, and Brigitte's horrifying crimes. And both of them were worried about Tallie. She joined them at night when she finished work, and then she and Max went home. Sam loved spending time with his "two girls."

Tallie was working on post-production on Hunt's last film now, so her schedule was less pressured and easier to adjust, and she could spend time with Max while she was home. There was still a lot to do on the film though, so she was busy, especially without an assistant. The film was due out by Christmas. She knew it was the right time to bring out that particular movie, and the distributors were counting on it being a huge success, even more so in light of Hunt's death.

"What's happening with Brig now?" Max asked her mother one night after they came home from dinner at Sam's. She knew that Jim Kingston had called her several times, but Max hadn't met him yet, and she was curious about him.

"They arraigned her for Hunt's murder, they're saying it was premeditated, so she'll stand trial for murder one. She's in custody now, and they're going to try her for both matters. The federal one for embezzlement. And murder for the state. Our embezzlement trial is set now for April 19. I'm not looking forward to it, to say the least. I'm sure she isn't either, but so far she's not willing to plead guilty. She has nothing to lose or to gain now. Between Hunt's murder and the embezzlement, she's going to be in prison forever. And we have the civil trial too, to try to get whatever we can back. I really want the house so I can sell it. But Jim Kingston says the IRS will want it too, for the tax evasion charges." It was unbelievable to think how Brigitte had destroyed her own life in a short time, impacted Tallie's, and ended Hunt's.

"Did she ever contact you again after the day she came by for her briefcase?" Max was curious about it. It seemed so weird to her, and to Tallie, that Brigitte

had never written to apologize and say
that she was sorry for anything she'd
done.

"No. I got a note from Hunt's girlfriend though, telling me how much he
loved me. Hard to believe, but nice of
her to say so, now that he's gone. And I
sent her one too." She had gotten a
note from Victor Carson too, expressing
his sympathy, and saying his wife had
left him and he was getting divorced.

The embezzlement trial was still ten
months away. It seemed like a lifetime,
and by the time they got there, everything that had happened would seem
so remote and unreal. In some ways it
already did. Tallie was trying to make
the most of Max's time in L.A. and they
spent time with Sam and went out
whenever they had time and Max didn't
want to see friends. They talked about
Hunt and Brig sometimes, but Tallie
wanted to try and forget.

Jim called her from time to time to
check in and see how she was. And the
day before Max left, he came by to
meet her. He dropped by for a few minutes on his way to pick up his son. He

was wearing a T-shirt and jeans, and he looked athletic and fit. It was the first time Tallie hadn't seen him in a suit, and Max looked impressed when she met him. He was good-looking and smart, and he seemed very relaxed and attentive around her mother. And Tallie seemed to enjoy talking to him. As soon as he left, Max pounced on her.

"He is *cute!*" she said the minute the door closed behind him, and Tallie hoped he hadn't heard her. "Now what's wrong with him?"

"I don't know. Why don't you ask him?" Tallie laughed at her.

"I mean, why don't you like him?"

"I do like him. He's very nice."

"That's not what I mean, and you know it. Why don't you go out with him?"

"For one thing, he hasn't asked me. For another thing, he is the FBI agent assigned to our case, and for yet another thing, I'm not dating. I don't even want to think about that now, and maybe never again."

"Why not?" Max looked disappointed as she glared at her mother.

"I think Hunt cured me. For a while anyway. I just found out that I spent four years being conned by the guy I was living with and my best friend. It doesn't exactly make me want to rush out and try again. I wasted four years of my life. I'd say the evidence is pretty convincing that my judgment sucks and dating isn't for me."

"Don't be stupid, Mom," Max scolded her. "Is he married or divorced? I mean the FBI guy." Tallie knew exactly who she meant.

"Widowed."

"Oh, that's too bad. Does he have a girlfriend?"

"I didn't ask him, and I'm not going to. At best, maybe we could be friends. I don't get the feeling he's dying to date either. I think he still misses his wife."

"That's pathetic. You're both ridiculous. Don't waste your lives." Max looked at her mother in frustration.

"Thank you for the free advice."

"Well, I think he's very good-looking, and he seems like a good guy. You should ask him for dinner sometime."

"Max! I'm not going to ask our FBI agent to dinner!"

"Why not?"

"He'll think I'm putting the make on him, and I'll look ridiculous."

"Maybe you should put the make on him," Max said smugly. And then she looked more serious as she met her mother's eyes. "How do you think Grampa is doing? He seems a lot weaker than the last time I was home. He doesn't want to use the walker anymore. He just wants the wheelchair." Tallie had noticed it too. He was fading.

"He just turned eighty-six, and you're right. But he seems livelier to me now that you're here, he loves spending time with you, but I don't think he feels well a lot of the time." He was so frail and seemed weaker and more bent every day. Tallie didn't want to think about it, but she knew that eventually he wouldn't be able to get out of bed at all. He seemed to be heading in that direction.

They had dinner with him that night, and they were all in good spirits, except Tallie was sad that Max was leaving again. She had to start summer school in two days, and wouldn't be home again until the end of the summer vacation.

Tallie drove her to the airport at the crack of dawn the next morning, and spent the rest of the weekend doing projects around the house and paying bills. It reminded her of what had happened the last time she paid them, when Brigitte showed up, and then went to kill Hunt. It still made her sad when she thought about him. It was such a waste.

The following week Tallie met with Greg Thomas about the civil suit against Brigitte. She now had a criminal attorney and a civil one, and Tallie had sued her for the million dollars that Victor was sure she had stolen, and he was checking their ledgers more closely for more. Tallie wondered what would happen to all Brigitte's things when she went to prison. Hers was another wasted life. It all seemed so senseless to Tallie.

And when she wasn't talking to her lawyer, Tallie was working on finishing the film. She finally wrapped it up, after Max left. And the final edit looked beautiful to Tallie. It was even better than she had hoped, the performances were strong, the cinematography was spectacular, even the score was impressive. She knew that Hunt would have been proud of it, and she was too. She had had them add a memorial line to the credits, in memory of Hunt. It was coming out nationwide on December 15. And the day she left the studio, after she finished, she stopped off to see her father. He was quieter than usual and looked like he was in pain.

"Are you all right, Dad? Is there something I can do? Do you want me to call the doctor?"

"No, I'm fine. My arthritis is bothering me, that's all." She tried to get him out of bed to move around a little, but he wouldn't. And Amelia said he hadn't eaten. Tallie had been thinking lately that she needed to find someone to spend the nights with him, whether he liked it or not. He was too unsteady on his feet now to leave alone. And she

was constantly afraid he would fall and
get seriously hurt.

She stayed for dinner with him that
night, and Jim called her with an update
while she was there.

"Can I call you later? I'm with my
dad."

"Sure. Just call me on my cell. It's
nothing important. I just wanted to tell
you that we proposed a deal to Brigitte
today. I'll give you the details later."
What deal could they possibly offer
her? Tallie wondered. A hundred years
instead of a hundred and fifty? Jim had
already told her that she was going to
try a temporary insanity defense on the
murder one, and Jim said no one was
going to buy it. She had been totally
sane, just pissed off, which wasn't a defense.

"Are you happy with your movie?"
her father asked her over dinner. He
was always interested in her work. Even
now, losing strength, he always wanted
to know what she was working on and
how it was going. And he still enjoyed
watching movies on TV.

"Yes, I am. I think it's one of my best

ones. It's a shame Hunt's not here to see it."

"That's a shame in a lot of ways. I hope that woman goes to prison for a long time."

"I don't see how they could do otherwise with her. Between the embezzlement and Hunt's murder, I think she is totally screwed."

"She deserves to be," he said strongly. He had no sympathy for a criminal like her. "Anything new from your attorney or the FBI?"

"The special agent on the case just called me. I told him I'd call when I get home. I'll let you know." Her father had given her lots of good advice on the civil suit. He still had a sharp legal mind. And he was always reminding her of things to tell her attorney. Greg Thomas laughed when she relayed messages from her father, and he was surprised by how often he was right. He still read the *Harvard Law Review,* and loved reading legal websites on his computer.

Tallie waited until her father was ready for bed that night, and didn't leave until she had tucked him in. And then she quietly left to go home. He was already dozing. And she called Jim when she got home, and he explained the government's offer to Brigitte. He was very diligent about keeping her informed.

"If she pleads, they're willing to cut her time down to five years on the embezzlement. If she doesn't, it's up for grabs. They want to put restitution to you in the deal, using the proceeds from a house sale, and the contents of the house, cars, bank accounts, whatever she has. It looks like the state will try her for murder one, and her defense lawyer is trying to work a deal with the state to serve both sentences concurrently, if she's convicted or she pleads."

"How much time would that give her?" Tallie asked with a worried look.

"Five or six years, for the embezzlement, maybe eight or ten for the murder. It's not a lot, but she's a first-time offender. And the prisons are very crowded. If she's acquitted of the murder, which she won't be, she could serve five years for the embezzlement, or the judge could decide to give her

more and not honor the deal, if he
thinks it's too light. And don't forget
she'll have an increase in her time for
abuse of trust with you." Five years
seemed very short to Tallie, given what
she'd done. Ten for the murder seemed
more reasonable, since she had taken a
life.

"It's too bad the electric chair is no
longer used, or the guillotine maybe,"
Tallie said in a merciless tone. "I don't
see why they should want to plea-bar-
gain with her, given the severity of her
crimes."

"Because it will save the taxpayers
money and you a lot of stress if she
pleads and we don't have to go to trial.
We'll do it, of course, if she doesn't
plead, but it just saves everyone's
time." Tallie had to admit she wasn't
looking forward to the trial, far from it,
but she also didn't think Brigitte should
get off too lightly. "We'll see what her
lawyer says tomorrow."

"If it reduces her time in prison, she'll
be crazy if she doesn't take the deal."

"I agree with you," Jim said firmly.
"But you'd be surprised how many de-

fendants want their day in court and to go out in a blaze of glory. They're much better off making a deal in these instances than going to trial. In this case, that would be an agony for everyone involved, including you. Anyway, we have plenty of time, the trial is still eight months away." Tallie wished it would hurry up. She felt like she had been dealing with this depressing situation for years. Jim assured her again that they were going to find a compromise that worked for everyone, not just the federal courts in avoiding a trial. And then they talked about Max in summer school in New York, and what ball game his son Bobby was playing that week. Josh, his other son, had gotten a summer job at a law firm, and he was liking it a lot. Jim said that if he didn't play pro football, he would love him to go to law school, like Max. They talked a lot about their kids, who were the hub of their lives.

"What are you going to do now that you finished the film? Have you got other projects lined up?" Jim asked her with interest.

"Yes," she said immediately. "Yoga class, shopping, sleeping late, going to movies, reading scripts, reading books. I'm looking for another movie to do," she said honestly, "but I don't want to rush into something. I want time to check it out. I need a break anyway. I'm not in any hurry to go back to work, particularly if there's a trial, or even two or three of them, including the civil trial to recoup the money. I have to be available for that." It was going to put her life on hold until they knew how the legal situation was going to evolve. It was a long time to sit around waiting, but there was nothing they could do to make it happen more quickly. The government, and to some extent the judge, were in control. Tallie had very little to say about any of it, even though she was the victim. "Are you going away this summer?" she suddenly asked him. It occurred to her that it gave her a level of comfort and security knowing that he was following the proceedings and giving her regular reports of what was going on. She would have been completely in the dark otherwise. No one else kept in contact with her to inform her or reassure her, but Jim always did.

"I'm taking my boys fishing in Alaska the last two weeks in August, but other than that, I'll be here." And they both knew that things moved so slowly that nothing would happen while he was away. There would be very little shift in the case for the next many months.

Tallie and her attorney were waiting for Brigitte's lawyer's response to Tallie's complaint in the civil lawsuit. Victor was going over all her ledgers again to see if there were additional amounts of money she'd lost, the FBI was gathering more evidence in the case against Brigitte, and now the state was examining all the evidence in Hunt's murder. It felt like it was going to take forever. Jim could sense what Tallie was thinking on the subject from the discouraged tone of her voice. "At least she's in custody now. She's not a danger to you or your family. That's a lot. You don't have to wonder where she is or what she's doing or how much of your money she's spending." One of Tallie's great concerns was how much Brigitte had taken

out in mortgages on her house. If Tallie
was to get the house, or the proceeds
from a sale, if Brigitte had bled it dry in
order to get more money, it wasn't going to do Tallie any good.

And Greg Thomas had hired forensic
accountants not only to double-check
Tallie's accounts and the missing cash,
but also to examine Brigitte's, when
they got them from the bank, to see
how the money had been spent, other
than on Rodeo Drive. It was a long
painful process. And ever since they
had discovered it, Tallie was feeling
broke. She wasn't, of course, and her
father had reminded her that she hadn't
even known the money was missing,
which was embarrassing, but that often
happened with an embezzlement, if it
was cleverly done. She had the feeling
that they had been spending a fair
amount of money, and in fact she had
been supporting a whole additional person who was pumping money out the
back door as fast as it came in. In the
long run, she would save money now,
but she had also lost a great deal while
Brigitte was in control. Looking back on

it, Tallie couldn't understand how she had trusted her so completely, and over the years developed so much faith in her, that she blindly did whatever Brigitte told her to do. She thought that Brigitte had been making her life easier and protecting her; instead she was the silent enemy in their midst, stealing everything she could lay hands on, materially and emotionally, even her boyfriend and her trust. It was a shocking experience, and Victor Carson was nervous about it as well.

Victor had admitted to Jim that he was afraid that Tallie might sue him for not discovering what Brigitte had been doing long before. And Jim had told him it was always a possibility; other lawsuits were often spawned from the original crime. Everyone got hurt. And in fact, Tallie had already discussed it with Greg. If Victor was checking her accounts, why hadn't he seen what Brigitte had done? There was no plausible explanation for why he hadn't except that he was negligent, or stealing it himself, which she now believed he wasn't, and the FBI had concurred. But none of

this felt good to her, nothing was reassuring; there was no one she could trust
anymore, no one to protect her. She felt
naked and alone in the world.

Jim promised to call her and give her
an update before he left for Alaska, and
Tallie hung up with a sigh. It all seemed
so complicated and overwhelming,
even with his help. And there were
never any simple answers, clear-cut decisions, surefire resolutions or results.
She had the feeling that she was in hell
or purgatory and would spend eternity
dealing with the embezzlement. And
Jim had warned her that most victims
got nothing or very little back. The em-
bezzlers spent it, hid it, or it all went to
the IRS for the taxes the embezzler
hadn't paid on the stolen money, which
sounded ridiculous to Tallie. What criminal lists stolen money on their tax return? What line was that supposed to
go on? Item 22B: fraud and stolen
funds.

It was infuriating most of the time, although she was grateful for the information Jim provided, the explanations,
sympathy, and consolation. He seemed

like a good person, but he couldn't change what had happened, or affect the end result. At least he had gotten Brigitte arrested, and brought the case far enough along to do that. Tallie had heard horror stories since then of people who had lost hundreds of thousands of dollars and the authorities had done nothing about it, or the criminal had destroyed all the evidence so there was nothing to build a case on. Jim kept reminding her that she was lucky. The proof of loss and Brigitte's MO were pretty clear so far, and he felt they had a viable case that they could prove in court beyond a reasonable doubt. Tallie's name and celebrity would help them, and the fact that Brigitte had murdered a potential witness against her in the case spoke volumes. She was a criminal to the core and had abused Tallie's trust in her in every possible way, which also didn't sit well with the courts.

One of the things that had unnerved Tallie was that she had received a "victim number" from a computerized information system, designed to keep victims of crimes informed. It was a very worthwhile effort and sent hearing dates and other information to the victims. But having a "victim number" had horrified Tallie. She didn't want to be a victim, part of a faceless herd of people who had been foolish, naïve, or abused. It felt so wrong and wasn't how she wanted to identify herself in the world. Victim. It had made her shudder when she read the form.

Her mind ran in circles all night, about Brigitte and the embezzlement, and she couldn't fall asleep. When she finally did, she had nightmares. In her dreams, Brigitte kept shouting at her and tried to shoot her, and Tallie woke up with a start at four in the morning and couldn't go back to sleep. Jim had told her that many victims of crimes saw psychiatrists for the trauma, but when he had suggested it to her, she hadn't had time, and she didn't know if she wanted to do that now, although Brigitte had certainly traumatized her with everything else she'd done as well.

When she got up and went downstairs, in the morning she read the paper, and then called her father to see how he was feeling. She hadn't liked the way he looked the night before. His housekeeper answered and said he didn't want to get out of bed that morning. He said he wasn't sick, she reported, but was feeling slow. Tallie decided to go over and check on him when she got dressed. It was a challenge having an elderly parent as frail as he was who lived alone. She wanted to respect his independence, but keep him safe at the same time. And he chafed and got irritable if she fussed over him too much. Until now, he had flatly refused to have anyone stay with him at night, but Tallie could see that her father was slowly going downhill.

She drove over to his house, and he was sleeping when she got there. She didn't want to intrude on him so she sat in a little study near his bedroom and read some magazines. She heard him stirring after a while and went in to see him.

"How are you feeling, Dad?" she asked him with a smile.

"Tired," he said, smiling back. "I was

thinking about your embezzlement last night, and everything that happened with Hunt. I'm so sorry, baby. It was all so wrong. And I always thought he was such a good guy."

"So did I." She sighed and sat down in a chair next to his bed. And now Hunt was dead, and all because of his own bad judgment getting involved with Brigitte. She had burned them all, and had looked like dedicated innocence itself. But that had been no excuse for him to have an affair with her behind Tallie's back. And the excuse that he'd been blackmailed into it, or Brigitte had forced him, didn't hold water with her, nor with the FBI. Brigitte and Hunt had been greedy, dishonest, immoral people, both of them, and in the end they had paid a high price. So had she, but her life wasn't ruined, and she wasn't dead like Hunt. It was something to be grateful for as she looked at her father with sad eyes. She hated to see him so exhausted and weak. "I'll be okay, Dad," she reassured him.

"I want you to get back as much as you can. Be tough about it, merciless.

You've already lost enough. I want you to put up a good fight." He made it sound as though he were leaving on a trip, or wouldn't be there when it happened, and that worried her even more. She was thinking of calling the doctor, and she noticed that her father was having trouble breathing. They had oxygen in the house for an emergency, but she didn't want to use it without a doctor's advice.

"Are you okay, Dad?" Everything she felt for him was in her eyes, and the way she gently touched his cheek.

"Maybe I'll get up for a while. I'm tired of sitting in bed." It was a beautiful day, and she wondered if he'd like to go out and sit in the garden. And when she asked him, he said he'd like that. She got him the navy silk dressing gown he wore. He put it on, went to the bathroom with his walker, and came out with his hair combed and freshly shaved, and she smiled at him. He looked very handsome, and she couldn't remember a single day in her life when her father hadn't looked immaculate and meticulously shaved. He had always teased her about her uncombed hair piled on her head and her ragbag look. She told him she didn't have time to think about things like that when she was working. She said she never wanted to take the time to do her hair or get prettily dressed, and now she realized that she should. Not to the extremes that Brigitte had gone to, but just enough to look like a girl. She'd always been afraid that the ideas would fly out of her head if she thought of anything else. She was beginning to realize, at thirty-nine, that maybe that wasn't true. Hunt liked to say she was a genius, which she knew she wasn't, but she did focus on her work, much of the time, when she wasn't thinking of Max. Some great ideas came to her when she least expected. And she never wanted to be caught short with a comb instead of a pencil in her hand.

She walked her father slowly out into the garden and sat him on a deck chair. She got a hat to shield him from the sun, and lay on the deck chair next to his, and she reached out and took his hand. They lay there in the sun, peacefully holding hands for a long time. She had her eyes closed, and she was wearing shorts and one of Max's old T-shirts, and she felt her father gently squeeze her hand.

"I love you, Daddy," she said softly with her eyes closed, feeling like a child again. She could remember all the times he had been there for her when she was young, all that he had done for her after her mother died, the endless support he had offered for her career, the wise advice, and as she thought of it, two tears slid down her face, and she wiped them away quickly so he wouldn't see them if he was watching. She didn't want to be maudlin just because he was tired and old, or having a bad day.

"I love you too, Tallie," he said gently, and then he drifted off to sleep and she could hear him snoring gently. She smiled to herself and fell asleep, lying on the deck chair near him. It was an easy, peaceful morning, and she felt as close to him as she always did, and so grateful to have him in her life. She woke up after a while, and gently took

her hand away. He had stopped snoring, and looked as though he were
sleeping peacefully in the deck chair,
and then with a start, she realized he
wasn't breathing at all. She put her fingers to his neck to check for a pulse,
and there was none, and suddenly she
felt frantic, with no idea how long it had
been since he had stopped breathing, a
minute or an hour. She shouted to
Amelia in the living room to call 911,
and then with all her strength, she
scooped her father up in her arms and
laid him on the grass, and began giving
him mouth-to-mouth, but he was life-
less. She gently tried to compress his
chest and continue breathing for him,
and after an eternity she could hear
sirens in the distance, and suddenly
there were men in paramedics' uni-
forms beside her and they took over, as
Tallie knelt on the grass watching them
and crying.

They stopped after a few minutes,
and the chief paramedic helped her to
her feet and took her inside while the
others covered her father. "I'm sorry. He
looks as though he died peacefully," he

said gently. Tallie was overwhelmed with wracking sobs as she listened. She couldn't imagine a life without her father in it. And she realized that everything he had said that morning had been a goodbye to her, even his last "I love you," as he drifted off to sleep forever, still holding her hand, and she had been able to say the same to him for one last time.

"He was asleep," she said, choking on a sob. "Thank you . . . I'm sorry . . ." The paramedic patted her arm and went back to the garden. They had put her father on a gurney, covered him completely, and were rolling him to a police ambulance outside. There was a fire truck and a rescue truck in front of the house with them. And her father's housekeeper put her arms around her and cried with her.

The head of the paramedics came back inside to ask her some questions. Her father's name, his age, what illnesses he'd been suffering from, but essentially it was just old age and what he himself referred to as "the machinery wearing down." He had never had any serious illnesses, and he had never loved any woman other than her mother, or anyone in the world as much as his daughter, and she knew it.

"Where would you like us to take him?" She looked at him blankly, with no idea what to say. "We can take him to the morgue until you decide," he said gently and she looked horrified.

"No! No! . . . please . . . just give me a minute . . ." She got her phone out of her bag and called information for the phone number of a funeral home where she'd been to several funerals. Her father had never been religious, but she wanted a church ceremony and a Christian burial, since he had been born Protestant, but first they needed a funeral home.

They were instantly attentive when they answered, sounded unnervingly calm, assured her they would take care of everything, and told her what to tell the paramedics. And she could come in and discuss arrangements with them afterward. They assured her they would do everything to help her. They had recognized her name immediately, and were used to celebrities and their families and assured her of their utmost discretion. Talking to them was the kind of thing that Brigitte would have done for her before, and now she had no one to help her.

When she finished speaking to the funeral home, Tallie went outside to speak to the paramedics and told them where to take her father. She gave them the name of the home and the address, and they assured her that they were familiar with it, and told her again how sorry they were. She could see his still form covered by a blanket on the gurney in the ambulance, and she stood for a long silent moment, crying. Just moments before he'd been next to her, telling her he loved her, and now he was gone. She had known this would happen one day, but she hadn't expected it to happen so soon and with no warning. She wasn't ready for it.

She watched the ambulance and the emergency vehicles pull away and walked back into his house. Amelia was crying too, and they held each other for a long moment.

"I thought he was just tired," Tallie said, blaming herself. "I should have called the doctor this morning."

"It was his time," the kind Salvadoran woman said. She had loved Tallie's father too. "He's been so tired lately. I think he was ready." Tallie didn't want to believe that, but she knew it was true. And now she had no father. She had lost so many people she loved lately, and he most important of all. Now Tallie had no one, not even her father, only Max.

"But I wasn't ready for this," Tallie said sadly as she went back to the garden to find her sandals, and she saw his hat lying on the grass and burst into tears again. She wanted to go home, it was too sad being here, and then she had to go to the funeral home to make arrangements. And she knew she had to call Max and tell her, and she was dreading it. She would be heartbroken too.

Tallie told Amelia she could go home, it had been upsetting for her too. She could come back on Monday and tidy up. Tallie would have to figure out what to do about his house, and go through his things. She felt as though she had nothing but painful jobs to do now, and she was glad she had finished the picture so she didn't have to worry about that too.

She and the housekeeper hugged again, and Tallie left. She felt so distracted she could hardly drive. It seemed impossible to believe that on the way there that morning her father had been alive, and now he wasn't. It had all ended so quickly, but painlessly for him at least. She was grateful it had been peaceful. But she felt devastated by the loss.

Tallie called Max from the car on the way home, but her phone was on voicemail, and then she remembered she had gone camping for the weekend and probably had no cell reception where she was. It made her feel even lonelier. Hunt was gone, Brigitte, her father— she had no one to call, no one to tell, no one to hold her or comfort her, and she had lost her father, who had been her best friend in the world and her staunch supporter. Tallie felt lost as she got out of the car, and her cell phone rang. There was no one she wanted to talk to. She looked and saw that it was Jim Kingston. She answered in a raw voice, and he could hear that she'd been crying. He didn't want to bother her but was concerned to hear her so distressed. He had forgotten to tell her something minor the night before, so he called back.

"Are you okay?" She shook her head, unable to speak for a minute.

"No, I'm not . . . I'm sorry . . . my father just died a few minutes ago . . ." She couldn't stop crying, and he was a voice to talk to.

"Oh I'm so sorry . . . was he sick?" She hadn't mentioned it, and he knew how close to him she was, from what she had said, but maybe she had been discreet about an illness.

"No, he was very tired . . . he's kind of been running down lately . . . he's . . . he was eighty-six." She couldn't bear the thought of using the past tense for him. Everything in her life was past tense now. Hunt, their life together, Brigitte, and now her father.

"Do you want me to come over?" he offered, and sounded sincere. He didn't know what else to say. *Sorry* didn't seem like enough. And he knew how much she'd been through lately. This seemed like one blow too many. She felt that way too.

"I don't know . . ." She sounded disoriented and scared.

"I'll be there in a minute . . . I'm just a few blocks away." He had gone to his office on a Saturday to fill out some forms he hadn't gotten around to. There was always a mountain of paperwork on his desk, and Bobby was away for the weekend, which gave him a chance to catch up.

They hung up, she got to her house, and couldn't remember how she got there. She walked in feeling dazed. She left the front door open by accident, with her keys in it, and a few minutes later Jim walked through it. He had gone to Starbucks and picked up lattes for them both.

He quietly closed the front door and walked into the kitchen. She was sitting at the kitchen table, staring at the garden without seeing it, and then turned her eyes to him with a look of surprise.

"How did you get in?"

"You left the door open," he said, handing her the keys. It illustrated to him why she shouldn't be alone, although with Brigitte in custody, Tallie was in no danger that he knew of, but she was in no condition to be on her own from what he could see. He was here as a friend this time, not for the FBI. He gave her one of the lattes, and she took a sip without thinking, like a robot. Her eyes looked glazed, and her hand was shaking as she held the cup.

"Thank you," she said softly, and then her eyes met his. "He was such a wonderful person. When my mom died, he became everything to me, just like you are with your kids," she said sadly. It had been a special relationship like no other. "And he was always so loving to her. He was such a good man," she said, with tears streaming down her cheeks. Jim said nothing, and just rubbed her shoulder, and then she leaned over to him, and he pulled her into his arms and hugged her. He

wished he could take the hurt and the
loss away for her, but he couldn't. She
just clung to him and cried like a child.
And then finally she looked at him with
red eyes. "Thank you for being here. I
didn't know who to call . . . everyone's
gone now . . ." He knew what she
meant and he said nothing. There had
been a lot of changes in her life lately,
and now this.

"That's what friends are for," he said
quietly. He liked the idea of being her
friend, and so did she. There was no
way he could have just hung up after
what she told him. He wanted to come
and see her. They sat in the kitchen,
quietly talking. He just wanted to be
there for her.

"Thank you for doing this," she said
again, and he smiled at her gently.

"I know what it's like. I was devastated when I lost my wife." Jim was
happy to be there for her, even though
they didn't know each other well. It felt
a little strange to her to be sitting in her
kitchen and crying with him. "At least
you know he had a good life, and went
peacefully. But I know that doesn't

make it any easier for you. Life isn't
easy sometimes."

"Not lately," she said with a tired
smile. "I wish all the other stuff were all
over," she sighed. It was so wearing
and so unsettling.

"It will be over soon, Tallie. I know it
feels like forever when you're going
through it."

"Yeah, like childbirth, only you don't
get any reward at the end of this."

"We'll try to get you what we can
from the embezzlement. Her house is a
solid asset. And I know the U.S. attorney is asking for a restitution order for
you if she's convicted or pleads. You're
going to win either way. You won't get
back all of what you lost, but at least
part of it." And as Max had reminded
her at one point, they weren't starving
or in the street, but it hurt to lose that
much money, for anyone, even Tallie.

"I just want it to be over," she said,
then closed her eyes and leaned
against him as he put an arm around
her and supported her. "I want it all to
be done, all the horrible stuff that's

been happening, and instead there's always one more thing."

"Bad things come in clumps, like grapes. Ever notice that?" he said, and she laughed.

"Yeah, very, very, very sour grapes. I've had a few too many lately."

"I know you have," he said, and rubbed her shoulder again. She barely knew him, but she appreciated his kindness to her. She was grateful not to be alone just then. She was relieved that he was there.

"I guess I should go over to the funeral home," Tallie said, and looked like she was dreading it. She couldn't think of anything worse. She was glad she hadn't gone to Hunt's funeral, and now she had to arrange her dad's.

"May I go with you?" he asked respectfully, and she nodded, appreciative of his help and support. She felt very lost. And it occurred to him as he looked at her that in the world she was a celebrity and important person, but all he saw was a sad woman who needed help, and he was more than willing to give it.

"I'd like that," she said quietly as she went to get her purse, and a few minutes later they left. She was thinking about it as he drove her there, how different everything was now. She felt very alone and vulnerable. Having been robbed and cheated on and lied to made her feel that way. It was a reminder of how fragile we all are and how fast things can change. "Brigitte used to do everything for me, or with me," she said quietly as they drove to the funeral home. "Having someone like that who takes care of everything is like having a mother, or an older sister. I never had a sister, and I lost my mother when I was very young, so having someone shield me and take care of everything was wonderful. It makes you feel very safe, and then I realized I wasn't safe at all. It was like being attacked by the person you trust most and think will never hurt you. I felt that way about Hunt too, but more so about Brigitte. She was with me for a lot longer. Seventeen years. It was like losing a member of my family when I found out what she'd done. I never even had

a close woman friend because I had
her. Now I'm on my own. It's not like I
can't do it," she said as though reminding herself, "it's just very hard." It was
why he had come over to be with her
that afternoon, because he understood
perfectly how she felt.

"That's why crimes like that are so
terrible," he said as he glanced at her in
the front seat of his car. Bobby's baseball shoes were on the floor at her feet,
and one of his baseball bats was on the
backseat. There was nothing glamorous about Jim's life or his car, but he
was totally at ease with her. "It's also
why they give people more time in
prison for abuse of trust. It's a big deal.
It's not just about the money—it's about
abusing someone who is totally vulnerable to you and trusts you."

"Maybe it's a lesson to me not to rely
on anyone," she said sadly. She had
learned the hard way just how big a target she was and how naïve. "I guess it
made me lazy about taking care of myself." It felt good to realize now that she
could fend for herself, although she had
been thinking lately of getting a new as-

sistant. Her life was too busy not to have one. But the thought of starting to look for someone else depressed her, especially after her experience with Brigitte.

"You have to trust someone in life," he said, and she shook her head.

"Maybe not." There were fewer and fewer people in her life now that she could trust. With her father gone, only Max, and she was very young. Tallie couldn't lean on her and wouldn't have wanted to, she was her child. But at a peer level, as an equal, she had no one, which made Jim's gesture of friendship even more meaningful to her.

They reached the funeral home then. He parked in their lot, and followed her inside. He was wearing jeans and a T-shirt and running shoes, but he looked solemn and dignified. She was still wearing Max's T-shirt, and shorts, and she didn't care. What she cared about was what was in her heart, not on her back. That hadn't changed. And Jim liked what was in her heart. She was a good woman, and he liked what he knew of her after their many conversations, time together, and everything he had learned in his investigation. He had come to respect her a great deal. She was nothing like the Hollywood film people he'd met before.

The funeral director on duty was helpful and polite. They looked at caskets and made plans. She selected a program that would be distributed by the ushers in church. And she had to pick a photograph of her father, but she already knew the one she wanted. She had to pick a suit for him to wear, buy a cemetery plot, write an obituary, pick music, speak to the church, and find a minister to do it. There were so many details to think about that her head spun.

She signed a series of forms, and an hour later they left, and Jim drove her to the cemetery, where they picked a peaceful spot under a tree and arranged to have her mother moved there afterward. Tallie bought four plots, to include herself and Max one day, which seemed awful, but she wanted to know that they'd all be together. She hated the things she had to plan now. Every-

thing in her life was about loss and
death at the moment. She couldn't
think of anything good that had happened in a long time. And afterward Jim
took her to the Bel Air Presbyterian
Church, to make arrangements with the
pastor there. Jim spent the whole day
with her. It was six o'clock when they
got home, and she had to write the
obituary that night. She was exhausted
as they walked into the house, and she
dropped her canvas plumber's bag on
the couch, and looked at Jim.

"Thank you. I could never have gotten through it without you." He could
see that she meant it, and her eyes
looked huge in her face. If he had
known her better, he would have put
her to bed, but he didn't, so he couldn't
suggest it. He made her a cup of tea instead and handed it to her, while she
sat on the couch looking decimated.
She smiled as she took it. It was exactly
what Brigitte would have done. "I'm so
sorry to eat up your whole day like this."

"I have nothing to do this weekend,"
he reassured her. "I'm happy to do it.
Do you want me to go and get some

groceries? You have nothing in your fridge again. Don't you ever eat?" he scolded her, and she laughed.

"I just buy at the deli on the way home if I'm hungry. Hunt was the cook."

"Well, maybe you should hire one. You're going to starve otherwise. You never have any food here." He was used to stocking a fridge for two growing boys. He couldn't have fed a canary with hers. Their hamster ate more than she did.

"I hate having people around," she said quietly. "I don't like all that fuss. Or sitting down to dinner all by myself. I used to cook when Max was home, until Hunt moved in. He was such a good cook, that nobody ever wanted to eat my food again, not even me." She smiled at Jim. "Do you cook?"

"Self-preservation. I had to feed the boys when Jeannie got sick, and then afterward. I'm better at barbecue, but I manage. I do really good takeout, mostly Chinese and pizza," he said, and she laughed. "Why don't I pick up something for you to eat tonight?" She looked blank as he said it. She wasn't hungry and she hadn't eaten all day.

"I don't think I can eat," she said honestly. "And I have to write that obit before tomorrow." She needed to go to her father's house to get the photograph of him for the program, but she didn't have the heart to go tonight after what had happened there only that morning.

"You have to eat something," Jim insisted.

"I'll grab something later," she said vaguely, and Jim laughed out loud.

"Yeah, like a lime. I've seen your fridge." She laughed too.

He left a little while later, and she went to work on her father's obituary. She was trying to remember all the important details of his life, and she kept thinking of Jim. He had been so kind to her all day, and she didn't even know what to say to thank him. And at eight o'clock as she was writing furiously on her computer and moving things around, the doorbell rang, and he had sent her a whole Chinese dinner. There was enough for several people and leftovers the next day. She called to thank him, and he told her to be sure to eat it, and she promised she would. It was midnight when she finished her father's obituary and was satisfied with it, and she ate the Chinese food then. She texted Jim her thanks again, and he didn't respond so she assumed he was asleep.

She lay awake for a long time that night, thinking of her father and everything that had happened. And she still had to tell Max when she got back from her camping trip. Tallie was dreading that and knew what a loss it would be to her too. She adored him.

Jim called her the next day and asked how she was feeling. She thanked him for dinner again, and he asked if there was anything he could do to help her.

"I don't think so. But thank you, Jim. You've been amazing."

"Just call if you need me. And don't forget to eat!"

She nibbled at the Chinese food that afternoon, and then went to her father's to find the photograph, get him a suit to wear in his casket, with a tie, shirt, and shoes. The photograph she was using was of him in his fifties, when she was still very young. It was how she always remembered him, and she realized that she looked a lot the way he did when he was younger. She found a box of photographs of her mother too and decided to take them with her. She dropped off the suit at the funeral home, gave them the obit, and went home. And Max called her the moment she walked in the door.

"Hi, Mom. How was your weekend?" She sounded excited and happy and said she'd had fun with her friends. They'd gone rafting in New Hampshire.

"Mine wasn't so great," Tallie said with a sigh as she sat down, dreading what she had to say. "Max . . . it's bad news." She started to cry as she said it. "Grampa died yesterday. In his sleep. He didn't suffer. He just drifted away." Max burst into tears the minute she heard her mother's words.

"Were you with him?" she asked through sobs.

"I was holding his hand," her mother

cried. "He told me he loved me, and then he fell asleep. We were in the garden, but he'd been very tired for the past few days."

"Oh Mom . . . I'm so sorry . . . I'll come home tomorrow." It was already too late for her to catch a plane then, it was almost nine o'clock at night in New York. "I'll catch the first plane tomorrow morning." Tallie had already booked her a seat on it and told her what time it was.

"The funeral is on Tuesday."

"Oh God . . . poor Grampa . . . and poor you . . ." Max was sorry she wasn't there to put her arms around her. Her mother had been through so much. "Can I do anything to help with the funeral?"

"No, I took care of everything yesterday. It's pretty much organized." And the obituary going into the paper on Monday morning would tell everyone about the funeral on Tuesday, and there was visitation at the funeral home on Monday night. Interment would be private, like Hunt's. Tallie didn't want anyone at the graveside with them at the

end, just she and Max. And she had realized that afternoon that people would
want to come to her house after the funeral and burial. She could tell people
about it at the church. She had to call a
caterer in the morning, but she didn't
think she'd forgotten anything so far.
She'd been very efficient.

She and Max talked for a while, and
Max was arriving in L.A. at eleven
o'clock. The time difference was in their
favor coming west, and Tallie was relieved that they'd be together. It was too
agonizing to face alone. It made her
even more grateful that she'd had Jim
with her the day before. It would have
been infinitely harder without him. She
didn't mention it to Max, it didn't seem
important. But he called her that night
to check on her.

"Did you tell your daughter?" He had
been thinking of her all afternoon.

"I did," Tallie said sadly.

"How is she?"

"Okay. Sad. Thank you for everything
you've done, Jim."

"Well, let me know if there's anything
else I can do. I'm just a phone call

away." She didn't have the feeling that he was trying to take advantage of her, or the situation. He was just a kind man, who was trying to be a friend, and she was grateful.

Max was home the next day at noon, and she and her mother put their arms around each other and cried. Neither of them could imagine a life without Sam in it now. Tallie felt as though she and Max had been shipwrecked together, and were clinging to the wreckage and each other for dear life. All Tallie could hope was that they would reach safe harbor soon. She felt as though she had been out in the storms for too long. It had been months, but at least the grief she felt was pure, clean, and uncomplicated. No one had betrayed her, they hadn't lied to her or cheated her, or stolen from her. She had just lost someone that she loved with her entire being. It was like having her heart sliced in two with a surgical knife. It was brutal.

Chapter 17

The funeral of Samuel Lewis Jones was elegant and solemn. Tallie thought he would have liked it. The flowers were white and looked lovely in the church, the casket was a dark mahogany, the church was full, and she had given the minister enough information about her father's life that the eulogy was meaningful and moving.

And Tallie spoke briefly about the extraordinary man he was. All of his peers and close friends had died before him, so there was no one to speak of his distinguished career, his accomplish-

ments, his victories, the kind of friend
he was, and the kind of father, except
her. But she did a good job. Most of the
people who came were old clients of
his, who had been much younger than
he was, and were now older people,
since he had retired ten years before.
Some of the people Tallie did business
with were there as well. She saw Victor
Carson in a back pew, alone; her father's beloved housekeeper Amelia was
there; and so were a few of Tallie's ac-
quaintances and friends. It was a respectable showing for a remarkable
man who had been much loved and
greatly respected. And as she and Max
walked out of the church holding hands
with tears running down their cheeks,
she looked up and saw Jim there, in a
dark suit, and he nodded solemnly at
her, and she nodded back.

They stood outside the church for a
few minutes, and she invited people to
come to the house later that afternoon.
She invited Jim too, who said he didn't
want to intrude at such a delicate time.

"You won't be. And at least you'll get
some decent food at my place for

once," she said in an undervoice, and he laughed and said he would come. He said a few words to Max too. And then she and Tallie left for the cemetery to say their last goodbyes to Sam. It was agonizing leaving him there, for both of them, and Tallie looked wrenched by it when they got back to the house. Several people were already there, and Max and Tallie moved among them, thanking people for coming. There were many Tallie didn't know well, who had only known her father, but she'd been happy to see such a big turnout for him, and she thought he'd have been pleased.

Both Tallie and Max looked very serious in two black dresses Tallie had found in her closet. She felt like a scarecrow wearing hers, but she wanted to honor her father as was proper. And she looked beautiful anyway, even in the somber plain black dress, and Max looked pretty and young. People enjoyed meeting her, asked where she went to school, and what her major was, and she was proud to say she was going to be a lawyer like her grandfather. Tallie was proud of her too.

And Jim came about an hour after they got back from the cemetery. He had brought an armful of white roses, and asked one of the waiters from the caterer to put them in a vase. Tallie was touched by the gesture, and she and Max chatted with him for a few minutes, and then they had to greet other people arriving, and he talked to several people before he left discreetly a little while later.

Max commented on it that night, as she and Tallie were foraging in the fridge. "Jim really seems like a good guy, Mom."

"He is. He helped me make all the arrangements on Saturday. He was a big help. I've never done anything like that without Brigitte." But it had all gone very smoothly, and the caterer had provided a very nice spread at the house. Tallie had used them before.

"When's Brig going to trial, Mom?" Max had lost track. They were sitting in the kitchen with their shoes off, eating leftovers. Talking about Jim had reminded her of it.

"Ughhh . . ." Tallie hated to think

about it. "It's very confusing. She goes to trial on the embezzlement in April. I think she goes on trial for murder with the state after that, and I think the civil trial will come up in about a year, or before that. She's going to be pretty busy next year," Tallie said ruefully, and Max nodded. It was still nearly impossible for either of them to believe. "I can't keep it all straight."

The FBI, their forensic accountants, and Victor were continuing to put evidence together for the embezzlement to tighten the case, and they didn't need much input from her at the moment. They had all her information. The murder trial didn't involve her, except to testify to Brigitte's phone call before she went to kill Hunt, and whatever she had said before that. And Greg Thomas was preparing the civil suit, which really only involved restitution, and getting back as much money as they could from Brigitte, but the civil trial was a long time away. Tallie talked to Greg Thomas about it regularly, but it was all still very distant. Both government entities were still hoping that Brigitte would plead guilty, but she hadn't agreed to do so. She had entered a plea of not guilty at both arraignments and was sticking to it, but that could always change closer to the trial dates. For now, it was all hanging out in space somewhere. And to Tallie, closure seemed like a long time away. She longed for the day when the court dates and formalities would be over and they could put it behind them, instead of having it looming at them from the distance. Tallie was dreading all of it.

"She was such a fool," Max said, as they went upstairs together after they ate. Max had gotten compassionate leave from summer school for a week for Sam's funeral. And then Tallie would be on her own again. She was so grateful to have Max home now. "She completely destroyed her life," Max said about Brigitte, "her work, her relationship with you, her career, her trust, her credibility. She'll lose her home, she'll be in prison for years . . . and for what? A bunch of clothes on Rodeo, some jewelry, a nice house? And she killed a

man. She destroyed everyone's life,
even yours."

"She didn't destroy mine," Tallie said
thoughtfully, "but she certainly impacted
it."

"I'll say. You wind up alone, minus a
million dollars, and your boyfriend is
dead."

"Yes, he is. But he wouldn't have
been with me anyway. He was already
with someone else."

"But you worked together, and you
could have wound up friends. And he
had a right to a life too." Max was justi-
fiably outraged and had been since it
happened.

"Yes, he did," Tallie agreed. It was all
very sad.

"What's happening with the movie?"
Max asked. "When's it coming out?"

"Before Christmas. December fif-
teenth." She had spoken to his office
and the studio recently, and there was
going to be a lot of hype about it being
the last movie Hunter Lloyd produced.
But with or without the hype, Tallie felt
good about the film. It was definitely
their best, and maybe the finest work

she'd ever done. She hoped it did well, to honor him. And it would be nice too to make back some of the money she'd lost when she was embezzled by Brigitte.

"I'll go to the premiere with you," Max volunteered, and her mother looked pleased. "I'll be on vacation then. Maybe you'll get nominated for an Oscar again," Max said hopefully.

"I doubt it, but it's a date for the premiere," Tallie confirmed, and the two of them got undressed and into bed together, snuggled, and watched a movie on TV. It had been a long day, but together it wasn't quite as bad for either of them. But they agreed about how terribly they were going to miss Sam. He would leave a hole in their life a mile deep.

Chapter 18

Before Jim left for Alaska, he brought
both his boys to the house to meet Tallie and Max. He wanted Tallie to meet
them, and she was impressed by how
mature and polite they were. It was
easy to see how devoted the three of
them were to each other, and how
close. They were a lovely family, and
both were handsome boys. And Josh
seemed older than his nineteen years.
Max had finished summer school, and
Tallie was amused to see that she
looked bowled over by Josh's good
looks. He was a great-looking kid.

The two young people talked about law school. Josh admitted that he was torn between playing pro football and studying law. And it was clear from the comments he made which choice his father would have preferred. Jim was hoping Josh would choose law. It would bring him more in the end. A career in football was enticing but would be arduous and short-lived. And Jim liked hearing what Max had to say about it. For her, the choice was clear. Her grandfather had convinced her years before, and she was enjoying pre-law at NYU.

Tallie made them all lunch, and they sat in her garden, before Jim and the boys left to do errands. They were leaving for Alaska the next day. And by the time they left Tallie's house, a budding friendship had been formed between the three kids. Josh told Max he'd call her before he went back to Michigan and she left for NYU. He had even invited her to come to one of his games in the fall. And both parents looked pleased when they said goodbye.

"Have fun in Alaska," Tallie said to

Jim as they left, and Max walked out to the car with the boys. "You've got great kids," Tallie said in an undervoice, and Jim smiled. He liked hearing it, and he thought so too.

"So do you. She's a lovely girl. And she's a knockout on top of it. She looks just like you." She was even taller than her mother, but there was a striking resemblance between the two. The meeting had been a success, and both families were impressed by each other. They were healthy, normal kids, in each case with a single parent who was entirely dedicated to them, and it had paid off.

After they left, Max commented on them to her mother, and she was obviously enthused. "They're cool, Mom. And Josh is really cute. I like Jim too. And Bobby is really sweet." She liked the way they obviously got along with each other, and had a relationship of mutual love and respect. "Can we really go to one of his games?" She liked the idea. "I could fly in with friends from school," she suggested, and Tallie smiled. Josh and Max had definitely hit it off.

"Maybe. Let's see what's happening in the fall." Tallie wanted to start reading scripts after the summer. She was looking for a new project since she had bowed out of the next picture when her relationship with Hunt fell apart, so she was open to new projects and ideas. She knew that the best way to recover from the trauma of the past months would be through her work, and she was anxious to get involved in something again. She had no idea how long it would take her to find the right script, and it might take a long time. She would be ready to start reading scripts soon. Despite everything that had happened, she already missed working since finishing the last film. And she knew there was also something else she had to do. She had to start looking for a new assistant, which was going to be a major adjustment after working with the same person for seventeen years. She didn't even know where to start, or how she would trust someone again, but she needed the help.

Jim called her twice from Alaska, just to check in, and she was happy to hear from him. She didn't say anything to Max because she didn't want to give too much importance to the calls. He was just being friendly, and he was concerned about her, but she didn't want to read too much into it. But she liked the idea of getting their two families together again. It had gone well when they met, and their children were so important to both of them that it was a major plus. She could easily imagine them becoming friends. She and Jim had a lot in common bringing up their children on their own.

By the time Jim and the boys got back from Alaska, Tallie had called two headhunters and begun the search for a new assistant. She had met several possibilities and didn't like any of them. They were too forceful, too brash, too meek, or too wrapped up in the Hollywood scene. And she and Max had both been unnerved when one of the women who came for an interview looked strikingly like Brigitte, and even had some of her mannerisms and a similar voice. Max had commented that they must have had the same plastic surgeon, which made Tallie laugh. But she didn't want another glamour-girl assistant. This time she wanted someone quiet and unassuming, who was down to earth. She didn't want a debutante, a trust fund baby, an ex-actress, or anyone too showy, or too impressed by Tallie's success. She wanted an unpretentious workhorse like herself. No bling.

The first interesting candidate showed up the day before Max went back to NYU, and she liked her too. She had studied English literature, and had put herself through school at night at UCLA while working as a nurse's aide. She was bright, in her early thirties, and more recently had worked as an assistant to a well-known screenwriter for five years. The job had ended when the woman she worked for got married and moved to Europe.

She looked neat and clean, and she came to the interview in a plain white T-shirt, jeans, and high-top Converse sneakers. She was divorced and had no kids, and she was pleasant to Max when they spoke for a few minutes. She had a motherly, nurturing quality to her, which was helpful in that kind of job. At the end of an hour, Tallie suggested she try out in the job the following week. She explained that her situation with her previous assistant had come to a traumatic end, but didn't go into detail. She suspected that the headhunter had probably filled her in. And Tallie realized that it was not going to be an easy task for someone new to step into Brigitte's shoes. She had done a great job, and Tallie was used to her. Working with someone new was going to be a big adjustment.

"I like her, Mom," Max commented after the woman left. They had both noticed that she drove a pickup truck, which Tallie liked too. No Aston Martin or glamorous cars. She was exactly what Tallie had requested, someone smart, capable, and down to earth. Her name was Megan McCarthy, and she had freckles and red hair that she wore in a braid down her back. And she knew a lot about the film industry from her previous job.

"I like her too," Tallie said quietly. "We'll see how it goes." She didn't want to get too enthused about her yet. And this time Tallie's bookkeeping was not part of the job. Victor was handling all that for her, and was sending one of his bookkeepers to the house once a week to gather information and pay bills.

And for the rest of the day, after the interview with Megan, Tallie helped Max pack the mountain of things she was taking back to New York. And they went out for dinner at the Ivy that night. It reminded them both of Sam, and Tallie fought back tears as they sat down at the table they'd sat at for lunch with him the last time they'd been there. She missed him terribly, and so did Max. His absence was sorely felt. And Tallie still had to go through his things and empty his house and put it on the market, but she couldn't face it yet. Amelia was still coming in every day and keeping things clean, although Tallie had suggested she look for a part-time job. She really didn't need her now more than a few times a week, if that.

When Max went back to NYU, as a

sophomore this year, Tallie started reading scripts in earnest, looking for her
next project. She finally felt ready to
think about it and go back to work.
There were several she liked, though
none she wanted to develop, but she
was enjoying the process of sifting
through them. Just doing that, she felt
better than she had in months. It was
distracting and fulfilling, and part of a
healing process for her. Work always
was, and had been, her salvation for
many years, particularly at tough times.

The week after Max left, Megan came
in and started organizing things for Tallie. She was unassuming and bright,
and Tallie liked her. The two women
were very much alike in some ways,
and Tallie had far more in common with
her than she had with Brigitte, who had
been the exact opposite of Tallie. And
after a week's tryout, they had accom-
plished so much, and Tallie was so
comfortable with her, that she offered
Megan the job. They were both
pleased, and when she told Max about
it on the phone, during one of their
lengthy conversations, she approved.

Life was slowly returning to normal, despite the enormous changes that had occurred. Three important people had disappeared from her life, Sam, Hunt, and Brigitte, but new faces were finally appearing, and Megan seemed like a good addition. And Tallie's conversations with Max had become even more fun than previously. Max had taught her to iChat before she left, and they could see each other on their computer screens while they talked. It was fun for both of them and made Tallie feel that Max was right there since she could see her. Max teased her mother that she was becoming high tech.

When Tallie wasn't reading scripts, she and Megan began sorting through Sam's house together, and Megan proved to be a hard worker as they packed up his belongings, which was emotional for Tallie. Megan was gentle and sensitive about it, and knew when to leave her alone, and do other things, when Tallie came across items that upset or touched her, some of them things that related to her mother.

Tallie's goal was to get Sam's house

emptied by the end of the year, and have it painted before she put it on the market. She didn't want to rush and just tear the place apart, and it was sad putting away all the objects, papers, books, and mementos that had meant a great deal to her father, or reminded her of him. He had left everything he had in trust to Max, including the house. He didn't have a lot, but it would be a nice nest egg for her one day, particularly once they sold the house. The money would be useful for her once she finished law school, which was several years down the line. And Sam had taken advantage of a generation-skipping tax by leaving it all to Max, and he knew Tallie didn't need the money.

Tallie and Megan were making good progress on it, and Megan was helpful and respectful, as Tallie slowly got used to her. She was very different from Brigitte, which seemed like a good thing. She had none of her predecessor's glamour and style, she had no interest in being in the limelight. She just wanted to do her job and help wherever she could, and she was resourceful and willing to work long hours.

Tallie heard from Jim occasionally, although she hadn't seen him since before his trip to Alaska with his boys. He called to check in but didn't have anything new to report about the cases. All the trial dates were still so far out that nothing had moved into high gear yet, and wouldn't for some time. Evidence was still being gathered on the criminal side, and Brigitte was in jail, awaiting trial. Jim had heard from someone in the probation department that she had no remorse whatsoever over what she'd done, not even about killing Hunt. She felt he had betrayed her so she'd been justified in what she did, and she seemed to feel entitled to what Tallie had, and had commented that she made better use of it than she did. And Jim told Tallie none of it surprised him. He said it was typical of the breed.

Tallie had always thought that she would hear from her at some point, apologizing for what she'd done, stealing from her and sleeping with Hunt, but she heard nothing, not a line, not a

card, not a word. It was as though they
had never known each other and Tallie
was a stranger to her. Jim said she fit
the classic portrait of a sociopath, with
no remorse, no empathy, and no con-
science. It was still hard for Tallie to believe or understand. But at least the
shock of the multiple betrayals she'd
experienced was beginning to fade,
and Tallie felt more at peace. And she
was enjoying working with Megan, who
was a hard worker but had a nice sense
of humor too. And sometimes after long
hours of work, they had a good laugh,
which did Tallie good. Things were light-
ening up a bit for her at last.

In November, Tallie found a script that
she liked, it was an unusual piece by a
young screenwriter, and she was excited about it. She wanted to produce
and direct it alone, and she began pulling together the project, and contacting
investors. The ones she called had
been excited to hear from her, and it
was exhilarating to reach out in her industry again. She stayed busy making
notes and calls until Max came home
for Thanksgiving, and then she stopped

working for a few days to focus on Max while she was there. And as always they had a good time together.

"So what's happening with you and Jim?" Max asked her the first night she was home, and Tallie laughed.

"Nothing, why? He calls in to report about the case from time to time, but there's nothing much going on with that right now."

"Josh called me a couple of times from Michigan. He says his dad likes you," Max said shyly.

"I like him too, but we've got bigger stuff to do right now. That's nice that Josh called." Tallie smiled at her.

"Yeah. He's going to try and come to New York after football season to check out NYU law school." He had invited her to a game too, but she hadn't had time to go, and he had promised to call her over the Thanksgiving weekend. Max really liked him, but for the moment they were just friends. They had agreed that long-distance relationships were too hard to manage. And Jim called Tallie the next day to check in and wish them a happy Thanksgiving.

They were going to relatives of his wife's. She had a sister in Pasadena, with kids the same age as his, so they often spent holidays with them.

"What are you and Max doing?" he inquired.

"It'll be a little quiet for us this year. We usually spend Thanksgiving with my dad, and this year will be very different without him." And for the past four years, Hunt had cooked the meal. This year she and Max were going to fend for themselves and spend it with each other. And Max wanted to see friends while she was home.

"I know how hard that can be," Jim said sympathetically. "Maybe we can get the kids together for a meal before they go back to school, although Josh usually stays pretty busy with his pals when he's home."

"So does Max," Tallie said as her daughter walked into the room and inquired who it was. Tallie mouthed that it was Jim, and Max looked instantly enthusiastic and started coaching her that they should see them. Tallie grinned as she got the message. "What about this

weekend?" she suggested. "Lunch or
dinner on Saturday?"

"Let me ask the kids and get back to
you. Sounds good to me." He sounded
pleased and called her back half an
hour later. Both boys had liked the idea,
and had suggested they go bowling together and have pizza there. Tallie ran it
by Max, and she loved the idea. Tallie
sensed a romance brewing, or a mutual
interest at any rate, between Max and
Jim's oldest son. Tallie thought it was
cute, and so did he. He wished Tallie a
happy Thanksgiving again then, and
they agreed to meet at the bowling alley
on Saturday at seven. Max seemed
pleased when Tallie told her. And Jim
had said Bobby was bringing a friend
too, a boy from his school. It sounded
like a fun evening.

Thanksgiving turned out to be pre-
dictably hard for Max and Tallie. It was
inevitable, it was bound to be a tough
holiday for them without Sam and Hunt.
They made the best of it, and Tallie and
Max went to a movie together after dinner, and to bed early that night.

On Friday, Max went out with some

of her girlfriends who were home for the holiday, and to a party with them that night, and on Saturday, Max and Tallie went shopping for some things Max needed, and at seven they met the Kingstons at the bowling alley, as planned. Tallie could see immediately that Josh's interest in Max was more than just causal. He was even taller than she was, they shared many of the same interests, and they were adorable with each other. And Bobby and his friend were sweet. They all had a great time and stayed at the bowling alley until ten-thirty, and Josh and Max looked reluctant to leave. Bobby teased his brother about it, and Jim and Tallie acted like they didn't notice, and chatted casually as they finally left and stood talking in the parking lot for a few minutes. The two families had had a great time together.

"Thanks, Jim," Tallie said easily. He had noticed all evening that she looked happier and more relaxed than the last time he'd seen her three months before. But that had been shortly after her father's passing, and everything else she'd been through. She looked like she had recovered some of her poise and good humor in the meantime, and he was glad to see it.

"We'll have to go skating when the kids come home for Christmas," Jim suggested, and his boys were quick to second the invitation. "They set up a nice ice rink near where we live, for the holidays. I'm a little rusty, but we always enjoy it."

"I haven't skated in years," Tallie confessed with a grin.

"Are you working on a new movie at the moment?" he asked her with interest.

"I'm starting to. I'm just doing the groundwork now. I finally found a script I like. And *The Sand Man* is coming out in a few weeks."

"I'll have to go see it," he said easily, and she nodded. Max was coming home just in time for the premiere, which was going to be a big deal, since it was the last film Hunter Lloyd had produced. Insiders were predicting a number of Oscar nominations. It was going to be a major film, and hopefully another box-office hit. As always, Tallie was modest about it and changed the subject. The six of them said goodbye to each other, and a few minutes later they drove home.

"He's cute, isn't he, Mom?" Max said with a look of mischief in her eye, and Tallie grinned. She could see how taken with Josh her daughter was, even without the comment.

"Josh? Yes he is, he's a very nice, handsome boy."

Max started laughing as soon as Tallie said it. "I meant his dad."

"Oh, for heaven's sake," Tallie said, and rolled her eyes. "Yes, he's cute too. He makes a very nice friend." Max said nothing, and smiled as she looked out the window as Tallie drove them home.

Chapter 19

The Sand Man opened to rave reviews, for the acting, direction, score, and cinematography. People were going nuts for it, and moviegoers of all ages were stampeding the theaters where it was showing. It was a colossal hit, and Tallie was thrilled. It gave her an enormous boost after a painful year. Max came home the night before the premiere and attended it with her mother, and the next day the house was filled with flowers, champagne, gifts, and messages of praise. And Tallie couldn't help wishing her father could have seen it. He had loved it every time one of her movies was a big hit. And he would have loved this one. It had all the action, complicated plot, and fine acting that he loved.

Jim Kingston called to congratulate her too. He said he was going to see it that weekend with Bobby. And Josh was due home in a few days for Christmas vacation.

"It must be a fantastic movie, from what the critics say," Jim said pleasantly, and then asked her if she was ready for Christmas. In truth, she was dreading it. It was going to be another important holiday without her father. The pain of his loss was still acute, for her and her daughter.

"As ready as we're going to be." She had already been to Maxfield's to buy everything she thought Max wanted. Brigitte had always helped her with her Christmas shopping, but Tallie didn't ask Megan to do it for her. She had made a point of being less dependent on her than she had been on Brigitte, and doing more for herself. She wanted their working relationship to be better

balanced and even a little distant. She
was keeping things more professional,
and getting less personally involved. It
seemed wiser after all that had happened, and Megan understood. She
had already become a major asset in
Tallie's life.

"What about you?" Tallie asked Jim
about Christmas.

"Christmas shopping has never been
my forte. These holidays are never quite
the same after what we've been
through and you have. And I know you
must miss your dad."

"I do," she confessed. "But at least
he was eighty-six, so even if I miss him,
there's a kind of natural order to it,"
which hadn't been the case with Jim's
wife.

"We have to set up that skating
date," Jim reminded her. "I'll call you as
soon as Josh gets home," he promised.
So she wasn't surprised when he called
her four days later. She'd been sitting at
her desk, thinking about Brigitte, wondering what her Christmas in jail was
going to be like. Tallie couldn't even
imagine it and didn't want to. She

picked up the phone, knowing it was Jim, and he sounded elated when she answered. Before anything else, he congratulated her on her latest film. As promised, he and Bobby had seen it over the weekend and loved it. "It's amazing!" Now that he knew her, he had been even more impressed by her skill as a director. The performances had been incredible, and Bobby had loved the film as much as he did. Tallie was pleased to hear it.

"Thank you," she said warmly. It was breaking box-office records, and so far was the smash hit of the season. "It's doing really well."

"I have a Christmas gift for you," he said, changing the subject. She didn't have one for him, and was suddenly embarrassed. "Brigitte's lawyer contacted us today, and the district attorney. She wants to plead guilty in both cases and get it over with and get the time running. And that means you'll be home free on the civil lawsuit too, because once she pleads, all you have to do is make a stipulated settlement with her lawyer for the amount she's willing to make restitution for, and you're done. You won't have to go to court or testify. There's no jury, no trial . . . it's almost over, Tallie," he said gently. It was a gift he was thrilled to be able to give her. Soon she could put it all behind her, and he knew how important that was for her. The upcoming trials had been weighing heavily on her, and Jim knew they would be traumatic. And until they were behind her, she couldn't really heal.

"Why do you think she did that?" Tallie asked him, surprised and pleased. It was major news.

"Probably because her lawyer's not stupid. She can't win any of these cases. She'll get a much better deal from the U.S. attorney and the district attorney if she pleads. Damage control. They'll agree to how long she spends in prison, instead of pushing it to the limit with a jury trial in both cases. She would have had to be suicidal to do that. She's doing the right thing, and it'll make the civil matter a lot easier for you if she's reasonable, which remains to be seen. But I hope she will be. This was really her only choice." He was de-

lighted, and as she began to understand it better, Tallie was too. "Merry
Christmas, Tallie," he said warmly.

"Thank you, Jim, for everything." She
really meant it. They both did.

"Let's set up that skating evening to
celebrate after the holidays," he said in
a friendly tone.

"I'd love it," she said with genuine
pleasure in her voice, since they'd had
fun with them before, when they went
bowling. And then she went to tell Max
what Brigitte had done. She wished she
could have told her father. The nightmare was almost over. Maybe it was
Brigitte's Christmas gift to her after all,
or maybe not. Maybe she had done it
for herself. Damage control, as Jim
called it. It was hard to tell. But it was a
good thing. And very good news for her.

Tallie and Max were having breakfast in
the kitchen on a Tuesday morning between Christmas and New Year. Tallie
was glancing at some e-mails on her
computer while Max read the paper,

and suddenly Max gave a scream, and Tallie nearly jumped off her seat.

"Oh my God, what is it? What happened now?" She felt constantly wary of bad news, which was the fallout of everything that had happened. Jim had told her it would pass, but it hadn't yet. "What's wrong?"

Max was grinning as she read out loud in a voice filled with importance. "It's an editorial about all the movies that came out at Christmas. They're predicting you're going to win an Oscar for *The Sand Man,* and the guy who writes this column is usually right. How do you like that, Mom?"

"It sounds great, but you can't believe all those predictions. He's just guessing. We'll see." The nominations weren't due out till February. And then she added, "I've been nominated twice before and didn't win." But even being nominated would be terrific and great for the picture, if it turned out later that she was, and she might be nominated for a Golden Globe Award too.

"There's a nice optimistic attitude," Max scolded her. "If you get nominated, can I go with you?" Max asked her. She wanted to get in her bid early. And it reminded Tallie that she had gone the last time with her father, but it would be fun to go with Max, and Max had been with her before, although it was a long, sometimes tedious evening. But it would definitely be amazing to win an Oscar, with Max attending the award ceremony with her. It gave her something to look forward to.

It was time to live again, and with Brigitte pleading guilty to all charges, at least Tallie wouldn't have the trials to worry about. Things were finally looking up. And there might just be an Oscar in her future. She didn't dare hope for that. It was just a silly prediction, Tallie knew, but it would be incredible if she won one. It was an exciting dream.

Jim called her that afternoon and congratulated her on the article too, and said he hoped she'd win, and he suggested a night for their skating date that they'd all been looking forward to and the date he offered sounded fine to her. It was later that week. "How was

your Christmas?" he asked her pleasantly.

"Small. Quiet. Nice. We missed my
dad a lot," she said honestly, "but we
had fun too. And we've been busy ever
since." The time always flew by when
Max was home, and he said the same
about Josh. He said he has taking the
boys skiing at Squaw Valley over New
Year's, and he had suggested their
skating date the night before.

Max and Tallie met the three Kingstons at the skating rink on Thursday
night. Max brought a tin of brownies
she had baked for them, and the five of
them spent several hours on the ice,
laughing and chasing each other
around. Josh was by far the best skater,
as he'd been skating recently in Michigan, and he tucked Max's hand into his
arm and glided smoothly onto the ice
with her and kept her from falling, while
Bobby speed-skated around the ice
with friends. Jim and Tallie went around
the rink more sedately, but talking and
laughing, until they finally sat down on a
bench to catch their breath after an
hour. They were having a lot of fun. Tal-

lie had worn pink earmuffs and match-
ing mittens, and she looked like a kid
with pink cheeks and bright eyes, while
Jim looked barely older than his sons.
They were a handsome group as people noticed them skating together.

"I haven't had this much fun in ages,"
Tallie said, smiling at him.

"Neither have I. I always have a good
time when I'm with you," Jim said, looking shy for a minute. "I hope you realize
that I don't normally introduce my children to the people I work with." He
hadn't wanted to say "victims," but she
understood   what   he   was   saying.
"You're a remarkable woman, Tallie. I'm
honored that I've gotten to know you. I
wish I could have achieved a better out-
come for you, or that none of this had
happened to you at all. But as long as it
did, I'm glad I was assigned to work on
your case, and have gotten to know you
now." In some ways, they felt like they'd
become friends, and he really had gotten to know her, through some of the
hardest events in her life.

"I feel the same way, and I think
you've done an amazing job. If it

weren't for you, we would never have caught Brigitte or been able to stop her. I'm just grateful it's behind me now." She had bounced back better than he'd expected, and she seemed stronger now every time he saw her. And she was a very attractive woman, and so gentle and kind that he liked her better and better and was more and more attracted to her. He had never spent personal time with a "victim," but he loved the time he spent with Tallie, and on every occasion he saw her, all he wanted was to do it again.

"I didn't want you to think that this is a usual occurrence for me. In fact"—he looked away for a moment and then back into her green eyes—"I haven't dated since Jeannie died."

"I understand," she said softly, took off one pink mitten, and patted his hand, and he gently took her hand in his own.

"Would you have dinner with me sometime, Tallie?" he asked her with a cautious look. He was afraid that she would say no, and he'd spoil what they were sharing now. She smiled at him and nodded.

"I'd like that very much." As she said it, he beamed at her, then stood up and pulled her to her feet. She had just given him everything he wanted, and he was afraid to say more. And for the first time, looking at another woman he didn't feel disloyal to his late wife. He felt sure that she would have liked Tallie, and how kind she was to his boys, and Max was a lovely girl. They all seemed to fit together, and the three times they had all seen each other had been innocent and fun. And Jim had already warned Josh not to misbehave with Max, and he had promised. Jim didn't want anything to go wrong. Tallie had been through enough, and so had Max.

For the rest of the evening, the kids skated together, and sometimes Jim and Tallie skated with them. And in between they sat on one of the benches and talked for a while. Jim said that sometime he wanted to take her to a restaurant called Giorgio Baldi, where they had the best pasta in the world.

They all hated to see the evening end, and reluctantly left the ice when the session was over. It was eleven o'clock, and they had been skating for four hours. The three younger members of the group didn't even look tired. And the Kingstons were leaving for Squaw Valley in the morning for three days of skiing. The boys promised to call Max when they got back, and Jim exchanged a long look with Tallie when they said goodbye and kissed her on the cheek. Tallie waved at them as they left the parking lot first. It had been a wonderful evening, and it sounded like there were more to come. She had had a lovely time with Jim and his boys, and so had Max, who was leaning back in her seat in the car with her eyes closed, listening to her iPod, which allowed Tallie to drive home in silence, lost in her own thoughts.

Tallie didn't hear from Jim for a week after he got back from Squaw Valley. He was busy at work with a flood of new cases that had landed on his desk after the first of the year. But he called her the day after Brigitte pleaded guilty to the charges of embezzlement, mail and wire fraud, abuse of trust, and tax evasion. She had pleaded guilty to all of it. And then to first-degree murder. The sentencing had been set for early April. And the probation department would be working on the pre-sentencing report and recommendation to the judge until then. Jim said that she would probably do ten years because she had pleaded. She could have gotten as much as twenty, or even life, if she hadn't. So she had done herself a big favor with the plea. And Tallie's civil suit would be a matter of negotation for restitution. Brigitte's guilty plea had included an agreement to make restitution in full to her victim. Jim warned Tallie that she might not be able to recoup that much, if Brigitte had hidden it or spent it, but she would get something. But except for the sentencing and the negotiations for restitution in the civil suit, it was over. And Tallie wouldn't have to go through the agony of a trial. She was enormously relieved.

"Were you in court for the plea?" Tallie wanted to know.

"Yes, I was."

"How was she?"

He hesitated and then told Tallie the truth, however hurtful. "She was cool, calm, and collected. Totally unemotional. She didn't look scared. She gave her guilty plea in an unwavering strong voice, not a tear, not a tremor, and she looked the judge right in the eye. She's a perfect sociopath, through and through. Her hair was even clean and freshly done, and she wore a very sexy dress that you probably paid for." It was shocking to hear. Tallie tried to envision it in disbelief.

"I don't understand," Tallie said quietly.

"You wouldn't. Most people wouldn't. That kind of personality is so foreign to the rest of us. That's why they get away with what they do. We can't even imagine it, so we don't suspect it, while they lie, cheat, and steal, and occasionally kill someone. It's pretty scary stuff. I feel sorry for Hunter Lloyd," he said quietly, "but I'm glad it wasn't you."

"So am I," she said, thinking about Max. It would have destroyed her if her mother had been killed.

"So what about our dinner? Does Friday night work for you?" he asked quietly, afraid she might have changed her mind.

"Perfect." Max had gone back to New York that morning, and Tallie was free. She wasn't going out socially, and since she wasn't working at the moment, she had time on her hands. All she was doing was talking to investors for her next picture.

"I'll pick you up at seven-thirty," he promised, and they were both smiling when they hung up.

And when Jim arrived promptly on Friday night, Tallie was happy to see him. Knowing that Brigitte had pleaded guilty really had given Tallie a sense of relief all week, and she felt freer than she had in months. And Greg was moving ahead with negotiations for a stipulated judgment in the civil suit, to get some of her money back. She was slowly putting it all behind her.

And she and Jim talked nonstop

through dinner about their kids, their work, their families when they grew up. The evening sped by and the food at Giorgio Baldi was as delicious as he had said. And when Jim took her home, he hesitated for a long moment as they stood outside her house, and he kissed her gently on the mouth, and then looked at her with concern.

"I just want you to know that I've never kissed a victim before," he said softly.

"I'm not a victim," she whispered back. "And I never will be again." She was definitely coming back. He smiled at what she said. She had told him at dinner that she had taken her most recent letter from the Victim Identification Program with her number on it and thrown it in the trash when it arrived that day.

"You know what I mean," he said. "I've never gotten involved with anyone through my work." He had already told her that when they went skating, but he wanted to be sure she knew it was true. "I don't want you to think that I go around hitting on the people I work with." But she had never thought that. If anything, she had thought they were friends, until he kissed her.

"I have kind of a problem too," she admitted, as long as they were being honest with each other, which she liked. It was essential to her, and always had been, but more so than ever now. "I'm not sure I could ever trust anyone again." She looked very serious, and he laughed when she said it, which startled her. "I mean it," she said for emphasis.

"I know, and I don't blame you . . . but if you can't trust an FBI agent, who can you trust?" She thought about it for a minute and then smiled.

"You have a point."

"This may be the safest relationship you'll ever have. I don't mean to be presumptuous, but . . ." Before he could finish his sentence, she kissed him back. He had forgotten what that could be like, and so had she. She had blotted everything out of her mind and heart, and he had thought he was dead after Jeannie, and now he realized he wasn't. He was very much alive, and so was she. And as she looked up at him, she had no idea what would happen, but what she did know was that she could trust him, and she was safe.

Chapter 20

One of the last of the formalities Tallie had to go through relating to Brigitte and the embezzlement was a visit from the senior probation officer assigned to do the pre-sentencing report to recommend the length of Brigitte's sentence to the judge. As it turned out, she was a friend of Jim's and he knew her well. She had called him as soon as she was assigned the case, and he filled her in on the details, without mentioning that he was dating Tallie. It was irrelevant to the case.

"What's she like?" Sandra Zinneman

couldn't resist asking him. She had been momentarily impressed when she realized who the victim was. Sandra was a big fan of her movies, and she wanted to stay professional about it, but a certain amount of curiosity got the best of her nonetheless. She had always liked what she'd read about Tallie, and when she went through the file, she was sorry about what had happened to her. "It sounds like she got a really rotten deal from her boyfriend and the defendant, to say the least," she commented to Jim.

"She's a very decent, down-to-earth person. She's been through a lot with all this. Are you having her come in to see you?" Jim wished he could somehow spare Tallie having to talk about it all again, but the probation officer's recommendation was important for the judge. He would base the length of Brigitte's sentence on what Sandra put in the report. She was a key person in the final result. She would also be interviewing Brigitte and everyone involved in the cases, in order to offer a well-rounded suggestion, based on all the elements of the case. And she was known to be thorough and fair.

Sandra sounded thoughtful for a minute. "I was actually thinking of going out to see her at her place, for a couple of reasons. I thought it might be less upsetting for her, and I kind of wanted to see where they worked together, and what the atmosphere was at 'the scene of the crime.'" She was referring to the embezzlement, not the murder. "The setting must be pretty grand," she said, sounding slightly in awe.

"Not really," Jim told her. "It's a nice house, but she's a very normal person. The defendant was the one who was 'grand.' Tallie Jones looks like anyone you'd see at the supermarket. Her success never went to her head. It's the defendant who got carried away and greedy." He liked the idea of Sandra going out to see Tallie. "What are you thinking, after reading the report?"

"That Brigitte needs to do some serious time." She had read the defense lawyer's request to have Brigitte do her sentences concurrently, and Sandra Zinneman didn't see why she should.

She had embezzled a fortune from her employer, committed a shocking abuse of trust, and pleaded guilty to murder. Sandra thought that consecutive sentencing was more in line with what she deserved. She wasn't inclined to go easy on her. "I'll go out and see the victim as soon as I can. I've got a couple of other big cases on my desk." She had another murder case, and a ring of pedophiles who had been doing business on the Internet, that she wanted to deal with first. As a senior officer with an excellent reputation, the department's biggest cases went to her.

"Let me know if there's anything I can do to help," Jim offered.

"I need to ask her how she feels about the sentencing, and what kind of effects she's had from the case." Jim knew the drill, and he knew it would be disturbing for Tallie to go through it all again, but this would be the last time, until the sentencing itself. Tallie was expected to make a statement to the judge there. Jim was planning to go with her to offer his support, and he had to be at the hearing anyway, since he was assigned to the case.

Sandra called her two days later. Tallie was pleasant, and they made an appointment for Sandra to see her the following week. When she did, the visit was less painful than Tallie had feared. Sandra was extremely skilled at what she did, and exhibited real compassion, which was sincere and heartfelt. She liked Tallie immensely when she met her, and was impressed that she put on no airs or graces, she didn't overdramatize, and she looked and acted like a regular person who had been the victim of a crime, and was severely hurt by Brigitte's betrayal. Sandra felt deep sympathy for her, and admired her even more than she'd expected. By the time she left Tallie's home, after three hours of serious conversation, Sandra had even more respect for her than before they'd met. And Tallie felt strangely at peace and protected. She could see that this woman, who saw so many truly shocking crimes, sincerely felt for what she'd been through. It had actually been a relief to talk to her. And Sandra had made it clear that she was going to recommend the maximum sentence, despite any deals Brigitte and her attorney might try to make. And she told Tallie that she felt fairly certain that the judge who had been assigned the sentencing would listen to her suggestions. He usually did, and her opinions were frequently followed by the court.

Tallie thanked her warmly, and when she closed the door behind Sandra, she went to sit in her garden with an enormous feeling of relief. It was almost over, and her case was in good hands. She could begin to turn her mind to other things now, and look to the happy times and better days that lay ahead.

Chapter 21

Tallie was frowning as she sat in the back of the long black stretch limo. She was wearing a red satin strapless dress Max had picked for her, and she looked like an angry four-year-old, while her daughter laughed at her. The dress was agonizingly tight, but Tallie looked spectacular in it, with her blond hair piled on her head, and red satin high-heeled sandals.

"I don't see why we have to go in this ridiculous car. And I hate this stupid dress. We could have gone in an SUV. And my boobs are falling out. I'm not going to make a spectacle of myself," Tallie said petulantly as Jim and Max exchanged a look. Max was glad he was there, and so was Tallie. She'd been sad all week realizing that her father wouldn't be. But it was nice having Jim with them. Jim and Tallie had been spending a lot of time together for the past three months. She spent time on the weekends with him and Bobby. And Jim had come to New York with her to visit Max. She had lined up the investors for her next picture, and they were going to start shooting in September. And ironically, Brigitte was being sentenced in a week. It was almost over. And Tallie was glad Jim had come with her and Max.

"I should have worn black," she muttered and Max laughed.

"You look great, Mom. And you're a star. You can't show up in an SUV when everyone else gets out of a limo."

"Why not?" Tallie said while Jim smiled at her. He was crazy about her, and so proud to be with her.

"We'll come in a truck next year," Jim

promised with a smile. "Or an FBI car. That'll work."

Tallie smiled then for a minute. She hated this kind of thing, with a wall of press in her face, shouting her name, showing off, all dressed up and wearing too much makeup. It felt so phony to her. She had the looks for it, but not the personality. She would rather have been at home, watching it on TV, but not if she won. She was sure she wouldn't anyway, which made it even more embarrassing to be so done up. *The Sand Man* had won four Golden Globes, but an Oscar was much harder to win and she never had before. She was sure tonight would be no different, although she had been nominated for best director and the film had been nominated for five other awards.

The long black limo slowed in the lineup, and finally it was their turn, as Max looked her mother over for a last time. She had worn a white strapless dress herself with a little white fox jacket and looked like a starlet. But Tallie looked magnificient. She looked regal as she waited to get out of the car. She didn't like playing this game.

"We're up next, Mom. Look at me." She checked her mother out for a last time before they got out of the car. "You look gorgeous. Don't forget to smile." Jim was watching the mother-daughter exchange, and he was touched. They were great together, and he was coming to love Max as much as her mother, and his boys were impressed that he was dating a Hollywood star, but she didn't act like one—that was the best part, and what he had loved about her from the beginning. She was literally being dragged to the Oscars, kicking and complaining, against her will. He thought it was funny. Tallie didn't.

"I'll just shoot them if they annoy you," Jim promised, and she laughed, a deep chuckle as she sat in the car in the sexy gown, with her hair perfectly arranged in the casual upsweep, the red satin sandals, and diamonds on her ears. He knew she would be the envy of every woman in the place or who saw her on TV. And he was wearing a brand-new tux he had bought for the occasion. He had never needed his own before, but he thought he might now, from time to time. And he had been very honored when she had asked him to escort them. He knew both his boys were watching on TV, he had warned them, and his sister-in-law, who was a fan. Jack Sprague was watching too. He was impressed that Jim was going to the Academy Awards.

And then they were out of the car. Tallie made a graceful exit, looking more like the actress she had once been than the director she was now. She was smiling, and the press started shouting her name as they started along the red carpet. Jim walked between them with Tallie and Max on either side of him. Tallie smiled at the photographers like the pro she was, answered a few questions, and laughed at something someone said. She posed for a picture with Max, another one with Jim, another with all three of them. Someone asked his name and he gave it. He felt dizzy as they made their way along, and he spotted major stars up ahead of them and behind them. He could see why she didn't like this, it was terrifying. But nothing showed on Tallie. She was totally gracious as she glided along, and then they were finally in the building being escorted to their seats as cameras panned the audience for major stars.

"Oh my God, facing a suspect with an AK-47 is less scary than that," he said under his breath to Tallie. She was right, he thought, it was the scariest thing he'd ever done. He'd never done anything like it before.

"I hate it," she said through clenched teeth with a smile, but this was her world, and she had to be part of it once in a while, whether she liked it or not, especially on a night like tonight. She loved the work, but not the show-off part. And Max looked like she was having fun as they took their seats in the second row.

"You look gorgeous, Mom," Max said as she checked her out again, to make sure she didn't have lipstick on her teeth or her hair out of place. Tallie looked perfect, and Jim was proud. He had never expected to be part of this, and it was still mind-boggling to think of how he'd gotten there, and how natural it all seemed to be with her now that he was here.

Several people came over and spoke to Tallie, and a number of them wished her luck. There were producers and other directors, major stars, and her agent. Tallie introduced him to all of them. Jim couldn't keep them all straight, but it was obvious how respected she was by her peers. It had to feel good, he thought to himself, even if she didn't win, but he hoped she would. As the lights dimmed, he leaned over and wished her luck, and she smiled at him, as a camera zoomed in on them, and neither of them could see it, but his sister-in-law was screaming hysterically when she saw them on the TV screen in Pasadena. To his family, he was suddenly a star, along with Tallie, and not in a million years had he ever thought it or dreamed it, but neither had Tallie. She had never expected to wind up here. She had just been doing her job, which was what she loved best.

"I've already had my good luck,"

she whispered back to him, and he squeezed her hand.

As always, the evening was interminable, as they hopped and skipped over categories, from best animated feature to best supporting actress to best song. It kept people watching throughout the evening, rather than giving them everything they were waiting for at the end. The first award *The Sand Man* won was best musical score. There were screams of delight as the composer went to get his Oscar and thanked the enormous cast, all the technicians, and everyone he'd ever known. Jim realized it was going to be a long night. Tallie looked serene as they held hands, and she and Max whispered exchanges from time to time. Jim thought Tallie seemed more relaxed as the evening wore on. And he was getting more anxious for her. She looked beautiful and calm.

They did best actress that night before best director, and everyone was excited as a Hollywood favorite hobbled up to the stage in an extremely tight dress that made her look like a mermaid, but she was a beautiful girl, and Jim was awestruck seeing her up close as she ran past them. She was so close he could smell her perfume, and Tallie smiled at him. She knew just how heady this all was. She had lived it for years. It didn't impress her but it was new to Jim.

And then finally it came. Best director. They read off the names, showed clips of the films. The TV cameras zoomed in on each of them and showed them on giant monitors as they waited. Tallie looked totally calm, as she smiled at Max and Jim, and squeezed their hands. She had already decided she wouldn't win and felt fine about it. Her life as it was now was enough. She didn't need more. And when she went to work on a new picture, she'd be happy. She didn't need an award for the last one.

Two of Hollywood's best-known actors had made the introduction, and the female star stayed to read the winner's name. They waited as she fumbled with the envelope in long white gloves and joked about it, and Tallie laughed and looked totally relaxed.

"Tallie Jones!" the young actress screamed with delight, as they played the theme from the movie, and Tallie didn't seem to hear it. It didn't register with her. Jim heard it first and Max was crying and clapping her hands as Jim was pushing Tallie out of her seat, and Tallie realized what had happened when she saw Max. She had won!

Tallie walked toward the stage with a dazed look on her face. She hadn't expected to win. She turned back once to look at Jim, and he was almost crying with joy for her, and then she moved forward, and ran gracefully onto the stage, held the Oscar in her hand for an intstant, and closed her eyes, and thanked God for the blessings in her life. She could feel her father with her, and her voice was a low sexy rumble when she spoke. The room went quiet to listen. All eyes were on her.

"I have two people to thank, my daughter Max, and my father Sam, for making my life and work so wonderful." And she looked serious then. "And I want to thank Hunter Lloyd, wherever he is, for giving me this extraordinary opportunity, and allowing me to make this beautiful movie. Thank you, Hunt . . . Thank you all!" She waved the Oscar high at them, and left the stage as gracefully as she had come, disappeared into the wings, and ran back to her seat, and Jim and Max, a minute later. The whole room had given her a standing ovation for what she said. Hunter Lloyd was missed there that night. He was an important Hollywood figure, gone forever, but his movies would live on, and hers. Her speech had been short and touching. She kissed Max and Jim when she sat down. Jim had never been so proud in his life. He was thrilled for her and to be part of it. It was a shining moment in their lives, and it meant the world to him to have shared it with her.

The Sand Man won Oscars for cinematography, editing, best director, best picture, and best supporting actress. The Academy had honored them all, and Hunt. They had shown a beautiful photograph of Hunt on two giant screens, and a famous actor had made a short and touching speech about him, that his work would never be forgotten, and that he had been one of the best producers Hollywood had ever seen. When *The Sand Man* won best picture, Tallie went back to the stage to accept the award for him. And the audience rose for another standing ovation, and this time there were tears in eyes and on cheeks.

Tallie made a short and moving speech about the extraordinary producer he had been, and the honor it had been to work with him. "His memory will live on with us forever, like his work. Never lost, never forgotten, never far from our hearts. Sleep on, sweet prince. Go gently into the night. You will be much missed." She spoke with astounding eloquence, and held the Oscar she was going to send to Angela Morissey for their son, and when she left the stage, there wasn't a dry eye in the house. It had been a noble farewell, despite what he had done to her. Jim admired her more than ever as he listened, and when she returned to her seat again, he put an arm around her and held her close. She was a remarkable woman. And Jim felt like the luckiest man in the world. Max was crying as she beamed at her mother.

It was a glittering evening, and Tallie was besieged by the press as they left. She was still clutching her Oscar and Hunt's, and Jim's hand. And Tallie thanked everyone who had been involved.

The three of them went to two of the after parties that night, and after the second one, Tallie told Max they were leaving and she'd send the car back for her. Max was having a great time with a bunch of young people she knew, and a handsome young actor who was flirting with her. She was the belle of the ball, and Tallie looked happy as she left on Jim's arm, still holding both Oscars. A last rush of photographers took their picture as they left, and she heaved a sigh of relief as she leaned back against the seat in the car and Jim smiled at her as they drove off.

"That was some evening," he said in

awe, "and you were *amazing,*" and then
he kissed her. "I'm so proud of you, Tallie." For an instant she thought of her
father. He would have been proud of her
too, but now Jim was here. He was a
blessing she hadn't expected, after all
the losses. And now the Oscar, which
would give her even more credibility as
a director. She was grateful for that, but
she wasn't thinking of her career as she
looked at him.

"I was proud of you tonight too," she
said, looking at him. "Thank you for
coming with me." He didn't know what
to say to that. What could he say? He
loved her modesty and simplicity, her
integrity, and the woman she was. He
kissed her again, which told her more
than he could with words.

"Thank you" was all he said, and she
kissed him back. And when they got
home and she got out of the limo and
sent it back for Max, she looked at Jim
and laughed.

"The coach just turned into a pump-
kin, and the coachmen into mice. I think
I like it better this way," she said, and he
laughed at her.

"I know you do. I love you, Cinderella."

"I love you too," she said as they wandered into the house. They were still talking about the evening as they walked up the stairs together. It had been an incredible moment in her life and a great honor, and the best of it was that all the liars and frauds were gone. A good man had found her at last.

Epilogue

A week after the Academy Awards, Brigitte Parker was sentenced to eighteen years in prison. Based on the recommendation of the probation department's pre-sentencing report, the judge refused to run her sentences concurrently, and ran them consecutively. She received a six-year sentence for her embezzlement from Tallie Jones and twelve years in the state system for the murder of Hunter Lloyd.

Tallie Jones was able to reclaim about a third of what she lost, from the sale of Brigitte Parker's possessions.

The proceeds of the sale of her home on Mulholland Drive went to the Internal Revenue Service for income tax evasion.

A year later, Tallie Jones and Jim Kingston were married on the beach in Hawaii, accompanied by their children.

A year after that, Victor Carson married a twenty-three-year-old Russian trade show model in Las Vegas.

About the Author

DANIELLE STEEL has been hailed as one of the world's most popular authors, with over 600 million copies of her novels sold. Her many international bestsellers include *Hotel Vendôme, Happy Birthday, 44 Charles Street, Legacy, Family Ties, Big Girl, Southern Lights,* and other highly acclaimed novels. She is also the author of *His Bright Light,* the story of her son Nick Traina's life and death.

Visit the Danielle Steel website at daniellesteel.com.